In Spite of Killer Bees

In Spite of Killer Bees

JULIE JOHNSTON

Tundra Books

Published in Canada by Tundra Books,
481 University Avenue, Toronto, Ontario M5G 2E9

Published in the United States by Tundra Books of Northern New York,
P.O. Box 1030, Plattsburgh, New York 12901

Library of Congress Card Number: 00-135460

National Library of Canada Cataloguing in Publication Data

Johnston, Julie, 1941–
    In spite of killer bees

ISBN 0-88776-537-8 (bound).—ISBN 0-88776-601-3 (pbk.)

I. Title.

PS8569.O38715 2001   jC813'.54   C2001-930265-7
PZ7.J6415 2001

We acknowledge the support of the Canada Council for the Arts and
the Ontario Arts Council for our publishing program.

We acknowledge the financial support of the Government of Canada
through the Book Publishing Industry Development Program for our
publishing activities.

Design by Sari Naworynski

Printed and bound in Canada

1 2 3 4 5 6   08 07 06 05 04 03

To the memory of Sarah Mae Dulmage
and for
Alexander, Connor, Mackenzie, Nicolas, Adam,
and Samantha Mae

ACKNOWLEDGMENTS

I would like to express my gratitude to Kathy Lowinger for her spot-on editorial comments and suggestions; and to Sue Tate for her patience and fine-tooth copyediting. May I also extend thanks to the following for their advice and encouragement, and for their much-needed comfort and cheer: Mary Breen, Jane Collins, Lea Harper, Troon Harrison, Patricia Stone, Betsy Struthers, Florence Treadwell, Christl Verduyn, Hugh Conn, Basil Johnston, Kathleen Jordan, Diane Matheson, Lauren Stiroh, Leslie Tralli. For occasional insights, inspired suggestions, and turns of phrase, I am indebted to Andrea Green, David Green, Mackenzie Green, Melissa Johnston, Frank Tralli, and Kevin Stiroh.

CHAPTER ONE

Looking out, Agatha says, "This could be in a movie." Helen and Jeannie ignore her. They usually do, even though she's fourteen now and believes she's becoming quite interesting. Agatha has never told anyone this (someday she will), but she sometimes thinks she is both in a movie and watching it. She has the feeling that sometimes she soars.

Helen paid for the car, but Jeannie's driving it. She's seventeen, so why not? Of course, to call it a car, Aggie thinks, is flattering the thing – the two hundred and fifty dollar bag of scrap metal on wheels. It groans up the last hill. Agatha leans over the back of the front seat. For a moment all three sisters are breathless as they take in the panorama. "It's the edge of the world," Helen says. And so it seems for the fraction of a second they are perched there, the rest of their lives spread before them. Straight ahead, below, is the lake – bluer than the sky, flecked with diamonds in the glancing sun. Off to the right nestles the village of Port Desire.

The car releases a series of relieved backfires as it starts down the other side of the hill. They can see more of the village now: a church spire dazzling, haloed in the westerly sun. Around it, roofs of houses huddle like toadstools beneath tamed forests of trees.

The highway leads right into town to become the main street, LAKE STREET, a sign says. It's lined with parked cars and on the sidewalks dozens of people in shorts and sunglasses amble along, eating ice cream cones, gazing into store windows. They cross the street wherever they feel like it, especially right in front of the Quade girls' vehicle. Jeannie slams on the brakes more than once, muttering hostile names through her open window until Helen tells her not to be any more appalling than she has to be.

Agatha has been on the lookout for cops ever since they left Sudbury for the simple reason that Jeannie has only a G-1. Jeannie said, when they set off, "Don't worry about it. It's okay as long as you have an adult with you." At twenty-two Helen counts as an adult, which is fine except that Helen doesn't have a license, either. Agatha has felt rattled for nine solid hours, with Helen in the navigator's seat telling Jeannie she's getting too close to the shoulder, telling her to stay in her lane, telling her to shut her filthy mouth whenever Jeannie's replies get a little too crass for Helen's hoity-toity ears. Agatha isn't used to her older sisters being quite so hostile. Back home in Sudbury, they pretty well ignore each other. She's surprised they've all survived the trip without resorting to homicide.

Agatha (Aggie is what she prefers) has eyes like fringed chocolate pies. She has her head out, ogling the sights, memorizing the sounds. She can smell the lake, or maybe it's the shore – hot sun on seaweed and wooden wharfs, with a hint of boat gas thrown in. The people here all look so nice and relaxed, some are even smiling. *Slam* go the brakes again as a jaywalking girl dripping ice cream jumps back out of the way of the car. "Oops!" says the girl, grinning. "Sorry."

Aggie grins back through her open window and thinks she'd like to be able to phone up that girl and tell her everything that happens and laugh for an hour. She's never actually done that with anyone. At her school in Sudbury, kids aren't particularly friendly. They have names for her – Baggie, or Shaggie, which she ignores, and sometimes Ditz, which doesn't even rhyme. Plus, she has to help in the deli after school, which doesn't leave much time for friends. Aggie senses the girl staring at her shaved head, but doesn't care. Something she had to do once in her life.

The Quade girls follow Lake Street as it curves past houses, a gas station, a store, a pharmacy, with little glimpses of the lake in between, boats on it zipping this way and that cresting the waves.

"Doesn't this look like something out of a movie?" Aggie repeats.

"Not much," Jeannie says.

"Start looking for house numbers," Helen says.

On the other side of the street Aggie peers at a hardware store, a grocery store, and a stone castle that turns out to be the post office. Glancing back to the water side, across the street from the post office, she finds number 32. "So this was Grandfather Quade's house!" Jeannie stops the car and they all bend their necks to get a good look.

"Could sure use a coat of paint," Helen says.

Jeannie says, "It's a dump."

"No, it isn't," Aggie says. "Predump, maybe. There's hope."

Aggie cranes her neck and takes it all in. It's tall, it's wide, it's redbrick with crooked, weather-beaten shutters framing fly-specked windows. Hollyhocks sway lazily at the side, and a rickety veranda in need of paint sags in front. It's a monster of a place and smack on the main street.

Jeannie puts the car in gear, pulls into a grassed-over driveway on the far side of the house, and follows it around to the back, where the car promptly dies in front of a pad-locked garage. They get out with their knapsacks, slam the car doors, and all three turn to make sure the impact hasn't dismantled the car's jigsaw puzzle chassis.

The house is closed tight, blinds down, curtains pulled. No point in knocking because who would answer? Helen has a door key sent by their grandfather's lawyer with his letter. First time they'd ever got anything by courier, which made them all feel important. They *are* important. Not very many people in Sudbury have a millionaire grandfather die and leave them a huge fortune, at least no one they know. They go around to the front, but the key doesn't work in the door.

"Wiggle it," Jeannie says.

"It's the wrong key," Helen says.

Looking for another door, and carrying their knapsacks for fear they might be stolen, they retrace their steps around past the car to the back of the house. Stone steps lead down to a low door cut into the foundation. Helen can tell by looking at the large keyhole that their key won't fit. Behind the house, what should be a back lawn is more like a hay field sprinkled with lacy white flowers they've never seen before, or noticed. It goes right down to the water's edge to a lopsided building, its eaves scalloped and scrolled with the same trim as the house – a boathouse. Aggie lopes down for a closer look and pushes open the unlocked door. She calls, "Come and see it!" Her sisters meander down, Jeannie practically dead on her feet, Helen frowning over the key.

Inside, in the boat slip, in the muted light coming through the cobwebby windows, they make out an old wooden rowboat, its oars resting on the seats.

"I'd like to jump right in and go for a little row," Aggie says.

"Underwater?" Jeannie says. "Better get a diving suit."

The boat has buckets of water in it. The older girls head back up to the house, Jeannie's yellow hair tangling in the breeze, Helen's swept back tightly, her dark head on an angle.

"You stay out of that boat, Aggie!" Helen turns and calls.

Aggie mutters one or two halfhearted insults. She hates when Helen sounds motherish, although she should be used to it. One of these days, she thinks, smiling. (One of these days is her motto. It means, 'wait for the future, things are bound to get better.' She always adds, 'once Mom comes back.')

Things are already looking up, she has to admit. With all the money they're going to inherit, they'll be able to go any-where, do anything. Their mom will come home and help them buy a nice little house somewhere and fix it up cute and she'll cook delicious dinners and they'll sit around watching videos, funny ones, and laugh till they roll on the floor, or sometimes sad ones, and they'll pass around the box of Kleenex. Once Mom comes back into the family, they'll all start liking each other, she's pretty sure.

Aggie thinks this is probably what it's like to have a religion. You always have some kind of heaven to look forward to. Aggie is a born-again family-girl.

The funeral isn't until tomorrow at two in the afternoon, according to the letter they got from the lawyer. They came a day early to get their bearings, Helen says; case the joint, Jeannie says; make plans for the future, Aggie thinks.

Back in Sudbury, when Mrs. Muntz passed *The Globe and Mail* across the breakfast table to them, they crowded in to read the death notice and the article about their grandfather. "*. . . considered one of the wealthiest men in Canada fifty years ago,*" it said, and went on to tell how famous he was for owning silver mines way back when he was young. Helen clipped the article and saved it because they were in it, too. "*Survived by two sisters and three granddaughters,*" it said. She pasted it into the scrapbook she's making about their family along with the letter they got from their grandfather's lawyer saying that they were among the beneficiaries. Under the newspaper clipping Helen wrote: "*Dad always used to say, luck is like an hourglass. When it runs out you turn it over and, before you know it, it comes pouring back in.*"

The key works in a side door almost hidden by the trumpet-shaped hollyhocks – pink and purple, clinging defiantly up and down a thicket of stocks. The girls let themselves into a dark passageway that is lit only at the far end by faded daylight filtered through dingy windows on either side of the front door. They stand still for a moment, chilly in the gloom, breathing the stale air. Huddling close, they creep toward the front of the house, past closed doors. An open one, they notice, leads into a vast kitchen, high-ceilinged, with crack-lines in the plaster. All the ceilings are high. Farther along, past closed sliding doors, Helen flicks a light switch. A staircase, its center covered by threadbare carpeting held in place with thin brass rods, sweeps up from the front hall. To the left and right of it are living rooms – one stiffly grand, awash with ornamental knick-knacks; the other smaller, padded with overstuffed chairs and couches, faded and sagging.

Aggie whispers, "Not your typical rich-people's mansion, is it?" Everything looks decayed and dusty, with dreary pictures on the walls of shipwrecks and sheep and waterfalls and more sheep. "Not exactly a fun palace."

Jeannie shivers. "Who'd want to live here?"

Helen says, "What did you expect? Our grandfather was sick in a hospital, or some place, for a long time before he died. No one has lived here for years, probably."

"Our grandfather," Aggie says. "Funny how we've gone through our entire lives without any relatives and, now that we've finally got a grandfather, he turns out to be dead."

Something makes them turn back toward the stairs, listening.

"What?" Aggie's eyes are wide.

"Listen." Helen frowns.

They hear the slow drip of a tap, a fly buzzing a window, a sigh in the floor under them – sounds of a tired house. They turn to head back along the passageway, but out of the corner of her eye Aggie thinks she sees a shadow move. She screams, making them all scream as they race to the side door, stumbling, bumping each other with their knapsacks to be the first out.

"What was that?" Jeannie says.

"This place is haunted!"

"Don't be ridiculous, Aggie," Helen says.

Nevertheless, Helen leads the way around to the back of the house, where their car is parked. They get in and Jeannie tries to start it. *Wa-wa-wa!* it wails halfheartedly. The car has no intention of going anywhere.

Aggie and Helen are walking back along Lake Street. They're looking for a motel, or a house with a room to rent, or a place selling tents cheap. Anything. They're not going inside that house again, ghosts or no ghosts. Jeannie's still back there behind the house, in the car, her head lolled against the window, sound asleep, not locked in because the car's locks don't work.

They aren't having any luck at all finding a place to stay. Helen looks hot in her black sweater, buttoned right to the neck. Aggie would like to suggest an ice cream cone, but Helen would just say no. Not as many people around now, not as many ice cream cones going down this close to supper time. Aggie's hungry. They turn down a short street, pass a booth selling ice cream, and go over a high bridge spanning the water. On the other side is a long weathered wharf, with boats tied to both sides of it – mostly houseboats and cabin cruisers in a variety of shapes and sizes. They read the names: *Mamma's Mink*, Syracuse, NY; *Ma Rêve*, Trois Rivières, Que.

"If we find an empty one," Aggie whispers, "we can sneak in after dark and spend the night."

"As if."

A squat houseboat, square-ended, in need of paint, casts off from the wharf and, churning slowly through the ropey weeds, heads up the shore in the direction of Grandfather Quade's boathouse. Aggie stares at the people on it, shielding her eyes from the sun. "Hey!" she says. "Hey, that looks like Mom! It *is* Mom!" She runs along the wharf nearly tripping over mooring lines. "Mom!" she yells. "Mom!"

Helen comes up beside her, trying to get her to calm down. People are staring. People having a five-o'clock beer on the afterdeck of their boat grin at the girls with shaded eyes. "That's Mom out there!" Aggie yells at Helen, nearly in tears. The woman has slipped into the cabin out of sight. They can see the man at the wheel taking the boat up the lake, not in any hurry.

"Come on," Aggie says, grabbing Helen's arm and pulling her back along the wharf and over the bridge. "We can take that old rowboat out and head them off."

"Don't be a *total* idiot," Helen says. Aggie is always seeing their mother – in crowds, in passing cars, buses. Helen jogs along beside her, though, just to get her to shut up. Up the street they pound, Aggie rounding the house ahead of Helen, heading to the car at the back. She yanks the door open and Jeannie screams in shock, grabbing the steering wheel for balance.

"Mom's out there in a boat," Aggie yells. "Come on, we're going after her." She runs down and disappears into the boathouse.

Helen is out of breath from running. "Go down and get her out of there, will you?" she asks Jeannie.

"Get her yourself," Jeannie says, slumping against the back of the seat.

"She's going to drown herself."

"Good. Two funerals for the price of one."

Helen heaves a big, worn-out, why-do-I-have-to-do-it-all sigh.

Jeannie sighs, too. "Okay, okay." She rolls out of the car and faces Helen. "I'm out of here, you know, the minute I get my share of the money."

"Well, that makes two of us, honey."

By the time Jeannie enters the boathouse, Aggie has the boat untied. "Get in," she says.

"We can't swim."

"We don't need to swim, we have a boat."

"That thing could tip."

"It won't tip." Aggie is in the boat now, more than ankle-deep in water.

Jeannie scowls, tells her not to be a jerk.

Aggie snorts her disgust. They can hear the *putt-putt* of the houseboat's engine.

Standing in the boat alone, gripping one of the oars, tee-tering, Aggie poles it out of the boat slip into the breeze. She sits down with her back to the pointy end and fits the oars into the oarlocks, not really knowing what she's doing. Push or pull? she wonders. She gives a mighty push and the boat lurches, blunt end first, out into the lake. *Push, lurch, push, lurch*, the water in it sloshes forward and back, over her feet and legs.

The houseboat is in sight now, quite close, its wake wedging out behind. Aggie stands up and yells, "Hey, Mom! Mom!" She pulls an oar out of its lock and waves it awk-wardly above her head at the passing boat. "It's me, Aggie!" She can't see the woman. The man steers the boat without even looking at her. She might as well be one of the swallows darting and flitting over the waves. She lowers the oar and stands there breathing in and out, shoulders drooping, rocking with the waves. The houseboat is heading up the lake. When its swells hit Aggie's unstable rowboat broadside, it's enough to send her toppling, thrashing, into the water.

Jeannie, openmouthed, crouches in the boathouse. Through the frame of the off-kilter boat slip door, she watches the lake swallow her sister. She's paralyzed with panic. She doesn't know what to do. Aggie's head comes up, but Jeannie can't reach her. Aggie gasps in air and chokes, her face distorted. "Grab the oar, grab the oar," Jeannie believes she calls, but no sound comes out. Aggie goes under again and Jeannie moans aloud. Her stomach heaves.

Aggie's eyes are open underwater. She sees nothing but brownish green and thinks it must be the color of drowning.

She's lost contact with her arms and legs. They flail and thrash with a will of their own. She only knows about her chest, burning; her lungs, bursting. Up, she thinks, air is up. Her foot touches something solid.

Aggie makes a strangled retching sound as her head and shoulders break the surface. She reaches for the oar angling out from the boat and wraps her arms around it, clinging, gulping air, her throat rasping noisily. She hacks out a cough and sneeze together, then a loud belch. Her head and neck are still above water, but her toes are on the muddy bottom. Now she can swear, and does.

Jeannie gets her voice working. "Are you all right?"

Aggie coughs again and croaks, "It's not all that deep." She stretches out an arm and pulls the floating oar closer to her.

"You could have drowned!" Jeannie's screaming, now.

"A lot you'd care!" Aggie's still coughing hard, but manages to choke out, "You didn't even try to save me." She plows through the shoulder-high water, dragging the boat – her shaved head glistening, her nose running.

"What was I supposed to do? I can't swim either."

"You could have thrown something to me."

"Like what?"

"You could have called for help."

Jeannie stomps out of the boathouse.

CHAPTER TWO

They can hear the *bing-bong* of church bells reminding everyone about the funeral. "This is so pointless," Jeannie says. "We didn't even know the guy."

Helen says, "He was our grandfather. We will go out of respect for our father's family."

"As if *they* ever gave us any respect! How many of them came to our *father's* funeral?"

"None" would be the correct answer, but no one feels like saying it. They walk along, spread out like three strangers, Aggie trailing, squishing along in her still-soaking combat boots. Her wet clothes are hanging on a bush near the boathouse, where she spent the night curled up on three boat cushions, a tarpaulin over her. It wasn't until the first light of day that she realized the tarp was home to a colony of cockroaches. She sat up and a family of six scuttled out of sight between the cracks in the boathouse floor. She was too tired to care. She lay down again and slept until noon.

Helen and Jeannie spent the night in the car, both still mad at Aggie for nearly drowning. "You know what your problem is?" Helen yelled at her, after she'd hauled herself out of the water, while she was rooting around in her bag, shivering, looking for dry clothes. "You're not in the real world. You know? You think nothing bad will ever happen. You think you're walking around in some kind of movie version of your life, where you can just goof off any way you like and the director or cameraman or scriptwriter will make the appropriate changes and everything will be all right. Do you know that about yourself? When are you going to wake up, Aggie?"

"No, I don't," Aggie muttered. She pulled a T-shirt, with a faded and sappy picture of angel faces on it, a ketchup stain drooling from one, out of her knapsack.

"Stop pretending Mom's going to come back."

"But she will."

Jeannie added her two cents' worth. "She won't. She's a heartless, self-centered bitch. She's forgotten all about us."

"All I'm saying," Helen said, quieter now, "is get in touch with reality, Aggie. In this life you make things happen. You don't hang around waiting for the scene to change. You get out there and turn things around for yourself."

Fade to black, Aggie was thinking. She found her jeans in the bag and some underwear and socks, and went back into the boathouse to change.

They all woke up at about the same time, and all three went warily into the house, just long enough to use the bathroom and slide into a change of clothes from their knapsacks. They left the house as two women drove up and started unloading trays of food onto the front porch. One of the women said, "Good afternoon," and the three of them mumbled something in reply, but weren't very coherent. Jeannie was wolfing down a melting chocolate bar, Aggie had her mouth stuffed with chips from a bag, and Helen was munching an apple.

They are hurrying now, trotting right along in the hot sun toward the church spire, two blocks from the house. They bunch together as they get closer to the church's cavernous front door, open, ready, Aggie thinks, to swallow them whole. Inside it is cool and echoey. It takes a moment for their eyes to adjust to the half-light severed into red and shades of blue by stained glass.

They're a little late, yet only a handful of people are here, clustered near the front. They slip as quietly as they can into a pew near the back, but Aggie trips over some sort of footstool attached to the back of the seat in front and brings it clattering down. A little wave of excitement is happening. A woman in the front row, wearing a hat the size of a beach umbrella, turns to stare at their grand entrance. Aggie feels overwhelmed by the doleful organ music coming from she doesn't know where – heaven, maybe. Or else from the big pipes at the front of the church.

Now others are turning. Oh-boy, Aggie thinks, they've never seen anything like us, especially me with my bald little head. She's wearing her crushed velvet jacket that flares just below the waist. Mary Poppinsish, she has to admit, but it was cheap – even for a junk store – and covers most of her angel T-shirt with its permanent ketchup stain. And she has on her swishy-legged pants that are cool, except they're too short and make her look gangly. Face it, she thinks, I am gangly. Helen said she and Jeannie looked like the dregs of the earth.

Aggie eyes Jeannie and thinks she looks pretty good, although maybe a tad slutty, in a short bum-hugger of a skirt and a skimpy top that shows her belly-button ring. Helen, in her black sweater and draggy black skirt, fits right in with the other funeral folk, but then she always wears black. Helen slides sideways to leave a gap between her and her sisters.

The hat-woman is still getting an eyeful, and now the man beside her scowls at the girls. People are tapping each other on the shoulder and cranking their heads around to get a good look. The whole place is buzzing with whispers. *Look!* Aggie thinks they're saying. *It's the wicked grand-daughters! They're possessed! Quick, run!* The girls are getting the flared nostrils and haughty eyeball from all directions. Helen was right. They do look like the dregs.

But, actually, I don't think we care that much, Aggie reminds herself, because we have just become very, very rich. And they have not.

The church part is over. Outside, there is a small commo-tion about cars. An elderly man says he'll drive the girls. For a frightening second Aggie thinks he means her and her sisters, but it's the hat-lady he's talking about and a possi-ble bag lady beside her. The undertaker wants her and Helen and Jeannie to get into the back of a big black funeral car to drive to the cemetery. Jeannie starts to say, "No way," but Helen mutters, "Keep quiet and do what you're told."

They drive along one or two quiet streets. Cars pull over and stop while the funeral procession goes by. A couple of people walking along the sidewalk stop and stand still, and a man takes off his baseball cap. The car hits the main street going out of town, but here, no one takes much notice of them. People are still smiling and eating ice cream and jaywalking. It's like being in two different towns.

The line of cars has filed through the gates of the cemetery and disgorged the mourners. Aggie stands back beside Helen and Jeannie on the fringe because they don't feel they rightly belong. We do, though, Aggie tells herself. A few people came up to them going out of the church and said, "Sorry about your grandfather." The minister told them he was glad that they had been welcomed back into the bosom of the family. News to Aggie.

A puff of wind lifts the minister's scanty hair as he drones on about how all is changed in the twinkling of an eye, and about from dust we come and to dust we must return. A few people are honking into handkerchiefs.

Watching her grandfather's coffin being lowered into the ground, Aggie remembers a letter they found that her father had written to his father but never mailed. Too late, she thinks, too late, now. A man she never knew but who, in a way, was partly responsible for their being in the world at all is inside that polished box, mechanically inching its way underground.

Her own father had wanted to be cremated. He would never have mentioned it if he hadn't known he was going to die, but he knew how sick he was. He knew he wasn't going to get better. He said, "Might as well get a taste of the flames right off because I'll be going straight to hell." He was a gambler and a thief for a large part of his adult life, that's why. But he straightened out before he died, so that must count for something.

It's hard for Aggie to see and hear what's going on standing back there, although she's tall. When she was a little kid, Helen used to drag her everywhere and show her off to her friends and treat her like a living doll. But then she started growing and never stopped. Now she's fourteen and looks like she's on stilts, and Helen treats her like the family idiot.

Aggie looks around at all the shiny marble tombstones – pink, gray, black – and some ancient thin slabs – dull white, blackened in places by the weather. *Holy!* She just saw her name on one. What an eerie feeling, she thinks, like witnessing your own death. She crouches down to look. AGATHA JANE QUADE, DEPARTED THIS WORLD AUGUST 16, 1901. Today is August 16! Crap! she thinks, I'm gonna die!

She tells herself to calm down, that it was only somebody else with the same name. She can hardly breathe, though. Imagine if this was a sci-fi flick and she really became that person and . . . Jeannie is tugging on the collar of her jacket to get her to stand up. *Oh, great.* She ripped it a little bit and now the collar's dangling over Aggie's shoulder. *This jacket is an antique. Jeannie should have more respect.*

The minister is saying they are all invited back to the family home for refreshments.

In the house, glancing around at the people who have come back, it looks to Aggie as if there are more people here than there were at the funeral. No kids. Oh, wait, she sees one. Some strangled-looking guy in a shirt and tie, with a headful of corkscrew curls. My-my! she thinks.

People are snooping around as if they haven't been in the place for years. Over their shoulders they eye Aggie's shaved head, Jeannie's belly button, and Helen's scary little black-on-black ensemble. Aggie has a feeling they'd like to come over and say something, but don't know whether those Quade girls would sink their teeth into them or not. A wide doorway leads from the fancy living room into the dining room, where she can see a polished table loaded with cups and saucers and glasses of wine and plates of little cut-up sandwiches.

The rooms are huge. You could get their whole apartment right into these two rooms. Plus the deli. They live over a deli in Sudbury, owned and operated by a friend of their dad's – Mrs. Muntz. Their dad had worked in it for three years before he got sick. When he died they inherited his job in the deli, and also Mrs. Muntz. They're always inheriting things, it seems.

Helen says they should mingle, but Aggie's just standing there thinking how bizarre this is. She doesn't know how poor dirt-poor is, but she thinks they're it. And they're orphans, or the next best thing. And here they are, standing among a roomful of alien beings, on a planet they've never even heard of, but where money is so plentiful they must have forests of it. They don't know how much they've inherited, but Aggie's thinking millions. One million,

Helen figures. "It would be enough," she says, "that we could all have our heart's desire."

Aggie watches Jeannie belly up to the end of the table where the wine is. They're all staring at her. People always do because, no two ways about it, at seventeen Jeannie's really beautiful. Good figure. Bleach-blonde hair, and plenty of it. Aggie would like to try for a sandwich. She's starved and has been most of her life. She wonders who's running this show as the home owner is somewhat deceased. I suppose we are, she thinks.

Helen is talking to a man with a face like a bulldog. Oh, no, they're coming over! Aggie thinks. Helen is glaring at her with that look she gets that means *be polite or I'll rip your heart out.*

"Ward Gorman," the man says, "your grandfather's lawyer." He has his hand stuck out for Aggie to shake.

Yikes! A bone-cruncher.

He grins at her with his snarly little bulldog teeth. "And you are?"

"Huh?"

"This is my youngest sister, Agatha." Helen is being all grown-up-sounding. Of course, at her age, why not? Jeannie sashays over clutching a wine glass, belly button all aglitter. Lots of handshaking going on. Gorman is going to introduce them to everyone, he says.

He clears his throat, and everyone stops talking. Some of these people, it turns out, are related to Aggie and her sisters; others are friends and neighbors of the deceased. A man nudges Aggie's shoulder. "Haven't clapped eyes on the old feller must be goin' on twenty years," he whispers, an "old feller" himself.

"He didn't go out very often," Mr. Gorman, the lawyer, tells everyone. It seems their grandfather, Bertrand Quade, became something of a hermit after his son took to a life of crime. Gorman doesn't come right out and say that, but Aggie knows what he means. She notices Helen looks uncomfortably pink.

Now he's talking about what a wonderful person Bertrand Quade was to remember his three granddaughters in his will, and even though his son, their father, left the family home many years ago, the old man was able to die in the peaceful certainty that he was doing the right thing by his son's children.

Left the family home? Try kicked out.

The woman with the huge hat, it turns out, is their great-aunt Margery Upton, their grandfather's sister. She and her husband are leaving, and so others want to leave, too. She says to Helen, "Now you be sure to call us if you need anything while you're here. We're in Kingston, less than an hour away by car if you're needing to shop for anything – something decent in the way of clothes, perhaps." She is looking at the girls' funeral attire with her upper lip pulled down and her nostrils ready to snap shut in case they turn out to be smelly besides being badly dressed. She says, "We have some very nice clothing stores for young women in Kingston."

Helen gives her a really phony smile and thanks her so much. How does she know how to do that? Aggie wonders.

Great-Aunt Margery leans in close to them and, in a loud warning whisper, says, "In Kingston they're very severe with shoplifters." She has bad breath. Great-Aunt Margery's husband worries a loose button on the sleeve of his suit jacket.

Helen looks wounded. Jeannie narrows her eyes into poisoned darts. Aggie, feeling like a smoke-belching volcano, stretches to her full height. "Listen," Aggie begins, hands on her hips. She steps up to the woman. "If you think, just because our dad had a criminal record, that we're all –" She stops because Helen sticks the point of her elbow deeply into Aggie's chest wall. Their father made news headlines, too, but so far, Helen hasn't found a place for those clippings in her scrapbook.

Now the woman's sister joins them, toting a canvas bag that advises people to recycle. Great-Aunt Lily, she calls herself. She pats the corner of her eye with a handkerchief, making her glasses bob up and down. Aggie noticed her earlier, wandering from room to room inspecting things. She even opened a drawer in a table in the front hall. Nervy, Aggie thought, already feeling possessive about the inheritance.

This woman isn't as old as Margery, Aggie guesses, but getting up there. Sturdy, she looks, like a tree stump. Her hat is the floppy canvas kind, with a string dangling down that she could tie under her chin if there were another string. She studies each of the girls in turn and frowns. "Can't say I see any resemblance to our Cam."

"Come along, Lily," her sister says.

"How do we know they're not imposters?"

"Now, don't start in, Lily." Margery takes her sister's elbow none too gently and turns her toward the front hall.

"Well, how *do* we know?" She slips from her sister's grasp. "Couldn't they have read about the funeral in the paper?" Lily looks intently up at Aggie, her head on one side. Aggie stares back, struck dumb by the woman's scrutiny. Lily says, "It is a well-known fact that imposters blink at a rate of fifty-two times a minute." She continues to stare at Aggie, and Aggie blinks.

"So," Lily sighs.

Margery tries again to manhandle Lily past a knot of people, but she's not cooperating.

"I've said this before and I'll say it again," Lily says. "A father who closes the door on his only son is a scoundrel! Our brother was the real criminal in this family." She shakes her head sadly at the girls and at the sea of artifacts and ornaments surrounding them. "We amass things in this family. Possessions are important to us. We hoard them."

Margery is behind her now, hands on both her shoulders, urging her along. "Never mind, Lily," Margery says, loud enough for the girls to hear. "You might just as well save your breath. What would they care about treasures collected over several lifetimes? I expect they'll make off with most of this and just sell it. And that will be the end of it."

Helen looks sick, as if she's been caught stealing everything and probably murdering their grandfather, too. "No, look," she calls after them, "take anything you like because —" Jeannie gives her a look that clearly says *don't be an idiot because who knows what we've fallen heir to?* But Helen is too upset to care.

Margery holds up a hand in protest. "No, no, don't trouble yourself," she says with the air of a martyr, and out they go with the elderly husband padding along behind.

Lily breaks free again and says loudly in their direction, "Objects, we treasure. People, we fling away. I don't expect you can understand that. Nor can I." Before they can react, Lily is gone, hustled out by her sister.

The girls glance around at the wealth of treasures they've probably inherited – rosy crystal vases, beaded silver bowls, carved figures, the type of thing their father had got caught with – except, at the time, he had been putting it back. That's the ridiculous part; he was a thief who had developed a conscience. He suddenly realized it wasn't fair to steal art objects that people found beautiful.

The girls watch people leave, and some even say goodbye to them. The shirt-and-tie teenager is leaving now with his parents, Aggie notices. Wait, they've stopped at the door. They're having a little conference and glancing sideways at the Quade girls. They're going to risk a handshake. Wow, Aggie feels honored. Someone recognizes them as fellow humans. The dad mumbles something and introduces the wife, Linda Quade, and the son, Cameron Quade. Aggie frowns. She'd like to ask how dare this pimply-faced, curly-haired youth steal her father's name. But she doesn't. Instead she blurts, "But that was our dad's name!"

"Your father and I were first cousins," the dad says. "We were buddies when we were kids. . . ." He pauses. Aggie knows why. He probably means they were buddies before Cameron Quade the First turned into a thief. He says, "We always said we'd name our first son after each other. Mind you, your father didn't get a chance, having all girls. My name is Bert, by the way, Bertrand, actually."

The same name as their grandfather. Jeannie says, "Must have been confusing at family gatherings with all those repeat names."

He says, "We haven't had a family gathering for years, except for funerals, it seems."

Aggie notices Cameron Quade, the gangly youth, eye-balling her in a brooding kind of way from beneath his curly locks. He's tall and skinny like Aggie. She decides it must run in the family. Now he's slouching, trying to make his head disappear into his shoulders. Now he's inching toward the door, willing his parents to leave through the compelling power of his eyeballs. It works. They're gone.

The funeral guests have polished off most of the tea and wine and all of the sandwiches, as well as three plates of little cakes, and now they all want to get along home. Some of them smile at the girls as if they are normal people; some look down at the floor as if the girls are an embarrassment; some say good-bye as if they mean *that's the last you'll ever see of us!* The two women who brought the refreshments clear everything away, and carry crates of dishes and glasses out to their car. "Bye now," they call.

And now it's just Jeannie and Helen and Aggie, stuck with each other in a place that looks more like an antique shop than anybody's home. They scarcely look at each other. Helen stares out the front windows at the street, wondering how long it will take them to sell the place. Jeannie picks up a silver bowl and looks at the bottom, knowing you can tell somehow if it's solid silver, or not.

Aggie wanders from room to room thinking about her father's childhood, wondering if he had had a favorite room, wondering what he had missed most after he'd left, after his luck ran out.

It's not that late, but all three have huddled into one big bed in an enormous bedroom upstairs. Jeannie and Aggie still think the place is haunted. Helen is above that kind of speculation. They poked around in scary cupboards until they found some clean folded sheets to make up the bed. Helen is propped up against the pillows – even though she thinks they smell like decayed hair grease – pretending to be asleep. Jeannie is sprawled on her stomach, taking up most of the space. Aggie is wrapped in a blanket, curled up at the foot of the bed. The light is off but she can't fall asleep. Her stomach is rumbling.

Jeannie mutters, "Keep it down, will you?" and kicks her.

"Ow!" Aggie kicks her back.

"Ow!"

"I'm dying of starvation," announces Aggie.

"Well, do it silently." Helen's hollow voice.

Aggie wishes she'd scarfed more of those sandwiches, or stowed a plate of them away somewhere. Even though they weren't very good. Most people don't have a knack with sandwiches. She does. It comes from working in the deli after school. You have to judge the right amount of stuff to put in. You have to have enough salt and pepper, but not too much. You have to make 'em thick, but not sloppy.

Mainly you need good bread. Good bread is the secret.
They learned that from Mrs. Muntz.

They've been living with Mrs. Muntz over the deli now for
three years and yet they've never got beyond calling her
Mrs. Muntz. They just wouldn't. Her name is Gertie.
That's what her close women friends call her. Not the
Quade girls, though. She's always been very strict with
them and goes around banging pots down on counters and
closing cupboard doors with a bang just to make sure they
don't take advantage of the kindness she showed them by
taking them in after their father died. Some days she makes
Aggie feel like a nervous wreck. Most days.

Helen manages to tune her out, which is easy enough
because Helen's hardly ever around. When her full-time
shift in the deli finishes, she escapes to the library to a series
of free lectures, or to the Y, where she learns how to weave
and make mosaics. And when Jeannie's not in school or the
deli, she's with one of her many short-term boyfriends.
Their dad's death set them adrift, sent them each floating in
a different but lonely direction.

Aggie would like to get a movie going in her head until she
falls asleep, but she's got other things to think about. Like,
what happens next? Helen can't wait to get to the lawyer's
office tomorrow to get their money, put a for-sale sign on
this house, and go away somewhere to university. She
wants to get out of the deli business. Jeannie says she wants
to be a movie star. Aggie thinks she's kidding, but Helen

wouldn't put it past her. Aggie hopes they're both kidding because what about her? If they both go off somewhere, what will happen to Aggie? Not that they haven't got a perfect right to go off, with all the money they are all going to inherit, but . . . if only their mother would come home. She's not sure, now, whether that was Mom in the houseboat. It could have been. Aggie hasn't seen her since she was eight.

The place is alive with noises. There's a tap dripping somewhere, and there are thumps every once in a while. The wind is rising outside. Aggie can hear it in the chimney and felt it on the staircase coming upstairs. There are multi staircases in this house, she discovered, branching off in different directions, depending on which part of the house you want to go to.

Before they went to bed, they explored all the downstairs rooms. They found a laundry room behind the kitchen, complete with vintage washer and dryer, and another room full of dead plants. Next to the smaller of the two living rooms, they found a study or library, home to not only walls of books, but to a large desk – shiny even under a layer of dust – some comfortable chairs, and a leather couch. On the wall near the desk, they discovered a rack with about a dozen keys hanging from little brass pegs. They started to explore the rooms on the second floor, but stopped when they found a few closed doors. They said, "What if there's a rotting corpse in that room, or what if there's someone with a big ax behind that door waiting to hack us to pieces?" That's when they all piled into the same bed.

Makes it handier for the ax-murderer, though, Aggie muses.

Aggie knows what she's going to do with her share of the money, although she hasn't told anyone yet. If she told Helen, she'd say, "Waste of time and money." And Jeannie would say, "She'd have come back before this if she'd wanted to." When they get their money, Aggie's going to hire a detective to find their mother. That is her heart's desire.

What is that noise? She listens. An overhead thump! There's a whole other floor up there, Aggie thinks, inhabited. Could be the wind.

After their father died, when they were packing up their belongings to move in with Mrs. Muntz up over the deli, they went through his stuff and found a letter from his father dated a few months before Helen was born. It said something like: *You have tested me to the limit. You have embarrassed me with your unruly behavior. You have lied to me, stolen from me, spurned an education, all for the sake of a girl who is nothing but trouble. If you marry that girl, do not expect anyone in this family to lift a finger to help you. We do not reward irresponsible behavior. You have broken my heart.*

Their father married her anyway and was cut off without a penny and without another word from his father. If he'd had a mother, things might have been different, but she died when he was a little boy. Mrs. Muntz said, "Crazy in love! That was your papa. Your mama, she was like a drug to him. She had him in her power."

In another envelope, addressed to his father but never mailed, was a letter from their dad. It was very disjointed and very emotional. One part of it, though, stands out in Aggie's mind. He said: *You live in a closed box with your eyes shut. You never heard my questions because you were too busy locking doors. You never saw my tears of rage. I'm sorry for what I did to you, but I figured you were already dead.*

When they read those two letters, they started to cry all over again. Maybe they needed their dad to be more of a hero, or maybe they just wanted a happier ending. They'd already been crying for three days and should have been drained of tears by then, but they weren't.

They loved him even though he'd been in jail. Their mother still lived with them at the time. After he got out, she used to yell at him and slam doors. Helen says she wasn't angry with him for stealing, she was angry that he got caught.

"It all went to her," Mrs. Muntz told them. "Never a thought for himself or you kiddies." When they were young kids, they didn't know any of this. They thought he had a job at the racetrack because that's where he went every day.

Aggie remembers the day he got out of jail. He said, "Never again!" That's when he quit going to the track and started working in the deli for Mrs. Muntz, and that's when their mom threw a screaming fit and hit him with a shoe. She left not long after.

Aggie never really thinks of him as a crook or a gambler. She prefers to remember him reading books he got from the library. She remembers he always paid his fines if the books were overdue. But she also remembers that every so often he and their mother would go away, leaving Helen in charge, even though she was just a kid – eleven, twelve, thirteen. And then they'd come back and their mom would be happy for a while and their dad would start reading again. And then they'd get a new TV or something. Once they got a car.

When she can't get to sleep at night, she makes up a movie about their dad and his family and their mom and how things could have been different. His father should never have kicked him out, for starters. And their mother should have loved them enough to stay with them. She didn't even come back for his funeral. Jeannie said, "Good thing she didn't," and Helen said, "How could she? She didn't know about it."

Helen put the letters into the scrapbook she's making about their family. Then they went on packing to go live with Mrs. Muntz. They didn't have much. You can't fit much into a three-room basement apartment.

The nice thing about living over a deli, Aggie believes, is the overview. She's familiar with every business on the street – what time they open, who works where, each with his own private little life going on. From a basement window, you feel locked in. She remembers they had bars on the windows of their little underground mole-hole so no one would break in and murder them in their sleep. In front of the windows, their father planted hollyhocks one spring to cheer them up a little. He said, "A place that has holly-hocks can't be all bad." But they weren't city flowers; they didn't survive. Between the bars on their window, all you could see were feet going by and legs going who knows where, but in a hurry to get there. "When you're in jail," their dad said, "you feel useless. You're worse than nothing. A drone occupying a cell." In their little basement lock-up, they knew they could at least open the front door and climb the concrete steps up to the street and join the feet and legs hurrying by.

Aggie feels as if she's falling asleep. She feels as if she's in a movie about somebody falling asleep. . . .

CHAPTER THREE

It's morning and they're at the lawyer's office surrounded by wood paneling and floor-to-ceiling bookshelves. Whole forests were destroyed to create this scene. The books are all the same – brown, trimmed with green and red.

Aggie is stuffed from breakfast, which they got at a restaurant they found down the street from the homestead. Two eggs any style, mounds of bacon, half a pound of butter spread all over the toast, three kinds of jam, juice, coffee. They ate to the point of severe bloat because today's the day they get rich.

The few villagers they met on the street on their way to the restaurant frowned at them and kind of cringed away. Helen muttered, "I hate the way they do that, like we're the scumbag element."

"Like we're going to lash out and attack them," Aggie said.

"Or we're going to be attacked by them. Look how we all bunch up together," Jeannie said.

Jeannie put on a little show when they first sat down inside the restaurant, flinging her arms back with her shirt half unbuttoned and her legs any old way, daring the locals to stare up her skirt. An old guy gumming toast got an eyeful. Everybody else looked away.

The girls noticed a deck with tables behind the restaurant, and so they moved out there for their breakfast. It was a little breezy, but they had it all to themselves with a view of the lake. Aggie chose to sit with her back to it. Under its sparkling surface, soggy arms longed to pull her down to the bottom and hold her there.

There were sun umbrellas over each table, and hanging from the umbrella shafts were jars with yellow liquid in them, half filled with dead bees. "We have a bee problem this summer," the waitress said.

"Tellin' me," Aggie replied. Bees hovered over the food, and Jeannie flipped her hands around trying to brush them away. Aggie picked up the empty toast plate and tried to whack one with it. The plate must have been made of concrete because it didn't break. Every time a bee came near Helen, she would freeze. "Don't do anything," she said, "and they won't hurt you." Some of them crawled into holes in the lids of the jars and couldn't get out.

There are only two extra chairs here in the lawyer's office, occupied at the moment by Helen and Jeannie. Aggie slouches against the windowsill behind them. They are waiting for Mr. Gorman. He comes in with his big bulldog chest puffed up over his belt. He crunches their hands one by one and then slides his tapered rear end behind his desk. "I have already met with your great-aunts," he says, looking up through woolly eyebrows. "They are aware of the contents of your grandfather's will." His mouth droops at the corners as he glances down again over the papers on his desk. He gets up and calls through an open door behind him, "Could you bring me those copies when they're ready, Mr. Hill?" To the girls he says, "My main office is actually in Kingston. I'm only here one day a week, but if you have any questions later on, Mr. Hill is here three days a week and would be happy to answer them for you."

In a moment a young man appears – Mr. Hill, his partner, Mr. Gorman says. He tries to introduce the girls, but he can't remember their names. Duncan Hill is the young lawyer's name, and he doesn't break their bones shaking hands. "Let me get you a chair," he says to Aggie. He smiles at each of them when he comes back in with the chair.

Duncan Hill, Aggie decides, is one hot dude, for a lawyer. Jeannie perks right up and gets a sparkly-eyed look going. Helen gets completely flustered and drops things out of her handbag. Aggie's happy to have been considered part of this family enough to have been given a chair. As the youngest, she tends to get shoved into the background, like dust balls or the family goldfish. Mr. Gorman is scowling at them, explaining the will.

They're all dressed a little better, today. Helen in black, of course (she'd make a good nun); Jeannie in a neon green skirt and wine-colored see-through top. Sounds terrible, but it really looks great, Aggie thinks. Aggie, herself, likes to wear things from other eras, which she gets in a store in Sudbury called Fred's Threads. Today's number dates from, well, she's not sure – say the 1940s – and is a faded dark blue dress, well wrinkled from being in her knapsack and long enough to almost cover her combat boots (still a little wet). It has a square collar trimmed with white and reminds her of a sailor suit. It makes her feel adventurous, as if she might yell out "land-ho" at any moment. Although, maybe not. From where she is sitting, she has a slim view of the lake between a house and a store. It's a deceptive silvery blue, flipped up into whitecaps, with a sailboat skimming along. She narrows her eyes at it and remembers the brownish green murk.

Aggie is now going to pay attention to what's going on here because her sisters are looking decidedly upset. "And so," Mr. Gorman says, "unusual as this may seem to you, your grandfather believed he was doing the best thing for all concerned. His only wish was to reunite the family, and to this end," he clears his throat, "you, uh, do not take full possession of the house and its contents until such time as his unmarried sister, Lily, is living under the same roof, that is to say, with all three of you, in her family home, where your father grew up – all of you together as, as a family."

Aggie's sisters gape at Mr. Gorman. "But –" Jeannie begins.

Mr. Gorman holds up a hand. He's not finished. "Provided this happens before freeze-up."

"Freeze-up?"

"Before the lake freezes. Your great-aunt Lily has lived for the past twenty-odd years in a cottage on an island, which your grandfather considered dangerous and unsuit-able for his sister – an aging woman, alone, and not always in full control of her mental faculties, in his opinion. Because she has never forgiven her brother for turning his back on his son, she would never listen to his entreaties to move back home. And so, in accordance with his final wishes, it so happens that you have four, possibly five months in which to be united with your great-aunt."

"And if this doesn't happen?" Helen asks.

"All of you, including your great-aunt, forfeit your interest in the house and everything will then be left to the nursing home where your grandfather lived in his declining years. Your great-aunts, as I say, have already been informed of this highly irregular bequest and are no less unhappy about it than you are. Your grandfather set up a trust fund to cover the upkeep of the house, pay the taxes, keep it heated, etcetera, but I'm afraid it isn't much. He had no idea how little money he actually had. Unless you are very careful with expenses, the fund will soon be depleted. Your great-aunt Lily fares a little better than you girls, having some investments in her name that will be enough to keep her in a retirement home, or some such thing, in her extreme old age. Margery, of course, is married and reasonably well-off."

Jeannie's face looks lethal. Helen's forehead is a ladder of lines. She asks, "How long is this arrangement supposed to last? Are we going to be stuck here the rest of our lives?"

Mr. Gorman taps the side of his head with a pencil, reads to the end of the page, and flips it over. "Your grandfather doesn't specify a time limit. I'm sure he believed that if a bond formed between his granddaughters and his sister, you would work things out together in a fair and equitable way. And of course there is a small allowance for your personal needs in a bank account that you may draw on in the event that you have no other source of income." He looks at each of them, expecting more questions, but is met with only stunned silence.

Mr. Hill is ushering them out now, and Aggie doesn't see any bags of money being handed over. She would like to ask about it, but doesn't want the lawyer to think she's too stupid to understand about wills. She should have been paying closer attention. People are always telling her she has to pay attention. She pleads with her sisters to explain everything all the way back to the house they apparently don't exactly own, but her sisters are mad as hornets.

"It's stupid," Helen says. "It's silly and senseless."

Jeannie says, "He was senile and selfish."

"But what did we get?" Aggie wants to know.

"What our grandfather in his wisdom left us," Helen at last answers, "besides the house, is a trust fund solely to take care of its upkeep. He bequeathed to his three penniless granddaughters a great big, dusty, old, rickety, monstrosity of a brick house – possibly haunted – and an elderly great-aunt – probably demented."

Aggie thinks about this. "You can't force people on each other just because they're related."

Jeannie says, "Who needs a run-down old barn of a place with a crap-load of junk in it, anyway? Let's just leave."

"I don't think it's junk," Aggie says.

Jeannie doesn't reply. Yesterday she didn't think it was junk, either.

They're back at the house. Helen is on the phone talking long distance to Mrs. Muntz, while Jeannie and Aggie strain their ears to make out the conversation. "As it turns out," Helen informs her, "we didn't get any money at all, not a dime! There wasn't any, or at least not much."

Aggie says quietly to Jeannie, "I thought our grandfather was rich."

"He may have lived like a millionaire, but he sure didn't die like one. Shut up for a minute!"

"This is bizarre," Aggie says. "Isn't there a movie about something like this?"

"If not, I'm sure it's on your list of ones to make. Shut up, okay?"

"So, what are we going to do?"

Jeannie's got her head inside a musty kitchen cupboard, looking for products that haven't gone beyond their best-before date. "Slash our wrists!" she screeches. "Will you shut up so we can hear what Helen is saying?"

"So what you're saying is, there's no room for us." Helen's forehead has twenty frown lines on it. "Well, of course I understand, Mrs. Muntz, but . . . I know she's your sister, but . . . I know . . . I know . . . I know. Well, thanks anyway, Mrs. Muntz. I'll let you know. Bye."

"What!" Jeannie and Aggie are on top of Helen before she can even hang up.

"How do you like that?" Helen says. "She's handed over our bedrooms to her sister's family because they've been evicted and don't have any place to go."

"How can she do that?" Jeannie takes jars of moldy jam and crusty ketchup and mustard out of the cupboard and slams them down on the kitchen table. "What right has she got to do that? I mean we live there!"

"Not anymore," Helen says.

"There's not one edible thing in this whole friggin' house!" Jeannie yells. Which is beside the point, Aggie thinks.

"It's not like we were paying rent," Helen says.

"What about all our stuff?" Aggie asks.

"She put it in that little storeroom off the deli kitchen. We can sleep in there, she said, if we go back. She'll give us a mattress."

"Thanks a lot, lady!" Jeannie says. "We'd actually prefer the gutter."

"What about our jobs in the deli?" Aggie asks.

"She thinks we're rich. We don't need to work."

"But we're not! Didn't you tell her that?"

"Of course – not that she listened. She said she'll send us the back pay she owes us. Mrs. Muntz's sister and her family have already started working in the deli."

"So what are we going to do?"

Helen looks at Aggie and away with what Aggie calls her middle-aged-lady look. "Rob places, I guess, like Dad." This is not exactly funny, and nobody laughs.

It's later the same day, and they still haven't figured out what to do. They can't leave because they have no place to go. They can't stay because there's no way Lily will move in with them, especially if she thinks they're imposters. Anyway, why would they want to shack up with the lunatic fringe?

"We can stay for a few months, anyway," Aggie reminds them.

"The joke is," Helen says, "we're stuck halfway between what we can't do and what we don't want to do."

"I'm laughing myself sick," says Jeannie.

Aggie can't stand the way they're all staring silently in different directions. It's a sure sign they're having desperate thoughts that don't involve all of them sticking together. She says, "Let's say we go back to Sudbury and look for jobs in some of the places near the deli."

"And live where, exactly?" Helen doesn't even look at her.

"In the deli storeroom until –"

Jeannie yells, "I'm not living in no storeroom!"

"Any storeroom," Helen says.

"Okay," Aggie says to Helen, "you and I can live in the storeroom and Jeannie can live with her boyfriend and –"

"We broke up," Jeannie says.

They don't really find any solution to the problem. It turns out Helen won't live in the storeroom, either. She says it smells like armpits. Instead, it's first things first. Food.

They're walking up and down the aisles of Port Desire's one and only supermarket – mini-market, they should call it. The more Aggie thinks about how little food they can afford, the hungrier she gets. Helen says they're not to touch the bank account Mr. Gorman mentioned unless they're really desperate.

"Why the hell not?" Jeannie says. "It's ours, isn't it?"

"Not if we're not staying."

Jeannie snorts. "Who cares? We can let on we're staying, can't we?"

"No, we can't! Everyone expects us to be dishonest, so that's the last thing we're going to be."

Jeannie shakes her head in disbelief that Helen can be so ridiculously scrupulous, and puts a large bottle of Coke in the cart. Helen takes it out, so now Jeannie has her own cart. "You're not pushing me around," Jeannie tells Helen. "I have my own little supply of cash, and I'll use it any way I want."

"Fine, just don't plan on sharing our food when you run out of Coke and chips."

"Why would I? I'm leaving."

"Good. The sooner the better."

Aggie drags along behind Helen, feeling sharp fingers of panic squeeze the back of her neck. If Jeannie can go, so can Helen. She thinks about the will. Didn't it state that Lily had to move in with all three of them, so they would all live together as one big happy family? She says as much to Helen. "Don't worry about it," Helen says. "You don't really think that's going to happen, do you?" Aggie doesn't answer because, in the private viewing room of her mind, she has already composed a quiet little domestic scene involving her sisters and Great-Aunt Lily all sitting around the kitchen table eating something hot and delicious when, suddenly, the doorbell rings and when Aggie opens the door, who should be standing there but her mother, smiling, arms wide-open.

She catches up to Helen again near the end of the aisle.

Helen looks at the prices of everything and puts almost all of it back on the shelf. So far they have spaghetti, Kraft Dinner, chicken noodle soup, and cheap sliced bread. They've been spoiled, Aggie knows, by the deli and by Mrs. Muntz's home cooking because everything in their cart looks either boring or stomach-turning. She'd love to see what Jeannie bought, but she's finished her shopping and has left the store.

They move into the checkout line and well, well, Aggie notes, look who's bagging groceries! The teenage funeral-boy – their cousin – and he's talking to Helen. The cash register lady scowls at Aggie and says, "Must be nice to be an heiress."

"What?" she says.

"Gettin' all that money your granddad musta had."

"All we got was the house," Aggie mutters. "And we're only living in it till we starve to death."

"Aggie!" Helen looks embarrassed.

"What?"

The bag-boy, their cousin, is staring at them with his big sad eyes. "So, are you staying for a while over at Uncle Bert's? . . . I mean your. . . ."

"For a little while," Helen says at the same time as Aggie says, "No place else to go." Helen gives her that look again. Meanwhile, Cameron Quade the Second looks as if he feels sorry for them.

They carry four bags each of mostly noodles and cornflakes along Lake Street to their very own rich-people's mansion. Aggie thinks Helen seems peeved. "What's up with you?" she asks her.

43

"Why do you have to keep telling people our business? Haven't you any sense of privacy? This is *our* problem. We don't need people butting in where they're not wanted."

"They just asked. I didn't see anybody butting in."

"I have a feeling this town knows everything about us."

"Maybe we're like movie stars," Aggie says. "I mean we *are* a little different from the average villager."

"Maybe we're the laughingstock."

Aggie shrugs. (Hard to shrug with four bags of groceries, but she does.) The way Aggie sees it, she bets they're just about as entertaining as a soap opera in this place. Helen is so private she gets dressed in the clothes closet with the door shut. And no light. Any secret would be safe with Helen. She'd take it to the grave with her.

As for herself, Aggie likes gossip, the juicier the better. When she can't sleep at night, she turns people's life-stories into movies and that puts her to sleep. Something wrong there, she tells herself. You watch my little movies, you end up in a coma. She thinks it's only fair, though, to let other people make up their own movies about her and her sisters.

The tourists and cottagers are out in full force today. They pretty much ignore the Quade sisters. Some of them glance at Aggie's prickly head, but some of them are a trifle skinheadish, too, so who cares? She's planning to let her hair grow, not as long as Jeannie's, which is – woo! – not only long, but big. They can hear the phone ringing as they come up the veranda steps.

Well, now, Aggie thinks, this is neighborly. They are walking along the street, going to their cousins the Quades' for dinner. Bag-boy actually phoned his mommy and told her their desperate poor-little-rich-girls' story because that's who was phoning when they got home with their puny rations. Linda Quade told Helen how to get to their place, which isn't very far from their mansion. Of course, nothing is.

As they get close to their cousins' house they hear, coming from some window at the back, the screeching of a tormented violin going over a random selection of non-musical notes. They knock on the front door, and the violin immediately stops.

The door is opened by Cameron Quade. What, Aggie wonders, am I supposed to call him? She would like to avoid calling him anything in case it feels like she's talking to her father. Nobody else is having this problem, she notices. She could say, "Hey Quade!" But that's their own name. She's never known any other Quades. She's always felt unique. Now they are overrun with them.

Linda, the mother, comes on scene now and ushers them into the living room as the boy makes an exit. There's a strong smell of paint in the house, which Linda apologizes for. Seems she's been painting a minuscule sunroom that opens off the tiny living room. The place is like a doll's house.

There's a little Quade sister in this family, named Susie. She's sitting on a kind of couch in their living room, sewing something with a thick needle and a long piece of thread. Aggie can't make out what it is – a rag, maybe. "Sit down," Linda tells them, "I just have to turn off the heat under the vegetables." So they sit.

"What are you sewing?" Helen asks the kid.

"Can't you tell?" Susie asks crossly. Aggie's sitting right beside her on this hard little couch thing, and she can't tell. Susie stares at her hair-free head and her Mary P. jacket, with the torn collar thanks to Jeannie, and holds the grubby little rag in front of Aggie's face.

"A patch for your jeans?" Aggie guesses.

"You're so stupid!" Susie says. With her elbow, she points to a doll on the couch between them. "It's for her, dummy!"

Her mother calls her from the kitchen, asking if she has washed her hands for dinner. "Yes!" Susie calls back. She notices Aggie looking at her hands, which are not what you'd automatically call clean.

"Ouch! Cripes!" Aggie jumps away from her. "What the . . ." Susie has stuck her needle into Aggie's arm. Now Aggie's looking at the kid as if she's maybe going to yank off her head, but the mother comes into the living room, so she doesn't. Linda asks them all to come into the dining room. Aggie is rubbing her arm, which she's surprised isn't leaving a trail of blood along the beige carpet. She'll probably die of blood poisoning.

"Susie, those hands aren't clean," the mom says. "Go now and wash them."

Susie says, "I already did," and sits down. The girls stand around, not sure whether they should sit down or what.

"Look at them!" her mother says. "They need a good scrub."

"They don't!"

"Susie, please go and do it."

"I won't!" she screams. "Stop picking on me!"

"Now, now," her mother says looking at the girls, a little embarrassed. "What will our guests think?"

"They'll think you're always picking on me. Make them wash *their* hands and see how they like it."

The dad, Bert, comes into the dining room and says, mildly, "Tut-tut, Susie, this is disappointing behavior."

Linda says very patiently and quietly, "I expect they washed before they left home."

Aggie slides her hands into her pockets because – guess what? – they aren't all that sparkling. The kid keeps it up and keeps it up, and Aggie notices that Jeannie's looking a little embarrassed, too, and has her hands in her pockets. Helen finally says, "Come on, Susie, let's all wash our hands. You can show us where to go." Typical Helen-tactic. The Quades' house is small, Aggie can't help noticing (compared to their château), and is filled with really spindly antique-looking furniture, grossly uncomfortable, and books everywhere. They see quite a bit of it on their way to the bathroom.

They all sit down to dinner with hands you could eat a meal off, as far as Aggie's concerned, and they're tucking into some pretty tasty home cookin'. Maybe Helen could come over here sometime, she thinks, and get a few pointers. And they're getting all kinds of information about the family. Turns out the dad is a professor and commutes to Kingston, to the university, when he has to. Usually he doesn't have to because he's on some sort of holiday called sabbatical. The mom teaches music.

There is even a loaf of homemade bread, which is as good as or better than Mrs. Muntz's. Aggie feels like praising it to the skies because she would love another piece – her third. "That's the most delicious bread I've ever tasted," she says. Helen pierces her with her pointy little eyeballs.

"Aunt Lily makes it," Linda says. "She often brings some to us when she bakes. Would you like me to cut you another slice?" Aggie and her sisters exchange a glance. Their inheritance has just become a little more appealing.

"Speaking of Lily," Linda continues, "she told us about the unusual stipulations in Uncle Bertrand's will. But, you know, the more I think about it, the more it makes sense. It could be a great chance for all of you. We worry about Lily; the whole town worries about her, especially in winter when she's stuck out there in her cottage until the lake freezes solidly enough to be safe to walk on. And it's just as bad in early spring, worrying about whether she'll venture out on foot and go through the ice. And, of course, her pills. She's so much less confused when she takes her pills on a regular basis. She needs someone to remind her. And you girls would have a lovely home and a loving family."

Aggie hears Jeannie gag. "Are you all right?" Linda asks her. Jeannie makes a little cough with her napkin over her mouth and nods.

Helen says, "We haven't made any definite plans."

The son, Quade, scarcely lifts his eyes from his plate. Once or twice he takes a gander at Aggie sitting across from him, but she doesn't know whether he can actually see her through the curly locks of hair that slide across his face into his eyes. She thinks he's a very glum, glowering sort of guy, not the type to get his mom to ask strangers for dinner. The dad offers to lend them some money, which

Helen, like a jerk, declines. "I think we'll be fine," she says.

Aggie's pondering the fact that they don't seem to be able to get the right attitude toward money in their family. In the old days, when they didn't have any, their mom and dad would go out and steal stuff and sell it, and now, when they still don't have any and someone offers to lend them some, her sister says, "Oh, heavens no, thanks all the same."

"Sorry?" Aggie says. Linda has been talking to her.

"School," Linda says. While Aggie was thinking about money and their lack of it, they were all talking about how she and Jeannie should enroll in the local high school until they settle their affairs and make some decisions.

"I won't be here long enough to make it worthwhile," Jeannie says. "I'm getting a job and as soon as I save enough, it's good-bye Canada, hello U.S. of A."

Helen is looking aghast (one of her favorite looks) mainly, Aggie thinks, for the benefit of the Quades. It's not as if this is the first time Jeannie has mentioned taking off.

"Oh, dear, an education is so important, though," Linda says.

"Yeah-yeah," Jeannie mutters under her breath. Out loud she says, "Just kidding. Don't worry, I fully intend to get an education." She tilts her head and smiles sweetly, a budding actress for sure. "I'm only taking a year off."

Everyone smiles, relieved, except Helen, who knows Jeannie inside and out; and Aggie, because Jeannie, in spite of being an A-student (believe it or not), is a rebel. If she took it into her head to join a motorcycle gang, it would not surprise Aggie. Up until now, Aggie hasn't worried much about Jeannie's movie-star chatter because up until now it's been more like a fantasy. It's like kids saying, "I'm gonna be a rock star, yeah!" And you just know they're headed for a course in dental hygiene. But she's starting to sound as if she has a plan.

Once again Aggie has missed the conversation. It seems that the Quades and Helen are planning to get her started in grade nine until her sisters decide what to do and where to go. As usual, no one consulted Aggie. Cousin Bert (the dad) says, "Cameron, you should take Agatha and show her the high school." Cameron looks as if he'd sooner face a pit of vipers.

Nevertheless, they set out after dessert (thick, juicy, spicy apple pie – *yum*): Aggie, the youth with his wrists dangling down to his knees, and Susie the Impaler. "How far is the school?" Aggie asks, just for something to say.

"Way the other side of town," Susie says.

"It is *not*," says her brother.

They keep trudging along. Aggie still doesn't know how far away the school is, but guesses she'll find out. "Two-point-five kilometers," Quade says, "door-to-door."

"Well," Aggie says.

"Expressed in miles, that would be . . . one-point-five-six-two-five miles."

Susie keeps running ahead and walking backwards so she can look back at them. "Or, in other words, twenty-five thousand meters."

Aggie cannot think of an appropriate reply.

"You've got a horrible name," Susie says. "Agatha! Wow!"

"Shut up, Suse," her brother says.

She's walking backwards, looking first at Agatha and then at her brother. "You two look sort of like twins."

"Suse! Go home."

"No, it's true. You're both tall and skinny, and you both sort of have the same eyes. Big. Like you can't figure anything out."

Can't figure anything out! Aggie rather thinks not. She has always thought her eyes were her most attractive feature – dark, mysterious, and full of passion. She doesn't know about Quade, but she would be happy to be scooped up by galactic aliens for scientific experimentation right about now. She sneaks a look at his eyes, what she can see of them under his curly mop. Yeah, they're dark, too, she notes. Wow! Twins separated at birth! There's a movie plot for you. One with hair, one without.

"That's the school," he says, after they turn a corner.

Aggie glances at it – two-storey, flat roof, wall of windows, asphalt parking lot.

"Holy," Aggie says, "ever different!"

Quade frowns as if she's serious.

CHAPTER FOUR

They've survived four days in the house and so far nobody's taken off. Each day they sleep in until almost noon, choke down a bowl of nourishing cornflakes, and then explore. "Did you know we have an entire miniature African village here, carved out of black wood?" Jeannie calls from a corner of the big living room. "It's on a little table. Kind of cute."

"*We* don't have it," Helen reminds her. "The estate has it. We're only here temporarily, remember?"

They've thrown out two garbage bags full of poisonous substances from the fridge and kitchen cupboards, and restocked – within limits. Jeannie has marked off a section of the fridge and freezer as her own territory, trespassers beware.

Helen has managed to get a job in the "bee" restaurant full-time until Labor Day, when all the tourists and cottage-owners go home. After that, "Who knows?" the owner said. "Maybe a couple of days a week."

Helen said she'd be happy to work on cash, she's had experience.

The owner said, "Yeah, I bet you have! Like your old man."

Helen got all huffy and asked him what he meant by that.

"Nothin'," he said. "You're waitin' on tables, that's all. You just keep your hands off the cash register. Understood?"

If Aggie had been Helen, she would have told him to stuff his job and walked out. But Helen says, "There is a logical solution to the problem we have of what to do and where to go, but until we figure it out, we have to eat. Ergo, the job at any cost."

That's Helen for you, Aggie thinks. Ergomaniac.

Jeannie's been asking around, but so far hasn't found a place that will hire her. "They give me this full frontal body scan as if I'm blind, while their faces scream *eek, young offender!* Then they smile and say, 'Sorry, not hiring.'" She and Aggie are sitting on the steps of the front veranda in the dappled shade offered by a kindly old maple whose roots have bumped up right through the sidewalk. They are watching tourists parade in the sweltering afternoon sun. Helen is at work.

Aggie says, "Don't worry, at least Helen has a job."

"That's not going to help me get out of this place."

"Out of this place? But what about Helen and me?"

"Helen is a free agent."

"Well, what about me?"

Jeannie doesn't look at Aggie. What to do about her is a situation both she and Helen have been avoiding. "Something will turn up," she says.

"I'm a mere child."

"Don't worry, Helen's your guardian. She has to look after you."

"What if she takes off, too?"

"She won't."

"But, what if?"

"What's-his-name, the lawyer, Gorman, will figure something out. Maybe Mrs. Muntz will take you back."

"No!" Aggie's heart swells and pounds like something doomed. She won't go back. She knows she can't survive in a rerun without the whole cast.

"Don't worry about it," Jeannie says. "I suppose there's always group homes or foster homes."

"What?"

"You know, they could place you in a home with a foster family until you're older."

"What if I hate it, and they're mean?"

"Then they'll move you to a different place. You might be lucky, though, and get a nice one right off."

"I don't want that. That would mean I'd have no fixed address. How would Mom ever find me?"

Jeannie gets up from the step. "Aggie, face the facts. She's not coming back. She's gone for good." She can't bear to look at Aggie's stricken face. She opens the door to go in. "Something will turn up. Don't worry," she says over her shoulder. The screen door slams behind her. Aggie's big brown eyes, forlorn as a stray dog's, haunt Jeannie all the way up to her room.

Outside, chipping paint off the veranda step with her thumbnail, Aggie says to herself, "Don't worry about it, don't play with matches, don't go near the water" – as if worry is something you have a choice over. She tries to stop thinking about what will happen to her, but worry hangs on to the back of her mind with sharp little fingernails. She tells herself that, after all, they are a family. It just makes sense that they stick together.

It's later in the afternoon, about five o'clock. Helen is still at work, and Jeannie is out somewhere, probably job-hunting. Aggie is inside now, looking around the room with all the books in it, and thinking about how comfy it is – dark but comfy. The walls are wood-paneled halfway up. From there to the ceiling, they're covered in wallpaper the texture of grass or straw, and may once even have been straw-colored. Now the wallpaper is dead-grass brown, except for a few lightish rectangles where, at one time, pictures must have hung.

Yesterday she and Helen were in here poking around, fingering the keys hanging from brass pegs, and wondering why there were so many. A lot of them were really old looking, some even rusted. "Maybe the old man had a key fetish," Helen said.

"Or maybe," Aggie said, "he was just crazy about keys."

Helen muttered, "Whatever," distractedly and pulled out a book from the shelf. They read for a while, both attracted to a selection of art books filled with pictures of famous paintings and sculptures. Helen said, "We should memorize the pictures and the artists so people will think we have culture."

"What people?" Aggie asked her.

Helen looked at her as if she were an underevolved mutant.

Aggie begins to shove aside the drapes nearly covering the windows to let more light into the study, and jumps back with a screech. Something has just moved on the other side of the glass; she isn't sure what – a person, maybe. Her heart is thumping, echoing inside the cave of her chest. It takes a moment to regain her nerve. She edges closer to the window and peeps between the drape and the glass, but only leafy bushes supporting giant white puffball flowers are to be seen, some broken. Beyond the bushes she sees only an expanse of unmowed grass, a board fence, a neighboring house.

Aggie speeds to the front door, swinging it wide in time to see Great-Aunt Lily in her canvas hat and a voluminous raincoat looking down at the veranda step on which she is about to place her foot. It is a moment before she looks up at Aggie. She stops short, startled.

Aggie asks, "Were you looking for something?" She believes it could have been Lily at the window.

Lily looks surprised by the question. "Nothing specific," she says, "although, one is always on the lookout. 'Seek and ye shall find.'" They are studying each other face-to-face, assessing each other's appearance. Lily's raincoat is buttoned incorrectly, Aggie notices, and there isn't a cloud in the sky. Lily thinks Aggie's clothes could stand a good wash. Aggie is now having doubts about Lily's Peeping Tom skills. Lily wonders if the child has had a bad case of lice, which would account for the shorn head.

Aggie doesn't know what she means by 'seek and ye shall find,' but says, "Would you like to come in?" She hadn't intended to invite her in; she meant to ask her why she had been peering through the window. Instead, though, this would be a good opportunity to discuss the idea of Lily moving in.

"I suppose we're to assume you are one of his so-called granddaughters?"

"Yes. I'm Agatha Jane Quade." Aggie tries to make her face friendly, but it's hard to do under Lily's glowering inspection.

"Very clever."

"It's true. Named after some dead person out in that graveyard on the edge of town."

"Some people are easily taken in. I am not."

Aggie holds the door back and spreads her palm toward the interior, invitingly.

Cautiously, Lily steps up onto the veranda and enters the house. Slowly, inspecting everything that takes her fancy, she makes her way to the kitchen and stands just inside it.

"Can I get you something?" Aggie asks, feeling as if she's watching a movie about some character whose great-aunt comes to call and who naturally asks her if she can get her something. She thinks, what am I going to get her – a slice of absorbent cotton bread? Crack open the last box of Kraft Dinner?

Lily says, "No, no, not really," in a thoughtful way, glancing around the kitchen, her glasses perched on the end of her nose, the front brim of her hat turned up. Hungrily, her eyes roam the cupboards with panes of glass in the doors that go right up to the high ceiling. Through them, you can see drinking glasses on shelves in different styles, and stacks of variously sized plates, as well as cups, saucers, eggcups, soup bowls, and mixing bowls.

The first time she saw the kitchen Aggie thought, you could serve up quite a feast here if you wanted. If you had any food.

Hanging on the walls are dusty copper pots, molds that look like fish and pineapples, and a framed picture of some oddly shaped fruit in a lopsided bowl. Aggie watches her great-aunt's eyes range the room like someone dropping into a museum ten minutes before closing, trying to see it all before they turn off the lights.

She blinks at Aggie staring at her. "Perhaps we could have tea," she says.

Do we even have tea? Aggie wonders, a finger pressed against her lip.

As if reading her mind, Lily says, "The tea caddy is in the end cupboard, and the teapot is up beside the stove. Always has been. That's where Mother kept it and that's where I kept it when I moved back to look after little Cam after his mother died. I'll make it."

Fine with Aggie.

Lily puts her big canvas handbag on a chair next to the kitchen table and fills the kettle at the sink. From a cupboard she takes a small black lacquered box, brightly decorated with pink and orange flowers, and from it extracts two packets of tea. They stand around awkwardly, not looking at each other, waiting for it to steep.

Soon the tea is ready, and Lily leads the way to the book-lined room. Aggie sits on the worn leather couch, brittle but comfortable in spite of its many surface cracks. Lily chooses a nearby chair.

Aggie gets up to pull at the drapes and looks back to see if Aunt Lily reacts in any way that could be construed as guilty. Lily, however, is too busy to take notice. She picks up one of two green-and-gold elephants sitting beside each other on a table. "My father brought these back from a trip he made to India as a young man. Made of the finest jade and the purest gold." She shakes her head. "What a shame," she sighs, "what a shame." She takes a big head scarf out of her coat pocket and gives them each a thorough dusting before replacing them.

Meanwhile, Aggie would like to fill the silence. She picks up one of the art books, a large one, and opens it, thinking maybe Lily would like to talk about how cultured the family is. She looks up to see her great-aunt frowning down at the book in Aggie's lap. It has opened at a picture of a great-looking Greek statue of some young guy, buck naked and no fig leaf. Snap shut it goes. Aggie thinks she'll pursue culture under more private conditions.

"I should have offered to hang up your coat," Aggie says to break the silence.

"No need." Lily pulls one edge across her knees. "It's always been so drafty here, I find. I came prepared." She looks over at Aggie, sweating in her swishy-legged pants and ketchup-stained T-shirt.

Prepared for what? Aggie wonders. To tell the truth, Aggie feels kind of sorry for the woman sitting in her old childhood home, looking at all the things she used to take for granted. She's staring at the walls, now – bare except for the conspicuous rectangles – at the uncluttered desktop, and at the key collection.

"So," Aggie begins, thinking she might as well get to the point. "Want to move in?"

"Move in?"

"With us. One big happy family, like your brother's will says."

Lily looks down at her hands in silence for a moment. "Bertrand is a jackass," she says at last. "Never listens to the boy, pays no attention to him, and the odd time he does, spoils him rotten and then wonders why he misbehaves."

"Um," Aggie says.

Lily glares at her as if she's to blame for Bertrand's being a jackass.

Aggie tries again. "Would you like to move in here with my sisters and me?"

There is a moment of contemplation before Lily replies. "With a band of hooligans? Certainly not. I'll have the police onto you first." She looks around fiercely, her fingers moving on the chair fabric, tracing a little knob on the wooden part of the arm, straightening a doily over the upholstered part. In a moment she's calm again. "It's sad," she says, "when your family disappears, one by one."

"I know exactly what you mean," Aggie says.

"My sister thinks I'm a fool."

"Mine, too."

"Your father was a sweet child."

Aggie's heart leaps. Very quietly she says, "You said, 'your father.'"

Lily stares at her. "Did I?"

Aggie nods hopefully, eagerly.

"Maybe I did. But then again, maybe I didn't. No way to prove it."

Aggie is crestfallen. She wants to ask if he stole things as a little boy, but knows it won't make any difference to her feelings for him.

"Thank you," Lily says finally, putting her cup and saucer on the table beside the elephants. "It was awfully nice of you to have me, whoever you are." She heaves herself to her feet and then stops. "Now what am I forgetting?" She looks around, looks down at her empty hands.

"Your bag," Aggie says and offers to fetch it from the kitchen. A great big canvas haversack of a bag it is, too, and pretty heavy for an old lady, Aggie thinks, handing it over.

"Thank you so much," Lily says as she reaches the front door. Soon she is away off down the street, the tails of her raincoat flapping behind her.

A nutcase? Aggie asks herself. Maybe she is. But then again, maybe she isn't. No way to prove it.

The next day is oppressively hot. Aggie's sisters have been bickering off and on ever since they got up. Jeannie asked Helen to give her money to get the car looked at, to see if it can be made operational, but Helen wouldn't. "It'll just break down again," she said.

"You don't know that."

"It also has a flat tire. Did you notice?"

Jeannie hadn't noticed. Now she's going around looking as if she's been awarded the death penalty.

Not a working day for Helen. She's been prying open windows to get some more air into the place, but the windows won't stay up on their own. They come crashing down behind her back, scaring the girls out of their wits and making them scream. Helen says to Aggie, "Why don't you go down cellar and see if you can find something to prop the windows?"

"Why don't you?"

"Because I'm asking you."

"Ask Jeannie."

"Oh, for cripes' sake, let's all go down. It's time we took ourselves into the bowels of this mausoleum anyway and had a look around."

"This what?" Aggie asks Jeannie on the way down the narrow cellar stairs, but if she knows, she's not saying.

The farther down Aggie goes, the more uncomfortable she feels. In one of the art books, she read that the Romans buried their dead underground in a series of galleries and chambers called catacombs. She stands at the bottom of the stairs, shivering, hearing her sisters' voices faintly as if they are far, far away. She hates this part of the house; it's suffocating her. She wants to scream, not because she's afraid, but because she's angry. *Pay attention to me*, she wants to scream. She would like to smash something. *I hate you*, she wants to shriek, but she doesn't know who the *you* is. She hugs her arms around herself to hold herself together.

Jeannie crosses the gloom of the cellar and goes through

a doorway. "Smells like moldy mushrooms down here," she calls, her voice muffled.

Her sisters are exploring all the little rooms, but Aggie can't move, overwhelmed by the chill, by a feeling that nothing will ever be right, that she is to blame, that her heart is black. Maybe this is what it's like to be dead. "Move," she tells herself, and then thinks about movies. What if this were really a movie and she and her sisters were down in this dungeon sort of place? She's starting to feel better, although her head hurts. It takes her a moment to realize she's pressing her palms hard against the sides of her head. "Why should Helen stay?" she asks herself. "Why should Jeannie?" No law says they have to survive as a unit. No law says anyone has to care how fast or slow Aggie's heart is beating. Nothing, she knows, is holding them together.

And so these three sisters are down in this dungeon place and Helen says –

"What a creepy little room! Look, firewood."

Aggie moves toward the voices.

"Here's the furnace. Wonder how you work it?"

"Jeannie, Aggie, come look at this!" Aggie is moving now, step-by-step, in the direction of Helen's voice. She's looking at shelves of jars of preserved fruit and picklelike things. They have little oval stickers on them with dates written in ink that's turned brown – 1934, 1942, 1950!

"Ptomaine city!" Jeannie says.

Aggie is breathing all right now, getting over it, whatever *it* was. Darkness pushing her down. All around them are pieces of old and broken furniture piled high, crippled bed frames, a caved-in baby crib, a wooden high chair with the tray hanging half off – parts of people's lives – flowerpots, cracked and chipped dishes – parts they don't want – heavy coats gray with dust, hanging from a pipe, a workbench littered with tools, sawed-up pieces of boards, lamp shades. Aggie's pretty well over the buried feeling, the blackness of a few moments ago. This could easily be a movie.

Helen says, "Let's take a few of these sticks up for the windows." They shuffle around in the sawdust finding scraps of wood and pieces of thick dowelling.

Upstairs on the main floor, they are busy propping open the heavy windows when someone bangs on the front door and twists the doorbell. They look out to see the backs of three kids about the size of Susie, their "sweet" little cousin. Aggie thinks one of them *is* Susie. The kids run across the street to the post office and hide behind a big tree in front of it. When the girls go out, they can hear them snorting, trying to smother their giggles. They have stuck a sign to the front door with masking tape: MY MOMS DIMUND RING IS GONE AND YOU MUST OF STOLE IT. GIVE IT BACK OR ELSE.

The three sisters look at each other, laughing a little but puzzled, too, frowning. And then Aggie just gets really mad. "Enough's enough," she says. After all the remarks they've been getting here and there about shoplifting and stealing from cash registers, she thinks it's about time to fight back. She jumps off the veranda and yells across the street at the kids, "Okay, suckers, get outta here and don't come back!" She forgets she still has a window stick in her hand, and she's waving it all over the place.

"Make us!" the little girls shriek.

Aggie storms across the street, her face contorted, eyes flashing. "I'll make you all right!" Her voice cracks with rage. The little girls scream and run up the steps of the big stone post office just as a lady comes out.

"What's going on?" she says in a voice that could mean she owns the post office and maybe half the street.

Aggie stops, breathing hard. "They're harassing us," she manages and knows immediately the woman doesn't believe her. Her rage subsides as quickly as it rose. Why would she believe her? Nice little eight-year-old girls, born and raised in the world's most innocent village. Aggie is still panting in the middle of the road, fists on her hips, clutching her big stick, feeling stupid and wondering what hit her. She probably looks like a homicidal maniac, shaved head and all.

"She's gonna beat up on us! She's gonna kill us!" the little girls shriek. They cluster around the lady for protection.

"Oh, fergawdsake," Aggie says, looking a little embarrassed now because of the window stick, which she had no intention of using. She turns around with a disgusted sigh and marches back up the veranda steps.

"Let's just go in," Helen says. She rips the sign off the door, and Aggie and Jeannie follow her in. "All right," Helen says, once they're inside. "From now on we say nothing to anyone, no matter what they say to us. We don't react. We freeze. Got it?"

"You mean we just sit here and let them treat us like scum? What good will that do?" Aggie wants to know.

Jeannie says, "Look at it this way, we bide our time. We'll get them back, don't you worry."

"We're not getting them back. The more we react, the meaner they'll get," Helen says. "If we mind our own business, they will get over it. They'll leave us alone, and eventually they will forget about us."

Jeannie says, "Helen, you are such a doormat."

Aggie thinks she would like to simply cut to the next scene.

They've been in Port Desire for a little over a week. Aggie is spending this rainy afternoon at the top of the house, on the third floor. There may be an attic above where she is, but she's not sure how you'd get to it. The stairs end in a narrow hallway with several rooms opening off it, smaller than the ones below. She's happy pushing open doors, peering into rooms – not frightened up here at all.

"Wow!" she says out loud. A room at this end of the hall is half filled with boxes and trunks and suitcases and old-fashioned clothes hanging on a rod that runs the full length of the room. Some are hanging in cloth bags and some in square bags made of see-through plastic. There are men's suits, military uniforms, ladies' dresses. There are hats – some in round boxes and some not – on a shelf above the clothes, and below, on the floor, is a row of old shoes and lace-up boots. Set for life, Aggie thinks. She could have a costume change every day of the week.

These clothes don't strike her as castoffs, as much as the things in the cellar did. Her ancestors actually wore them while they were starring in their own lives. She exchanges her combat boots for a pair of thin-soled, soft-leather boots with floppy tops, and they actually fit her pretty well. She doesn't want to pull too hard on the laces as they're rotten enough to break.

There's a cramped little bedroom up here across from the costume room. A narrow iron bed hugs one wall. There's a dresser, chair, chamber pot in the dresser, or washstand, or whatever – empty? she wonders. Yes. Gloves, soft as skin, once white probably, now tinged with yellow, lie folded in the top drawer along with some bent hairpins. Wait! Something's stuck at the back of the drawer. She forces it open, pulls. What is this? she wonders. A secret compartment. Bunch of paper in there, like a school book. Pages out of a scribbler. She sits on the side of the bed and tilts the pages toward the light coming through the dusty window.

"Agatha! Would you kindly get your butt down here for dinner – such as it is."

She can hear Helen calling her from two floors below. She's been bellowing for some time, she thinks, but Aggie's been wrapped up in this story she's reading. She guesses it's a story. It's very neatly handwritten on lined paper.

"Coming," she screeches back. Take it with her or leave it? Leave it, she decides. She shoves it back into the drawer. Down she goes by a different set of stairs, winding and very narrow, and ends up outside the laundry room behind the kitchen.

"I have to be at work in twenty minutes," Helen says. They fork their Kraft Dinner into them at the kitchen table. Jeannie is dining on Coke and chips in front of a television they discovered hidden behind cabinet doors in one of the many living rooms. Only two channels available – one

French, one English. Aggie can live without TV reruns in any language and is, in fact, loving her Kraft Dinner, so she's happy. She keeps saying "yes," and "oh, really," to Helen, but she's thinking about the handwritten story she found. It must be old because the paper is yellowish and the ink has faded in places. She wishes she could find the beginning of it.

There's a person named Amanda (luxurious hair, Aggie decides, and a little stuck on herself) and someone named Eliza (perky, funny, sarcastic) and someone else named Jane (who might be like her, inquisitive, smarter than she lets on). Just before the thing ends, they are setting four places at the table for tea and keep looking out the window for someone. *It's very late. I do hope nothing has befallen her,* Amanda says. Eliza says, *She has been away too long. Perhaps she won't come at all.* And then Jane, who seems a lot younger than the others, says something like, *I can't remember her. If she comes, she will surely be a stranger to me.* And then they hear horses' hooves outside their cottage window. They push the curtain aside and see a horse-drawn carriage with someone inside, her face pressed against its window. But Aggie doesn't know who it is because that's all there is. It ends right there.

She could make that into a movie, she thinks. Those characters could turn into real people.

"For dessert," Helen says, "we can have one cookie each or split an apple."

"Let's go berserk," Aggie suggests, "and have both."

Helen gives a big sigh and reminds her yet again of their financial situation. Helen hasn't been paid yet, but Aggie can't help wondering what she does with the tips she must make. Maybe salting some of it away for her escape into higher education. Helen is determined not to break down and use money from the trust fund. "We have no intention of staying," she says. "It would be like stealing."

"Rot," Jeannie says, but Helen's signature is the only one the bank will honor because of some clause about the girls having to be over eighteen to draw on the account.

They end up going berserk.

The rain stopped a couple of hours ago. Aggie is out walking off their hearty meal and "extravagant" dessert. She wants to check out the rest of Port Desire – the seven streets she hasn't been on yet. She's actually looking for a movie theater, but imagines she'd have seen it by now if it exists. She walks past the "bee" restaurant and notices that it is really packed. Lots of action on the main street tonight, too; many scoops of ice cream going down and bottles of pop. Cars patrol the street; boats buzz the lake. On the deck at the back of the restaurant, she sees someone swatting away bees with a napkin. She catches a glimpse of Helen in a big green apron (so not her style!), balancing a tray of food.

She crosses the street, turns a corner, and thinks about Amanda, Eliza, and Jane in that story. She thinks she has a few ideas about who they are waiting for and what happens next and what happened before. She can almost see this whole movie going on in her head when, for some reason, she looks up and notices where she is – the Quade cousins' neighborhood, the last people in this town she really wants to hobnob with since Susie and her friends turned her into a monster. She had thought she was going in an entirely different direction. Who knows, maybe all roads lead to Quades. She makes a quick about-face right here and . . . *oops!*

"Well, Agatha, how fortunate. I've been wanting to have a little talk with you." It's the mom, Linda, out of breath from jogging.

"I guess I've been sort of wanting to talk to you, too," she lies. She would have been happier avoiding the whole issue. "Did your diamond ring turn up anywhere?"

"Why, yes!" She looks at Agatha, frowning, as if she's thinking, how would you know about it? "I took it off to do some painting last week," she says, still puzzled, "and thought I'd left it on a windowsill. But I couldn't find it. Did I tell you any of this?"

"No, not really. Word gets around."

"It turned up in my jewel box."

"There you go," Aggie says. "Nobody stole it, after all."

"Of course not," she says. "Why would anyone think that?"

"Some kind of local preoccupation, I think."

Linda gives a big sigh as if she doesn't want to delve into any of this, and then she changes her tone and the subject. "Now, Agatha, I've been hearing some terrible things about you – that you threatened Susie and two other girls with a baseball bat. Why would you do that? Maybe that's what teenagers do in the city, dear, but not here, not in Port Desire. Now, I can't believe you would really have harmed them, but you must learn to control that temper of yours. A friend of mine witnessed the whole –"

"Wait a minute, Linda, whoa, hold on."

"Now, Agatha, don't deny it. Mrs. Brownwell saw the whole thing."

"It wasn't a baseball bat."

"What was it?"

"A stick. For propping up the window."

"What window?"

"The kitchen window. Look, what difference does it make? Susie accused us of stealing your ring."

"Susie! Oh, now. Susie wouldn't do that."

Aggie just stands there with her face hanging out. Facts are facts.

Linda stands in the middle of the sidewalk, shaking her head as if she half believes her, and half doesn't want to. Another pause and another big sigh. "Agatha, Agatha, she's only eight years old. Little girls make mistakes. But we don't try to beat them up with a baseball bat every time they do."

"It wasn't a baseball bat."

Linda gives her a fed-up look. She says, "If she accused you of something, I will send her over to apologize, if that will make you feel better."

"Don't bother. It won't." Aggie steps off the sidewalk to go around her and, as she does, out of the corner of her eye, sees Bert, the dad, coming up the street. Regular family reunion, she thinks, but decides not to hang around for it. She wants to get quickly and safely back to the family fortress, where she could happily spend the rest of her life. As she sprints back up the street, she hears Bert say, "What's going on? Anything the matter?"

Linda says loudly enough for the entire village to hear, "I'm afraid she is every bit as bad-tempered as her father was."

My father was not bad-tempered. I hate this place.

CHAPTER FIVE

Last week Jeannie and Helen moved into their own rooms. It wasn't Aggie's idea, although she has to admit it was cramped with all of them thrashing around in the same bed. They have looked in every room, and have not encountered a single ax-murderer or rotting corpse. She has the same room they all started out in that first night. It looks out on the back lawn – meadow, she should say – and the boat-house and, of course, the lake, which she contemplates from time to time, brooding over her fear. Helen's room is across the hall, and Jeannie's is beside Helen's.

Helen spent half of one morning scrubbing and polishing her new room, humming snatches of tunes. She stood back from it when she had finished cleaning and smiled at the fine job she had done, feeling a little proud, maybe even (she had to admit) a little attached to it.

Apart from stacks of newspapers, magazines, and flyers heaped on every available flat surface in some of the downstairs rooms at the back of the house, the place is remarkably tidy. A thick layer of dust covers everything, and the bathrooms aren't the cleanest, but on the whole, they can't complain. Actually, Helen complains. "We have to all pitch in and clean the place," she says.

"Why would we? We're not staying," Jeannie says.

We may not be staying, Aggie thinks, but we're not going, either. School will be starting in a few days.

Jeannie has landed a job! Not much of a job, but she thinks it may have possibilities. She's been hired to sweep up at the As You Like It hair salon. The girls are actually all sitting down at the same time at the same table to the same meal – canned pork and beans and taste-free bread, toasted.

"You won't make much doing that," Helen says.

"Just wait. When the owner finds out what fantastic styling ideas I have, she'll take me on as a stylist."

Helen, of course, tries to deflate her ego by telling her she can't do that without training, and Jeannie rises to the bait, aiming her fork at Helen and giving it a dangerous-looking twist. "Yeah, well, just watch me." Helen makes a remark about Jeannie's rat's nest head and how one look at her and the customers will take off, and Jeannie screams "shut up," and that's about all that is said on the subject.

They are experiencing their first Sunday night minus the tourists in downtown Port Desire. Tomorrow is Labor Day, and they've all gone home. Village of the dead, Aggie thinks. She wonders what the local teens do here for fun and frolic. She keeps looking out the windows, but nothing continues to happen. A couple of little groups go by, boys on one side of the street and girls on the other, and the girls yell smart-ass remarks at the boys and the boys go *har-har*, and then everybody goes home. She's not sure if one of the boys was Cameron Quade or not.

Yesterday Aggie went to the grocery store with a short list of essentials – spaghetti, cornflakes, Kraft Dinner, the usual power foods they've come to know and love. She thought she might be able to get an after-school job and was hoping Cameron Quade could put in a good word for her, but he wasn't there. "Oh, he was just working here for the summer," the woman on the cash register said. "Yesterday was his last day."

"Could I have his job for the winter?" Aggie asked.

"'Fraid not," she said. "We're not hiring."

"So who's going to bag the groceries?"

"Gotta bag your own, baby."

What a jerk-water town! Aggie thinks.

They have no phone now. They've been disconnected because the bill-payer is deceased. Jeannie says they could at least pay for that out of the fund, but Helen refuses. "We are not taking handouts from anyone, not even the bank."

Right now Aggie is up on the third floor, looking for the rest of the handwritten story she found. No luck, so far. She thinks maybe she should write her own story.

There's a bathroom up here, in two parts – a toilet in one little cubbyhole room and, beside it, a long narrow room containing a long narrow claw-footed bathtub and a sink. This is the only place she hasn't searched for the rest of the story. She's checked every other room up here – the costume room, the little bedroom, a room with an old-fashioned sewing machine in it along with some rolled-up carpets and a rocking chair. And a big room that must have been a playroom because there are still a few toys in it – a really old doll's house with no furniture, and a train track with no train.

She's looking in the bathroom cabinet up over the sink, but it's empty except for dust. She closes it with a click. *Wait*. In the mirror behind her she glimpses something. Turning, she sees a little door, about shoulder-high, in the wall behind the sink – probably someplace to store towels. The knob turns, but nothing happens. "Wiggle it," she tells herself. She pulls hard, but it's locked. Why would anyone lock a towel cupboard? she wonders.

She's sitting cross-legged on the floor, the back of her head under the sink, staring at the stupid little locked door. It occurs to her that her father would have found a way to open it in the blink of an eye. Too bad he didn't pass on his skills. Oops, she thinks, slap my wrists! Well, there's a big keyhole here, she reasons, so she should start looking for a big key to fit it. She gets her head down to see if she can see anything through the hole. Nothing. "Give it up," she says to herself. "Go to bed and read."

It's Labor Day and Helen's job in the "bee" restaurant has terminated as of one hour ago. Aggie hates the owner of the "bee" restaurant, Mr. Skint. When he reminded Helen that it was her last day working, Helen almost cried and told him she really needed the job. He said he'd phone her if business picked up, and she said, "We can't afford a phone."

"Yeah, well," he said, "things are tough all over."

He's the kind of guy, Aggie thinks, you'd like to see

something really awful happen to. You'd like to see him poisoned by his own cooking and throwing up all over himself and writhing in agony – ripping at his throat and belly with clawlike hands, his eyes rolling up into his head.

She might put that in her movie.

It's been raining off and on most of the day, but it's stopped now. Aggie has spent it searching for a large key. None of the ones hanging in the study fit the lock in question. She has searched every drawer and cupboard for a big key, but without luck.

Aggie comes down from the third floor to find Helen standing in the doorway of Jeannie's room, staring pointedly at her through the open door. Jeannie is now the sole breadwinner. She pays no attention to either Helen or Aggie, but sits staring crossly into the mirror over her dressing table, probably devising some outrageous hairstyle.

"Jeannie," Helen says, "you *have* to share with us! You know I've been slaving in that damned restaurant just to keep food on the table, and now we're out of laundry soap. And we're out of deodorant." Her voice is getting higher and louder. "And we're going to stink," she screams, "all because you won't cooperate. I'd just like you, for once in your selfish little life, to think about how we as a family are going to survive here in this situation."

"I don't give a rat's ass how *you're* going to survive," Jeannie says. "I need money to get out of here."

Helen and Aggie just stand quietly, staring at Jeannie staring at herself in the mirror, hearing echoes from the past. "I don't give a rat's ass" is something their mother used to say. Aggie wants to believe Jeannie is only testing them, trying to get a reaction. Helen says, "Okay, fine, *Mom*," very quietly. She turns and leaves with a resigned shrug. Aggie watches her go downstairs, but Helen doesn't even look back.

Aggie takes one last look in at Jeannie. She isn't actually staring at her reflection in the mirror; she's staring at nothing. Tears are rolling down her cheeks, dropping from the angle of her jaw onto her clenched hands. Aggie says, "Jeannie?"

"Get out!" she yells.

So Aggie does.

Downstairs Aggie tries not to think about the way her little "nonfamily" is losing whatever loyalty it may once have had back in Sudbury, back before their father died. She says to Helen, "Laundry soap isn't worth worrying about. As soon as Mrs. Muntz boxes up our clothes and sends them on the bus, we won't have to wash them as often. Anyway, we can always use hand soap. Actually, people used to make their own soap. If we could find out how, we could. . . ."

Helen walks out of the room.

Aggie follows her. "Why don't you ask Duncan Hill if they need anybody to work in the law office? You'd be good at that."

"I already did," Helen says. She's taking a pad of paper and a pen out of her purse.

"What did he say?"

"Maybe in the spring." Helen goes back into the over-stuffed living room, followed by Aggie.

Spring. By then they'll be shriveled little starved corpses, Aggie thinks, lying in state in their private mausoleum (she looked it up). Wearing dirty clothes. And then she remembers they won't be here in the spring. The house will belong to someone else by then, a nursing home or something, and the costumes will probably be ditched or sold along with everything else.

She sits across from Helen watching her write and looking around, thinking about how she's almost becoming fond of their little château, even with its wall-to-wall doom and gloom. Jeannie comes clumping down the stairs, anger in every footfall. From the living room doorway she says to Helen, "If you would get off whatever high horse you're on and use the bank account that's sitting there begging to be spent, all our problems would be solved."

"No, they wouldn't. They'd be increased because we'd be stealing."

"That's crap and you know it!" Jeannie's threateningly close now.

"If we take the money pretending we're staying, it's as bad as stealing, and I think we've all had just about enough of that in our lives. We've made no attempt to lure Lily into moving in, and she's made no attempt to make friends with us. It isn't going to work."

"I made an attempt," Aggie says, but they're not listening or don't hear her, which amounts to the same thing.

"How can you be so gutless and brainless?" Jeannie yells.

"The same way you can be a selfish little dishonest slut!" Helen yells back.

Jeannie whacks Helen on the side of the head, and Helen, at first, looks too stunned to do anything, but a moment later, she jumps up from the couch where she's been writing and takes off after Jeannie, who is up the stairs in a flash. Jeannie escapes into her room and slams the door, and Helen gives it a good kick and starts to cry.

While Helen is upstairs kicking Jeannie's door in, Aggie glances at the letter she's been writing. Sneaky, she knows, but how else is she going to keep abreast of things when no one tells her anything? The letter is directed to someone at a university asking about student loans. Anxiety attacks the inside of her head with masses of sharp points. Now she knows for sure. They're both going to fling her away – maybe not tomorrow, maybe not next week – but it seems that the flinging is inevitable. Helen is limping when she comes back into the living room.

Stung, Aggie escapes outside.

She leaves through the side door before she remembers she should avoid it. This afternoon, after the rain stopped, she gave up her search for the key to the bathroom cupboard and came out for some air. At the side of the house, she encountered a big cluster of strange-looking bees swarming around the hollyhocks and sweet clover and wildflowers growing in profusion. They didn't look like the sluggish bees, or wasps, or whatever they were at the "bee" restaurant. These looked and sounded mean, so she ran back inside. She thought, what if they're killer bees! What if they've flown all the way up from South America because this is such a great town for bees? I mean, how would you know? One day you're walking around going about your own business and then suddenly, *zap*! You end up stung to a swollen bloody pulp. Tonight, however, they have disappeared. Perhaps they sleep at night, the way people do. She feels a little safer.

This evening she picks her way in the twilight through long wet grass and tangled weeds in the backyard. On one side of the lot, behind a fence, she sees lights dimmed by blinds in the tall old house next door, where people sell antiques. On the other side, a cluster of trees separates them from the next house. Aggie dares herself to go down closer to the water's edge, where a willow tree sways its swishing branches out over the water as if it wouldn't mind taking a dip. She stops, just about as close to the water as she wants to be. Tonight, the lake is calm and flat as a dish of soup. She would like to feel calm and flat, too. Bathed in moonlight she takes deep breaths. There are two full moons – one behind a gauzy cloud, and the other reflected in the water.

Out on the lake, a houseboat turns away from the shore and putts softly up the golden path of the moon. Watching it makes Aggie's heart pound, partly because the sight of it causes her to relive her underwater panic, and partly because she thinks it's the same houseboat on which she thought she saw her mother. But of course it isn't. Or maybe it is, but the woman wasn't her mother. If she were making this into a movie, it would be, though, and her mother would jump off the back of the boat and swim to this very shore to escape the kidnappers who own the boat. She watches the boat until all she can see of it is a tiny light.

Her mother probably can't swim, either.

Aggie's feet and legs are soaked from the grass, and she's shivering. Time to go in. Reality is a big house filled with warring sisters, not worthy of one of her movies. The back of the house looks so different in the moonlight, she thinks, wading through weedy clusters toward it. She lifts her eyes to the third floor where there are more windows than she remembers, although that's hardly possible.

CHAPTER SIX

THE FIRST DAY OF SCHOOL. Large fancy letters in white on a black screen. It isn't going too badly, really. It's a small place; everyone knows everyone else's name, except Aggie. She ambles along from class to class and tries to pay attention. She's on her way to her last class now – English.

She got up early this morning to choose something first-dayish to wear from the costume collection on the third floor. Her idea was to camouflage her nervousness about starting high school with a bunch of strangers, although, when she thought about it, she was the strange one.

When she came down, Helen looked horrified, and Jeannie shrieked with laughter. They're not speaking to each other, only to Aggie. The image Aggie was trying to achieve was Scottish Highlander off duty, with a kilt she found. She bunched it up at the waist and strapped a leather belt around her middle to hold it up. The kilt had no belt loops, so things, she thought, could get dicey. Hanging down the front was a white furry pouch thing, and over her T-shirt with the ketchup stain, she wore a short khaki jacket. A trifle unusual, maybe, but cool, in her opinion.

Bit of a skirmish took place. Helen got all worked up and yelled, "What are you trying to do? Get yourself thrown out of school or arrested or something?"

"I don't think I'm breaking any law," Aggie said.

"No one will even speak to you," Helen replied.

"Now, there's a tragedy!"

Jeannie said, "They'll probably search you for drugs."

"Well, good luck to them."

Aggie loves it! They're fighting with each other, but they still have enough family spirit to gang up on her. She hates to admit it, but they won this morning. She changed. She took off her T-shirt with the ketchup stain and wore the one with the hole in the back.

Walking up and down the halls of the school, she cannot deny it, the teenagers do stare at her. At least they aren't ignoring her. In math, the teacher asked if there were any questions and someone said, "Yeah, what do you call that white furry thing hanging down?" And everybody got a good laugh. But the math teacher said, "You call it a sporran; it's a purse. The Highlanders wore kilts just like this one that . . ." he looked at his class list ". . . Agatha is wearing. Kilts don't have pockets. This is the original fanny pack, worn in front to avoid pickpockets." Aggie tells herself, "You have to like math with a knowledgeable teacher like that."

All day long the other teachers never tire of staring at her, especially when she speaks with a little bit of a Scottish burr, which she almost can't help. They have been going around looking worried most of the day.

Oh-oh! Here we go, she thinks. The big guy, the principal, is beckoning her over to the side, out of the mainstream
of kids moving along the corridor to the last class. He is one
powerful-looking guy. He says, "I know you're from the
city, young lady, and I'm willing to make allowances for a
few little idiosyncrasies. However (cough, cough), let's get
one thing straight. We may not have a uniform in this
school, but we do have a dress code. We find that if people
conform to the norm, everyone benefits."

"Conform to the norm," Aggie repeats, rolling the *r*'s,
and he nods, biting his lip suspiciously. She likes the way
he's made a little rhyme and doesn't even know it. She says,
"That is so cool! Like a little motto."

His glasses are glittering at her so hard she can't see his
eyeballs. His mouth is bunched in anger. "Take heed!" he
says into her face.

She's in English class now, but is not sure what the
teacher has been saying because she was thinking about
the principal and the way his face spelled out the words *I
hate you*. Or maybe it was *I have this irrational fear of you,
and so naturally I will hate you until I find a substantial
reason for doing so*. She has not done anything wrong that
she knows of, and so tries to put him out of her mind.

The teacher is asking if there is anything special the
class would like to do this year – such as read books not
on the curriculum, or recite an epic poem, or act out a
Shakespearean play. All the kids are squirming and groaning quietly. They're looking at the clock and scratching their
armpits. So Aggie says, "I would like to make a movie."

She notes that they are now experiencing dead silence.

"A movie?" the teacher asks.

Aggie's not sure if she has to explain to her what a movie is. She is fairly old, Aggie realizes – gray hair in a bun – but no, she has encountered movies during her lifetime it seems because she says, "We would need equipment."

Silence envelops the class again until a kid at the back of the room says, "We have a camcorder." Someone else pipes up, "So do we," and Quade, Aggie's second cousin – who happens to be in each and every one of her classes – says, "My great-uncle has . . . I mean had . . . an actual movie camera and projector and a screen and a thing for editing films and splicing the ends back together."

"So did my grandfather," Aggie says. Quade turns on her the stunned look he's good at, as if he doesn't know what she means, and then he does, and looks embarrassed because he forgot that they share the relative in question, although deceased.

The teacher says, "Well, it's something to think about. I have no idea where we would even start."

"At the beginning," Aggie says. People laugh, but she means it. She continues, "First we write a script, then we cast the parts, then we learn the lines, then we film it, show it, charge admission, rake in the millions, pick up our Oscar, and that's all there is to it."

There is an excited buzz now, some of it even enthusiastic, although at the same time possibly a little scornful. The final bell goes while the teacher tries to quiet everyone. "You can be thinking about it during the week," she hollers over the tumult of teens trampling over each other to be first out. "On Friday we'll take a vote."

Outside, eyes drill into Aggie, trying to figure her out as she hurries away from the school to get back to the safety of her fortress. Someone calls out, "Hey, Walt Disney!" She doesn't care. Better that than Billy the Kid, for instance.

Aggie has found an alarm clock with a deafening ring that she sets to go off every morning to get her up in time for school. Jeannie and Helen have been threatening to throw it in the lake because they need a little more time in the sack. Beauty rest, Aggie supposes. God knows, they can use it.

Jeannie is definitely not happy in her sweeping-up profession and has not yet been promoted to stylist. Each day she ambles over to the As You Like It before noon and is finished around five.

Helen spends her days making lists of things that should be done in order to move her life forward, but then she crumples them, so nothing much changes. She managed to find a pay phone near the drugstore, though, and put through a call to Mrs. Muntz, kindly requesting her to box up their clothes and paltry possessions and to send them to Port Desire on the bus. While on this mission, she noticed a sign in the drugstore window offering a steady baby-sitting job. She phoned the number and the woman seemed eager to interview her until she asked, "What did you say your name was?" When Helen told her, she said, "Oh, well, on second thought, I don't really think so, thanks all the same." Helen spent the rest of the day close to tears, leafing through art books and memorizing the artists.

Aggie is trying to tone down her choice of costumes in an attempt to more readily conform to the norm. Today,

Wednesday, she has put on her very average jeans. Above the jeans, however, she is radiant in a yellow peasant blouse, she thinks you would call it, with long puffy sleeves that almost fall off her shoulders. It is covered with small, richly painted beads in shades of red, orange, and fuchsia. The beads, annoyingly, start falling off in math and go spinning all over the floor and, by the time geography rolls around, she has scarcely a bead left on her blouse. "Rotten threads," she explains, when classmates stare at her. They are generally fairly helpful, though, and scramble around on the floor with her to retrieve them. Some of the beads simply disappear, and from time to time people skid on them, losing their balance. No one, so far, has broken any bones.

In the music room a girl named Rachel helps her move the piano because a whole sleeve's worth has rattled across the floor and vanished beneath it. "They're gorgeous," she tells Aggie as together they gather a handful each. They put them down inside Rachel's open flute case to admire them against the blue plush before Aggie places them in her jeans' pockets. "I know where I first saw you," Rachel says. Aggie's eyebrows rise in puzzled peaks. "Driving along in the back of an old car."

Aggie grins, remembering. "You were dripping ice cream down your chin."

"You nearly ran over me."

"And the car died of shock about two minutes later."

"So, I was just wondering," Rachel begins, but hesitates. "Um, why did you shave your head?"

Aggie shrugs. "Something I've always wanted to do, I guess." Rachel eyes her, waiting, thinking there has to be more to it. "Wanted a change," Aggie smiles. Rachel frowns quizzically, her chin tucked in.

"Okay, okay," Aggie says. She takes a breath. "Sometimes . . . you just get to a point in your life where about the only thing you can do is shave your head because otherwise, nothing else is going to happen."

"Wow!"

"So there you go."

"That is so profound."

"'Course I may let it grow in." That's when the bell rings and they have to run for their last class – geography.

Aggie is home now, after school, her jeans' pockets bulging with beads. The front door is locked; it usually is. She turns the doorbell, but her sisters must be out. We need to hide a key under a rock, she decides. For some reason they usually forget to lock the side door, probably because they rarely use it now that the killer bees have moved in, swarming near the hollyhocks, biding their time, waiting for a signal to attack. Going around to the side door, she can hear them humming close by, but can't see them. Quickly, she pulls open the door and is inside before they can rally their forces.

She heads for the kitchen to check the refrigerator, hoping for a miracle supply of soft drinks or cake or pizza, but before she can even make her way across the room her nose is assailed by the aroma of – is it? Yes, it is – a big elegant loaf of freshly baked bread, exactly like the one she'd nearly demolished single-handedly at the Quades. She has to sit down. This can only be the work of Great-Aunt Lily. She must have brought it before Helen went out. She leans across the table to smell the bread at close range and she feels she could faint with joy. She picks it up; it's hefty. No absorbent cotton lightweight this. No sirree, this is a serious bread product. What am I waiting for? she thinks.

She paws through a drawer of kitchen implements until she finds a big knife with a serrated edge, places the bread squarely on a cutting board, and then she's into it like a starved maniac. She had no lunch again today. They like you to eat lunch at school so you can conform to the norm every minute of the school day, but she couldn't find anything to take except cornflakes. But this is heavenly. This is the best bread Aggie has ever experienced. *Mrs. Muntz, eat your heart out*. She could have bought a sandwich in the cafeteria because she still has a little money from her Sudbury days, but they were beginning to curl at the edges and quite possibly were left over from the year before.

She can't stop eating bread! It has a crisp almost salty crust, and the interior is soft and buttery and a little dense, but not too dense, and *yum!* She adds a small dab of butter and thinks, I could become a bread addict. I could be out on the streets robbing innocent bystanders, brutalizing small children and old ladies for the price of a loaf of bread. It's a disease; I can't help myself. Quick, get another slice into me!

"What in hell are you doing?"

Gulp.

Jeannie's home and is looking at the bread and at Aggie as if she's committed a felony. Nevertheless, Jeannie picks up the bread knife and sizes up the half-eaten loaf while Aggie explains that it just appeared, heaven-sent, possibly, or else Lily-baked. Helen comes in and sees the two of them stuffing bread into their faces like they're on death row. So now Helen's addicted and the three of them sit around complimenting the bread for being so tasty and grinning at each other as if they've always been on the best of terms, and they divvy up the last of it and wipe crumbs off their clothes, just like one big happy family. Boy, Aggie thinks, it doesn't take much to solve our problems.

"How often does she bake?" Jeannie asks.

"Who knows."

"I wonder if this is the start of a trend."

"We can only hope."

A little later, after supper (soup only, stuffed as they are from bread) eaten by all three of them at the same time around the same table, Jeannie slaps down two twenties and a ten on the kitchen table and says, "Don't say I never did nothin' for this family."

"Anything," Helen says.

Aggie doesn't say a word. Just sits with her feet up on her chair, hugging her legs tight and smiling into her knees.

CHAPTER SEVEN

And so it's Friday, end of the first school week, and in English class the movie has been given the official nod by the teacher, Miss Greenwald. They voted on whether to make a movie or a stage play, and the movie won, even though Aggie voted against it. It was a secret ballot, so no one knew. Rachel, who sits behind Aggie in English, thumped her on the back and said, "Congratulations, dahling, you have won the Oscah."

Faced with the reality of actually producing a movie, Aggie has developed a case of nerves. She has no more idea of how to make a movie than swim. What the future holds for her right now is death by failure. Miss Greenwald tells the class they must divide into groups to write the script.

Aggie pipes up, "It's already half written."

The teacher looks surprised, but says, "That's wonderful. Perhaps you would be kind enough to bring what you have for our next English class, and we'll brainstorm it."

The script is half written, all right, but only in her head. She doesn't want to think about this.

She hurries home worrying, wondering why she always has to open her big mouth. As she comes down the street toward the house, she can see someone straddling a bicycle, long spider-legs stretched out holding it stationary, lying in wait for Miss Muffet. She approaches and then wary, stops, eyeing her cousin with distrust because she knows his family thinks she's a mean little child-basher. "What?" she says to him as sullenly as possible.

He's all jittery and doesn't really look at her. He has earphones hanging around his neck and a Walkman for CD's in a pouch on his belt. "Do you know where the movie stuff is, the camera and everything?"

"No."

"I could show you, if you like."

"What for?"

"In case . . . you know, if you want to make a movie or something."

"Listen, boy, aren't you afraid I might bonk you over the head with a baseball bat?"

"No." Eyes downcast beneath the hair.

"Didn't you hear about me and your little sister?"

"Well, yes, but she exaggerates. She can be a very stupid little girl at times." He risks a glance. "If you want me to show you the stuff, I will." He looks at his watch. "Then I've got to get going. My lesson's in half an hour."

"Ah, the violin player."

"Yes." He sounds defensive.

"Do you, um, like that sort of thing?"

"The violin? Of course."

She's thinking of giving him a look that will convey the impression that he and his violin are just a little too precious for words, but before she can figure out how to do that, something else occurs to her. Oops, she thinks, I'm typecasting him the way the principal did me. So instead she says, "I wouldn't mind hearing you play it sometime." His face is one big expression of astonishment before he hides his eyes away again under his snaky hair.

She picks up the key from under a stone near the veranda steps, where they now keep it, unlocks the front door, and he follows her in. He goes ahead of her down the hall past the kitchen, past the room full of dead plants, and slopes off to the right into the cozy book-lined study. What can she say? She follows him.

Quade flicks the light switch, even though the drapes have been pushed back as far as they'll go. He stands in the middle of the room looking around. There are fireplaces in many of the downstairs rooms in the house, and this one is no exception. Quade is frowning at the mantel and the bare walls. "There used to be a lot of pictures in here," he says. "I wonder what became of them?"

"No idea," Aggie says. "Maybe the old man put them someplace else."

"Maybe."

He opens a built-in cupboard under the window behind the desk. Apart from dust balls, the shelves are almost empty. Aggie could have told him that. She has explored this room thoroughly. "That's funny," he says, scratching his head. On one shelf, there's a stack of magazines called

The Home Moviemaker and an empty reel. That's it. "Where did all his stuff go?" he says.

He sits on a swivel chair at the big desk and opens the bottom drawer. One by one he opens all the drawers, paws through the stuff – stamps, envelopes, a chess set scattered all over the drawer, pens, a dried-up bottle of ink. No movie camera. "Wait a minute," he says. "It might be in the back room. We borrowed it once and when we brought it back he said, 'Just put it in the back room for now.'"

They hurry across the hall, go past the laundry room, and open the door of a room that seems to be primarily a storage room for old newspapers, magazines, flyers, empty envelopes, pots of dead plants, and a whole collection of walking sticks and umbrellas. It's dark with the blinds down. They've never bothered to put them up because it's not a room they ever use.

Quade turns on the light. He shifts newspapers, looks under chairs, under the table holding the dead plants, in all the musty corners of the room, but finds nothing. "This is crazy," he says. "His camera, his projector, everything should be right here where we left it about, I don't know, three years ago – before he got sick, anyway. It would have been perfect for this project. Uncle Bert," he looks at her, "– your grandfather – showed me how it works. He showed me everything about it." He looks up at her as she stands there, shrugging her shoulders, holding up empty hands.

Quade says, "I wonder if somebody took it."

She feels hot in the face imagining how, in half a second, he will turn on her suspiciously and accuse her of stealing a camera that she doesn't know how to operate, but never-theless must have stolen because STEALING IS IN HER BLOOD! It doesn't matter that she is innocent; her face is crimson anyway, imagining what he might be imagining. He's looking at her now, noticing the guilty look on her face.

Suddenly red-hot anger prods her. Her hackles are up. If she were a dog, she'd be growling. And then a new thought comes into her head. Maybe Quade stole it, never brought it back, and this is all a subterfuge so he won't look guilty, even though – "Whoa," she tells herself. She's watched way too many movies in her life.

She says, "So, it's gone. . . . Who cares. It just doesn't matter." This is mostly for her own benefit, so she can stop thinking about it.

"Of course it matters. How are you going to make a movie?"

"Well, I guess I won't."

"We'll have to hunt for it."

"I don't even know how to make a movie."

"But you said –"

"I just said it for something to say. I'm a smart-ass."

He looks disappointed. "I thought it was a good idea."

"You would, you loser."

He turns his dark eyes on her with a look that makes her feel a little heartless, a little like a bully with a baseball bat. Very quietly he puts down a stack of papers he was looking behind.

What an insulting thing for me to say.

He turns swiftly on his heel and leaves the room.

"Hey, Quade," she says, turning off the light and

slamming the door behind her. He doesn't stop. He strides to the front hall and lets himself out. "Hey, I didn't really mean to sound like that," she calls. But the door shuts quietly behind him. She opens it and says through the screen door, "I'm sorry." But he is already on his bicycle, already has his earphones on. He doesn't even look in her direction before pedaling away.

If I toted a gun, she thinks, I'd be what they call trigger-happy. I'm a child-basher. I'm a reckless crusher of thin-skinned youths.

The next Monday Aggie looks for an opportunity to tell him she didn't really mean what she said, but he's in a little world of his own. Just him and his music. When he's not in class, he's got his earphones on. She tries to talk to him after school, but off he goes on his bike, earphones in place, his eyes all dark and serious and his lips tight to his teeth.

Rachel walks partway home with her, and they stand on Rachel's corner talking about homework and teachers and other kids. At any other time Aggie would be thrilled because this feels so much like having a friend, but her mind is still on Quade. Rachel looks at her watch. "Yikes!" she yelps. "Gotta go take my brother for a haircut!" And she takes off down the street yelling, "I'll phone you!" She's gone before Aggie has a chance to tell her they don't have a phone.

At home she goes up to her favorite third-floor hangout to try on costumes, but nothing fits. Everything looks stupid on her. Something along the lines of Attila the Hun attack-wear would be appropriate, she thinks, but nothing like that is available.

Eventually Helen bellows at her to come down for dinner. They are all having the same meal tonight – boiled wieners and stale buns – although not all in the same room. Even though Helen still hasn't managed to get another job, her mood is on the upswing. Duncan Hill met her on the street this morning and asked her if he could drop over and take her out for coffee.

When the doorbell rings all three emerge from their separate salons, but it's Helen who opens the door and asks him to come into the grand living room, leaving him in the clutches of Jeannie and Aggie while she does some last-minute primping. Aggie thinks he really likes Helen, but when Jeannie says one or two things that crack him up, he seems pretty interested in her. He's way too old for Aggie, she realizes, but given half a chance she'd bat her passionate eyes at him, not that he'd pay much attention if she did. Helen returns in a moment and casts a suspicious eye on Jeannie before they leave.

Later in the evening when Helen comes back, Aggie, from her bedroom, hears her telling Jeannie off for flirting with Duncan Hill. She goes downstairs to watch the fireworks.

"You don't own him," Jeannie says.

"But it was me he invited out for coffee, wasn't it?" Helen, for once, is asserting herself. Jeannie has a way, though, of raising her eyebrows and half-closing her eyes that says something like *how little you know!* Helen grinds her teeth and sails up the stairs, her black skirt swishing angrily against her black-stockinged legs.

Aunt Lily is ringing the front doorbell. It's after school, almost a week after the missing movie camera episode. Alone in the house, Aggie opens the door. Lily holds out something that looks suspiciously like a loaf of bread wrapped in waxed paper. "Another one!" Aggie squeals, delight in her voice.

Lily doesn't reply, just keeps holding it out in front of her, smiling.

"Bread?"

"Bread," she says. "When you get right down to it, bread is the answer."

Well, Aggie doesn't have a ready response for that, but she's not about to argue.

"It's just a little something for you and your sisters," Lily says, pressing it into her eager hands. "I baked again today and thought you girls might like a loaf."

Aggie is overwhelmed. Firstly, she's overwhelmed by the delicious aroma floating up from this welcome little treat, and secondly, because . . . well, she's touched that Lily seems to be softening toward them. She's got a kind heart, even if she *is* short a marble or two. "That's so nice of you. Really. I appreciate it. Would you like to come in for a cup of tea?" Lily shakes her head in its floppy hat with the one string hanging down, and says she can't because she has things to do. As she turns to leave, Aggie says, "But we have to talk about you moving in with us!"

"Oh, my dear, I could never do that. Move in with strangers – complete strangers?"

"But we're relatives. You are our great-aunt."

Lily stands on the sidewalk in front of the house gazing up at Aggie cradling the loaf of bread in the open doorway. "Perhaps it's true and perhaps it isn't. I do things based mainly on intuition, and my intuition tells me to move with caution. Strange for me, I know, coming from a family of risk-takers as I do."

"Risk-takers?"

"My brother made a great deal of money taking the right risks and then lost most of it with the wrong risk. I, myself, play a game of risk with the ice every winter and every spring."

Aggie says, "I guess you could say my father was a risk-taker."

"My nephew Cam risked his happiness for the false love of a bad woman."

Aggie stiffens, feeling defensive. "She isn't bad. You can't say that about my mother." Right now Aggie would like to smack Great-Aunt Lily on the side of the head for talking that way about her mother. Her mom has her faults, God knows, but to call her a bad woman is going too far.

Lily looks down at her comfortable walking shoes, worn down around the outer edges. "Sorry," she says, "I spoke out of turn. You're attached to that woman, I can see." She looks down the street as if she's about to leave, but turns back to Aggie. "There was a time when I used to throw caution to the wind and get attached to people, too. Oh, my, yes. But no longer, not now. People have a habit of dis-appearing, of disappointing, of disrupting my peace of mind. No, an island comes with its own risks, but they're ones I'm willing to take. I'll stay where I am."

Aggie pictures Lily clinging to her island, no bigger than a rock in the midst of stormy house-high waves, a log hut behind her – her only shelter – all but blown away.

Lily says, "I'm very snug where I am, and I have my garden and my baking to keep me busy and a host of other things. I do all my own repairs – the roof, the plumbing; I'm a model of self-sufficiency."

"But in the winter . . . the ice."

"Pooh, the ice. People worry far more than is good for them."

"But –"

"I must run. 'Time waits for no man' – or woman either for that matter. Toodle!" And she's off down the street, stumping briskly along, her hat string swinging. Aggie is left feeling deflated in spite of the bread. She takes it inside and puts it on the kitchen table. "Bread is the answer," Lily said. But what, Aggie wonders, is the question?

Time is passing too quickly for Aggie – already more than halfway into September and things are not going well. She doesn't feel like thinking about all that's happened, although she will anyway; it's in her nature to brood. She thinks it would be safe to say that she is a failure as far as writing a movie script goes.

What she ended up doing was taking the scribbler pages she found to school and showing them to her English teacher. "Did you write this?" she asked. Aggie had to confess that, no, she had found them. Miss Greenwald got all excited about the pages, anyway. "Three ready-made characters," she said smiling, "Amanda, Eliza, and Jane.

Now," she said to the class, "I will divide you into groups, and each group must come up with a story line. Then we'll vote on the best one."

Aggie stood beside Miss Greenwald, frowning, thinking, that's a stupid idea. Miss Greenwald asked her what was wrong. "That's a stupid idea!" she said. While her fellow students laughed, Miss Greenwald frowned and told her to sit down until she could contribute something positive. She wasn't trying to be funny, though. She simply thought it was a stupid idea because she *knows* the story. She knows how it has to go.

Anyway, there they were in their stupid little groups. Everybody just sat there and no one could think of a story, so Aggie began, "Okay, listen. There are these three sisters, like right now, in modern times, and their mother left them a few years ago and went off in the middle of the night without even saying good-bye. So they don't know what happened to her – where she went or anything. So they are always on the lookout for her. They get on a bus and travel everywhere looking for her, but without any luck. And then, one day, they are at a funeral and –"

"Who died?" someone asked.

"I don't know, we'll get to that, doesn't matter. Anyway, one of the sisters sees her own name on a tombstone, dated about a hundred years ago, and gets a creepy feeling all over that she's actually dead. And then the other sisters find their tombstones, and they all get the shivers, and it is very spooky at this point."

"Agatha, um . . ." This was the teacher.

"What?"

"Does this story have an end point?"

Aggie stared at her. Could she not see it? *It's so obvious.*

At home after school, safe in the confines of her third-floor tower, Aggie can't stop thinking about it. Why couldn't Miss Greenwald get the point that the three sisters are going to time-travel and, when they get back into the past, the mother is actually going to turn up? This is giving her cold shivers just thinking about it. Because they find out that the mother was kidnapped and didn't simply up and leave. And that she managed to escape from her kidnapper and find her way home to her daughters, but in a different century. And there is this big scene where they are all brimming over with happiness, and crying and laughing. Oh. My. God. This is so stupid, Aggie thinks. She's actually crying just thinking about it.

Big snuffle. No Kleenex. She can't afford it.

Anyway, she didn't get to tell the whole thing because everybody started finding fault with it and coming up with different ideas, like how the mother could be kidnapped by aliens (fergawdsake) from another planet, and asking stupid questions, and saying her idea really wouldn't work (bunch of defeatists). Aggie wipes her eyes on her sleeve. Let them make their own crappy movie. She doesn't want to think about this anymore.

She goes outside to check the bee situation and yes, they still have their own private flock of killer bees, living among the hollyhocks at the side of the house. The girls are still reluctant to use the side door for fear of getting stung to death.

Some of the bees, it seems, have set up business under the little roof at the back of the house that covers the cellar door.

Jeannie said, when she saw them, "Do you think the gods are trying to tell us something? Like, get out of town?"

Helen said, "No. We are just experiencing a bad year for bees."

Aggie said, "It's a good year for bees; it's a bad year for Quades."

Aggie would put bees into her movie if she were still making one, but she's not. And she's not thinking about it, either.

With each passing day, Aggie's concern about getting Aunt Lily to move in mounts. In spite of the movie situation at school, and in spite of the fact that her cousin Quade hates her, she wants to stay in this town, in this house, with both of her squabbling sisters. There's something about the place that feels right – the corner where she and Rachel stand yakking every day after school, the smell of driftwood and seaweed on the shore, and the flowers. Not just their own crop of hollyhocks, but it seems that every house in the village has a flower garden. All of it makes her want to nestle in.

It's Saturday, and Aggie has decided to take matters into her own hands and find out where Lily lives, or at least get her phone number. She goes through the phone book, *M, N, O, P, Q* – no Lily Quade. Of course she could have been married once and have a different last name, Aggie reasons. The Quade cousins would know, but that is not an option she wants to take.

They might know at the post office. She throws a cape she found up on the third floor over her shoulders because it's getting chilly these days. The cape is long and black, made of some fine wool material and lined with mauve satin. It even has a hood. A wide green-and-purple band trims the two front edges and it's really cool! She feels like the evil queen in "Snow White." *Mirror-mirror-on-the-wall, who has the shortest hair of all?*

Not Aggie. It's growing. She could make it stand up in tiny spikes if she could afford gel, which she can't. Instead, it goes in teeny-weeny curls all over her head. A pixie-headed evil queen.

Up the steps of the post office / castle she goes, tripping a little on her cape, and pulls open the heavy door. Should be a drawbridge, she thinks. Inside, there's a long counter with a man behind it and a wall of tiny silver doors with numbers on them. There is a lineup of two people. On another wall there are notices about this and that. BINGO AT HANLON HALL. FALL FAIR NEXT WEEKEND. Here's a good one: LOST, STOLEN, OR STRAYED! A HIVE OF BEES. IF YOU FIND IT, CONTACT CLARKE'S APIARY. And a phone number. How can you lose a hive of bees? she wonders. I suppose the guy will drive around in a truck and call, "Here, bees-bees-bees," and all the lost bees from all over town will line up and file aboard.

Her turn at the desk now. "Um, I wonder if you would know how I could get in touch with my great-aunt Lily?"

The postal worker looks at her face, at her hair, at her cape, and back at her face. "Lily Quade, that would be," he says.

She nods.

"She just lives out there on Goat Island."

"How would I get there?"

He looks a little surprised. "Boat," he says. "Swim, maybe."

"I mean, where is it?" she says, looking embarrassed because she must sound like such a dimwit.

He points at the front door of the post office and says, "Straight out from here, straight out from the back of old Mr. Quade's about, what, quarter mile? Not much more than that. First island you come to is Lily's. She's your aunt, is she?"

"Great-aunt."

"Let me tell you, she's some lady is Lily Quade. Putts in to the town dock nearly every day in her shiny little inboard skiff, no matter what kind of weather. Fancy little craft, and her sittin' right there in the middle to steer it. Even older than Lily is, I suspect. Or sometimes it's a canoe she uses – whatever strikes her fancy, I guess. She's been out there on that island for years now, summer and winter. Walks over on the ice all winter. Never been in her place, but I hear it's pretty snug."

"Is there any kind of mail boat that goes over there?"

"To Lily's? No special treatment for her, even if she is a Quade. Nope, she has to come in here to collect her mail like everyone else in town."

"Do you know her phone number?"

"No. Can't say as she has one. You could ask around, though. Bertie and Linda Quade would know. They're related."

She thanks him and leaves and votes against asking Bertie and Linda Quade. Maybe, she thinks, as she crosses the street, the way to get through to her is to write her a letter. But what would she say in it? That she's just on the very brink of being happy here, even though her little semi-family is drifting apart? That they need an anchor?

At home she is greeted by the familiar sound of Helen and Jeannie screaming at each other.

"This place is a pigsty."

"Well, that must make you feel right at home."

"Why don't you get off your fat ass and help me?"

"I like it the way it is."

Aggie sweeps in at this moment and removes her cape with a flourish. "Do we have to have this constant bickering?"

"No," Helen says, "not if you would both just work with me for one hour, so we could have this place looking half decent."

"You're so anal," Jeannie says.

"Look, already we have mice and cockroaches. It'll be rats next, unless we clean up our act."

"How do you know we have cockroaches?"

"What do you think those brown bugs are, stupid?"

"How disgusting!" Jeannie says.

Well, the place is a little cleaner, but now everybody is in a bad mood. Including Aggie. Jeannie said she was only going to clean the rooms she used, and Helen said, "Fine, that means you get to do the bathroom, kitchen, your bedroom, and the big living room." So then they had

another fight about a fair division of labor. And then Aggie
yelled, "Could you both just shut up and show me how to
work the friggin' vacuum?" And Jeannie yelled back,
"Anencephalic moron! Figure it out!" And all of a sudden
Aggie got it to work, only it sucked up the fringe on the rug
and it roared and Aggie screamed and she's still wondering
what "anencephalic" means. She wishes they had some of
that good bread.

Back at school, Aggie's being a little stubborn about the
movie. In fact, she's washed her hands of it. Miss Greenwald
has found a book about how to write a screenplay, and she
is just so enthusiastic it's embarrassing. The class ended up
with four different groups and four different story lines, all
more or less stupid, and then they had a vote to choose one.
Of course they chose the stupidest, in Aggie's opinion. This
was all way too democratic for her. The teacher kept
saying, "What do you think, Agatha?" She just shrugged.
She liked her own idea originally, but they've just taken it
and sucked all the good out of it.

Cameron Quade is still not talking to her, but he's
always nearby, somehow. She gets the feeling he loiters on
the edge of her personal space. He is only marginally
involved with the movie, even though he thought it was a
good idea. He offers the occasional suggestion just often
enough to keep the teacher off his case. She's very definitely
on Aggie's, though. Aggie is sitting in the classroom after
school, waiting for Miss Greenwald to lecture her about
her surly behavior. Here it comes.

"Agatha, I thought we should have this little talk, not

because you're doing anything really wrong, you see, but because you are spoiling things for yourself."

"Yes, Miss Greenwald."

"You have really good ideas and everybody appreciates that, but we are a class; we do things together."

"Yes, Miss Greenwald."

"We work together to achieve the same goal."

"Yes, Miss Greenwald."

She pauses and heaves a big, stressed-out sigh. "Don't do that, Agatha."

"What?"

"Must you keep saying 'yes, Miss Greenwald'?"

"No, Miss Greenwald."

Another sigh while she turns her head away, so Aggie won't see her looking up for divine help. When she turns back, Aggie watches her taking in all aspects of her appearance: her close-cropped little mop of curls, her navy blue 1940s sailor dress – back for a return engagement – right down to her feet clad in a pair of ancestral, soft, white leather button boots that are too tight. She's been in pain all day.

Miss Greenwald looks into her eyes with a kindhearted smile. "What's wrong with you, Agatha? I would so like to be able to help you."

"My boots are too tight."

Thrown a little off balance, her eyes are drawn again to Aggie's boots, and then back to Aggie's woebegone face. After a moment she suggests, "Well, take them off, then."

So Aggie does, button by button, and she wiggles her bare toes – none too clean, she's embarrassed to notice –

and immediately she feels better. Neither of them says anything for a minute or two. The long silence gets on Aggie's nerves, although she can't really stand the earnestness in Miss Greenwald's voice, either. Or her kindly eyes. Or the way she asks her what's wrong and means it. Where would she start? It's partly the movie disaster, but it's more than that. What's wrong with her is that her life is in a tatter of uncertainties. Helen says they have to leave and yet they stay, and now that they've stayed this long, she doesn't want to leave. But to stay, she needs Aunt Lily to move in. And to get her sisters to stay, she needs some kind of magic miracle.

"Nothing's wrong."

"Being standoffish gets to be very lonely, after a while," Miss Greenwald says gently, "like being a queen bee."

"I'm not trying to be a queen bee."

"No, I didn't mean that. You're not trying to queen it over us. It's just that you are so intent on being an individual that you don't see that the rest of us are individuals, too."

"You all conform to the norm."

"True in some ways, I guess. But, I think you might notice that other people have pretty good ideas, too. And like your original idea, theirs could also use some help."

"Tellin' me." Aggie stares sideways out the window to avoid Miss Greenwald's eyes, which are way, way too sympathetic. She takes a couple of breaths to keep from . . . *crap!*

Miss Greenwald waves a box of Kleenex in Aggie's direction. "One big blow," Aggie says to herself, "and I'm out of here."

"Agatha," Miss Greenwald calls, "wait!"

But she's gone. There are kids still hanging around the school. Quade is one of them, she thinks. She doesn't know for sure because of tears half-blinding her, and because she's trying to run in her bare feet, and if she makes it home, she believes, she'll be crippled the rest of her life. "Ow! Ow! Jeez!"

Little Agatha, home at last, running past the bees swarming the side of the house, and now she's down at the lake sitting on the dock beside the boathouse, with her feet in the water – something she thought she'd never find herself doing. But she's desperate. Might even fling herself in, who knows? The water is freezing, but she keeps on dipping her bruised and scraped feet until, little by little, she becomes used to it. Amazing, she thinks, how much you can put up with if you try. Big sigh. Could turn this into a little lecture on per-severance, she thinks. Life's little lesson.

She hears something, or possibly somebody, rustling through the long grass trying to horn in on her private sulk. It would be nice, she thinks, if she could have even five measly minutes to feel sorry for herself. Big sniff. She rubs the palm of her hand across her cheek.

"Hi."

She looks over her shoulder into the dark-eyed face of Quade. Complete with violin.

He stands there looking concerned, looking as if he has something to say, but can't get it out. "You . . . you said you wouldn't mind hearing me play, sometime."

She nods, but it's more of a shrug and not very enthusi-astic. He doesn't say anything else, but he's on his knees opening his case. He tucks the violin under his chin and runs his bow over it, twisting a knob or two. She takes her feet out of the water and leans against the boathouse in order to watch him. Violin in one hand, bow in the other, he strolls over to lean against the willow tree, where leafy sprays hang down, swaying a little in the breeze. Nothing awkward about him now.

He tosses his head to shake his hair back, and soon the notes come tiptoeing cautiously, seeking a way through the tree's leaf-bead curtain. A wistful piece. It moans down from the sky. It rises richly from the earth or the water, deepening, gathering strength. It flows and spreads around Agatha, wrapping her in its sadness – a lament for things lost, stolen, or strayed. Quade's shoulders sway away from the tree trunk, sway with the music and with the willow leaves, while she scarcely breathes.

And now he stops. In the silence, before she can find her voice, the violin takes on something new – a dancing, cheerful ditty, a toe tapper for sure – which stupidly brings the tears streaming down all over her face, but she doesn't really care anymore because she's just been listening to a foreign language and understanding almost every word. Who would have thought?

He's packing up his violin now and saying he has to go. She sees him looking at her wet face. He doesn't know what to say and neither does she, so they don't say anything. They smile just the tiniest bit at each other, though, and off he goes.

CHAPTER EIGHT

Once again it's Saturday afternoon. Aggie is over her pity-poor-me drama. At school she finally had a suggestion for the movie they're making. "There should be background music in it," she said, and Miss Greenwald said, "Excellent idea." They actually do other things at school besides make movies – science, math, French, and all those appropriate things. In English, besides making the movie, they read novels and poetry, which Aggie knows she's pretty good at deciphering. When she reads a novel, something curious takes over: she thinks she's both in the book and shaping it, helping it happen. She can't explain it. Well, she wouldn't want to explain it. When you look too closely at things, they become blurred. Her midterm tests reveal that she's a genius in English and a moron in everything else. *What else is new?*

She has been trying to tone down her costumes so that she looks more average at school, but average just doesn't seem to suit her. She thinks more imaginative thoughts when she adds a little touch of color to her otherwise drab jeans and sweatshirt ensemble. On the days they have English, she sometimes flings an old fur stole around her neck, with its hard little triangular fox head resting on her shoulder, its glassy eyes looking accusingly at her classmates. It makes her talk with an English accent. Or, sometimes she wears a tuxedo coat if she's feeling formal (although it makes her walk like Charlie Chaplin), or plaid golfing pants that end just below the knees if she's not. People at school still stare, but they seem more curious and fascinated than scornful. At least that's what Aggie believes. The principal, Mr. Pye, still glares hostilely at her through his glittering glasses. Aggie never fails to smile back warmly.

It's a mild Saturday afternoon for late September, a perfect day for the Port Desire fall fair. Sun filters through the leaves, exaggerating the colors, turning yellow to gold and pink to deep red. Aggie tried to get both Jeannie and Helen to go with her, but no dice. The air is filled with canned music from the rides, encouraging shouts from the game booths, and the smell of grilled hot dogs, which makes her believe that if she could have even one bite, she would be content to die right on the spot.

She is walking around the outside perimeter of the fairgrounds. When she reaches the back of the horse barns, she sneaks in behind them without paying. She cranes her neck to watch the Tilt-a-Whirl rioting through space and the Ferris wheel whipping its swinging seats high above the crowds. She has no money, so watching is about all she can do.

Beyond the midway are stalls and tables laden with the produce and artistry of local farmers and villagers. Aggie ambles along examining everything, marveling at the displays – cakes, pies, aprons, hand-knit sweaters, chili sauce, apple jelly, even pickled watermelon rind. She would like to ask why anyone would eat pickled watermelon rind, but is too polite. And there is bread, she notices. Also maple syrup in tins, fat succulent pears, rosy apples, and a pyramid of honey in jars.

CLARKE'S APIARY, the sign says. He must be the man who lost his bees, she thinks, and wonders if he'd like to take their swarm of killers off their hands. Could use them as guard bees.

Huge, sparkling clean potatoes are displayed on a table, along with shiny cabbages and scrubbed carrots and beets. She stops to ponder. How could you cook and gobble up a potato, with all its eyes looking at you, that just finished winning first prize in the fall fair? Enough, she thinks, to make you want to be a total carnivore.

Aggie follows her nose back to the bread table because it smells divine. The contest is on right now. Three judges are sitting in a tent behind the table, chomping away on little hunks of different kinds of bread and making notations on a piece of paper. Her stomach is rumbling so loudly, it's a wonder people don't run away screaming because it sounds like a volcano about to erupt. At least it does to her. There, somebody must have heard it. A woman has turned to stare at her. And guess who? It's Great-Aunt Margery Upton, last seen at the funeral wearing a large hat. Today she's queenly in a sky blue coat and matching hat, shaped like a flying saucer. She's looking at Aggie as if she's trying to remember what rock she last saw her under.

"Agatha Jane Quade," Aggie says, to jog her memory.

The woman looks startled. "Oh, yes," she says, after a pause. "Of course, now I remember you. You took me by surprise for a moment. You see, Agatha Jane was my great grandmother's name."

And now here's Aunt Lily, toddling up and darting looks at each of them over the top of her glasses. The two sisters greet each other. Both are a little portly and can't really get their arms around each other, but they manage to exchange little smacks on the cheek. Aunt Lily recognizes Agatha and bobs her head at her. She seems to be interested in the clothes Aggie is wearing, which today are a kind of safari suit – Bermuda shorts that actually come down below her knees, as they're a trifle large, and a jacket, also large, belted in back and with a zillion pockets everywhere, and brown-and-orange diamond kneesocks. She had hoped to find one of those soup-bowl helmets, with a little knob on top, in the trunk where she found everything else, but had no luck.

Aunt Lily and Aggie are into a little conversation now in which Aggie is telling her how much she and her sisters enjoyed her loaf of bread. "I meant to bring you another one," Aunt Lily says, "but something happened. What? . . . Oh, yes, I had a bit of a cold and I didn't get out for a while, you know how it is." Margery knows exactly how it is, and now she and Lily are deeply into a comparison of symptoms and cough syrups and the inadequacy of modern health services.

Aggie nods and smiles in a very Helenish way, thinking she should interrupt and tell Lily again how great her bread is, or would that sound like overkill? Instead she says, "We . . . we were wondering if you could let us have your bread recipe, or, even, um, show us how to make it."

"Bread recipe?" Margery asks.

Lily says, "Oh, my, yes – certainly. I'd be delighted."

"What bread recipe?" Margery asks.

"Great Grandmother Quade's."

"She would never give out that recipe to anyone. You know that."

"Yes, but I mean, well, you know she's been dead now for years and years."

"Lily, Lily." Big sigh. Big negative shake of the flying saucer. "Well, if you don't have any sense of privacy, any sense of upholding family traditions, then go ahead. Go right ahead and give away the recipe. Publish it in the newspaper, why not? Give it to every Tom, Dick, or Harry who asks."

Lily looks perplexed. "But, after all, you know –"

Margery breaks in. "I know what you're going to say: 'they're Cameron's daughters and part of the family.' Well, as far as I'm concerned, Cameron left the family under a cloud, and I see no sign of that cloud lifting. Well, you'll do as you like, I expect. You usually do. Very nice to see you again, Agatha. Do look us up whenever you're in Kingston." To Lily she says, "Philip and I will be having tea at the restaurant at four, sharp, before we leave for home. We'd be delighted to have you join us."

She steams off in the direction of the main gate, leaving Lily stuttering about not liking to leave until after the judging, and she has a few things to get done this afternoon, and "oh, my goodness me, look at the time," and calling after her sister, "I may be a few minutes late." And then Lily and Aggie are left standing face-to-face.

"*She* certainly believes we're part of the family," Aggie says, looking Lily squarely in the eye.

"I've discovered two things about my sister over the years," Lily says. "She's wrong more often than she's right and . . . I can't remember what the other thing is. Anyway, whenever she tells me not to do something, I find myself going ahead and doing it anyway."

"Does that mean you'll let us have the recipe?"

"If you like."

"Will you come and show us how to make it?"

"I'd be delighted." She turns back to the bread table then because someone is calling her name, excitedly. It seems she has just won the bread-making contest. Before she hurries off, she reaches across the table and hands Aggie a loaf of her prize-winning bread.

Kindhearted, evenhanded girl that she is, Aggie leaves the fairgrounds by the main gate and carries the bread home to share with her sisters. It's not even wrapped up. The temptation to chomp into one corner of it is nearly overpowering. *Oh-boy!* She has just licked the crust a little bit and it's sugary this time. It has raisins in it. She can hardly wait. She skips along the street toward the house with lips tightly shut over her more than eager teeth.

The smell of fresh bread wafting along with Aggie makes people on the street stare as she hurries along, her bread held out carefully in front of her. As she nears home, she notices that the bees are out in full swarm. Actually they look as if they are on the move. *Oh-my-goodness-me!* A few of them are coming toward her. A little welcoming party. This is no laughing matter, she thinks, and stands perfectly still the way Helen recommends, but they continue to come. All of them. They are not attacking; they're hovering. Aggie walks backwards, slowly, and they follow her. They're all around her. She has cold shivers. Slowly, she turns and walks back along the street, retracing her steps, hoping they won't want to stray too far from home. "Yikes!" she says. They're following her. She can hear them buzzing their little hearts out, but not landing on her. Maybe they love me, she thinks, like little stray doggies. Only lethal.

She decides to cross over the street, and yup, they're still with her. Maybe if she walks up the middle of the road, they'll get scared and take off. Cars are honking at her – and at her pet bees. Let 'em honk, she decides. *Yes, I know, lady, this is stranger than fiction, but what are you gonna do when your bees fall in love with you?*

An old man on the other side of the street calls something to her. Hard to hear with bees buzzing in her ears. He repeats it. "Bob Clarke's up at the fair, there. He'll take 'em off yer hands fer ya."

She would like to say, *great, thanks for the tip*, but she doesn't dare open her mouth for fear of bees flying in. The fair is exactly where she's going to go, though, because she feels she doesn't really have a lot of options open to her in this situation. Straight along the middle of the road is a lot safer in many ways than the sidewalk, where her buzzy little friends might take a notion to lash out and destroy the local villagers.

A one-woman parade. Well, one woman and about four thousand bees, give or take. People are coming out of their houses to watch. Cars are pulling over to the side to let her stay in the middle. People here and there along the sidewalk on their way to the fair stop and gape. They're fascinated by her storm cloud of bees but, she senses, they're also looking in wonderment at her oversized Bermuda shorts and her garish socks and all her handy-dandy pockets.

"Well done," someone calls. Kids are following along beside her, not too close though, she's happy to see, because these suckers are hazardous to your health. At the corner she has to stand and mark time, until a tractor pulling a hay wagon goes past. *Come on, come on, move it, buddy. This ain't no Santy Claus parade.* She marches on the spot, holding up the bread like a baton to signal the bees to wait. And they do. They're pretty good at this. Everybody ought to have their own little bee experience at least once in their lives, she thinks. It builds confidence.

At the fairgrounds, people in line for admission tickets scramble out of her way, and the ticket man waves her through like a visiting dignitary. She grins broadly. She could get to like this. She looks over her shoulder and sees that the kids and other people who followed her little parade are getting in for free, too. *Gotta love bee-power.* Straight on she goes, making a beeline (ho-ho) for the honey table and the sign that says ROBERT CLARKE, HONEY. People start calling out, "Hey, Bob, somebody here for you." They all move back out of the way, and a moment later a man comes over from where some pick-up trucks are parked.

Aggie thinks the bees are starting to get a little nervous, and, as a matter of fact, so is she. They're getting louder, and they are not as clustery. Bob asks people to please stand well back, and could someone bring him a pail of water and some soap if there's any to be had. "Are these killer bees?" Aggie asks him.

"They wouldn't out-an'-out kill you," he says. "They're just your garden-variety honeybee. I guess they went a little crazy. They sometimes do, this time of year, I've noticed. They'd sting you pretty bad if they took a notion. They seem darned attracted to you and your bread, though. Only certain people they let near them. You must be sumpin' special."

In a moment someone appears with a pail of water, and a lady who makes soap and has some on display at a nearby table holds out two bars. "Lavender or Evening Primrose?" she asks.

"Don't much matter to me, or the bees," Bob says, stripping off his shirt and undershirt. He takes Lavender and has a good scrub in the pail, villagers peering at him from all sides, but he doesn't seem to care. Somebody from the 4-H display tent brings him a brand new T-shirt, x-x large, with a big clover on it and the 4-H motto – HEAD, HEART, HANDS, HEALTH – and he dries himself with it and pulls it on over his head. "Now, young lady," he says to Aggie, "would you be so kind as to put the bread on the table?"

When she does, the bees seem a little confused, flying this way and that, as Bob comes around the table and picks up the bread. In a moment they refocus on the bread and desert Aggie for Bob. He says, "Thanks a lot, there, little lady. 'Preciate what you done." He's on his way with his bees in full formation, and that's the last Aggie sees of them. And it's the last she sees of her bread.

People are staring at her and smiling, some of them. "You're a very brave girl," the soap lady says. And Aggie just gives a very humble shrug and ambles toward the bread table, hoping to wangle another loaf, but Aunt Lily has already left, someone informs her.

She feels a little lonely without her bees.

At home she tells the whole saga of her bee adventure to her sisters. They seem properly amazed at first, but after she retells it with more and more details – for instance, what people said and how they looked when they said it – they drift back into the books they're reading. That's all they ever do, read books. At least Aggie's out there living a life fraught with danger and mystery. Maybe she'll go buy more cornflakes so she can tell it all over again to the cash register lady.

It's evening. They've finished a fine supper of canned beans and Styrofoam bread, during which Aggie has been trying to convince her sisters to go to the fair tonight.

"Na," Jeannie says.

Helen says, "I don't think I'm really interested in looking at a lot of grotesquely oversized pumpkins, or at somebody's prize cow."

"Come on, it'll be fun."

"You go."

But she doesn't feel like going alone at night, not after

this afternoon. Too many people know her around here. It's easier to hang out by yourself when nobody knows you, she reasons, because you can make up little fantasies about yourself to go along with whatever costume you happen to be wearing, and you can imagine people saying, *wow, what a strange but fascinating person she must be*. Once they get to know you, though, they treat you as if you're just an ordinary joe-blow wearing funny clothes, which ninety-nine percent of the time is what she is, but she doesn't like to come right out and admit that.

Someone is twisting the front doorbell. Duncan Hill! Helen and Jeannie are all smiles and chuckles, now.

"Want to go to the fall fair?" he asks. The question is directed at Helen, but Jeannie says, "Sure, why not?" At the same time, Helen says, "That would be fun." Meanwhile, Aggie's standing behind them with her hands on her hips and her mouth open, feeling a little like Cinderella.

Duncan says, "Come on, we'll all go." And Aggie gives him top marks for diplomacy. The two ugly stepsisters grab jackets, and off they all go, walking even though Duncan drove his car. "Too hard to find a parking place at night," he says. "People come from all over the county for this fair, you know." They walk four abreast on the road, probably, Aggie thinks, to avoid pairing off. They pass the high school and go out to the north end of the village, her parade route, which gives her a chance to retell her bee story. Duncan loves it.

A fair is better at night. As they get closer, they can hear the hurdy-gurdy sound of the merry-go-round and someone announcing a harness race. High above them, the Ferris wheel – lights atwinkle – stops briefly, its seats swinging. When it starts up again, people scream with joy and excitement. Aggie has a little thrill happening in her stomach just watching it.

Duncan says it's his treat, fortunately; otherwise they would have to sneak in. Two bucks for Jeannie and Aggie because the guy at the gate figures they're both students (ho-ho), and five for Helen and Duncan, the two adults. Aggie can't help grinning. *Is Jeannie's butt burnt, or what?*

Aggie can't remember when she's been happier. She has a greasy hot dog in one hand and a sticky cone of candy floss in the other, and she's loving them both, alternately. "You just don't know," she observes to her sisters and Duncan, although they're not listening, "how much your system cries out for junk food until you've been away from it for a long time. I feel like I've been rescued from a dungeon, where I've been locked up since the Middle Ages."

There are plenty of rides, although Aggie only wants to go on the Ferris wheel. On their way to it, they pause briefly to watch the little kids on the merry-go-round, and sure enough, they run into someone they know. Linda and Bert Quade are watching little Susie bound past on her musical horse. Helen starts up a conversation with them. Linda seems a little distant at first, but Bert is friendly. He knows Duncan, and Aggie thinks they must look like a nice little friendly group, which indeed, they are.

Bert says to her, "I hear you're making quite a name for yourself as a bee lady. Must have taken a lot of courage to get those bees back to their owner."

Aggie nods and shrugs and pretends it was nothing much, really, and would launch into the whole drama for them except that Helen starts nudging her to move along. "Be sure to watch the step-dancing competition," Linda calls after them. "Cameron is one of the fiddlers for it."

Aggie has to admit, Duncan is very generous the way he keeps encouraging them to spend his money. Helen tries her best to save it for him by saying "no thanks" to things, but Jeannie and Aggie have no scruples about it. They say "why not" and let him lavish on the treats.

They're in line for the Ferris wheel. "Next," the guy steadying the seat calls, and Jeannie steps up dragging Duncan with her. The safety bar snaps into place and they swoop backwards with an ecstatic little shriek from Jeannie. Helen and Aggie step up next and away they swing with a cheer from Aggie. Helen is not looking very cheery. Soon they're rising up to the top of the world. Jeannie and Duncan are directly above them, as over the top they go, Jeannie's laughter ringing out over the whole fair. Aggie catches a glimpse of her clinging close to Duncan, who has his arm across the back of the seat and on her shoulder. Not a peep out of Helen when it's their turn to go over the top, dropping with heart-stopping speed to the bottom of the loop and back up.

"You could have grabbed him just as easily as Jeannie," Aggie says.

"I don't know what you're talking about," she says.

"Yes, you do. You shouldn't just sit around waiting for things to come your way. Get out there and encourage them."

"Thank you, Miss Landers, for that piece of entirely unasked-for advice."

Their ride goes on forever, almost. "You really get your money's worth at this fair," Aggie says. As they come down for the last time, she catches sight of a stage with people on it, dancing – pointing their toes and kicking up their heels. And sure enough, there's Quade, his fiddle tucked under his chin. She points him out to Helen and says, "Let's go watch." For once, Helen agrees.

They go down the ramp from the Ferris wheel at a brisk pace, Helen dragging Aggie along by the arm right past Jeannie and Duncan. "The step dancing!" Aggie calls out to their surprised faces.

They find seats all in a row in the bleachers – Helen, Aggie, Jeannie, Duncan. Jeannie is laughing and making smart-ass remarks about the dancers. Duncan isn't saying very much. Helen sits mute, a stone. Up on the well-lit stage, Quade perches on a high stool, his bow a blur of activity over his fiddle, playing music that sounds a little like the second tune he played for Aggie's private concert-by-the-water.

The dancers come on, one by one, or in pairs. Right now it's a family of six boys and girls tappety-tapping their way to fame and fortune, all in matching green-and-white costumes. They're really good, Aggie thinks, but what does she know? She wishes she were one of them. Must be nice to have all those brothers and sisters all tapping their shoes to the same beat and smiling at each other as they dance shoulder-to-shoulder or face-to-face. She glances down at the proud mommy and daddy, sitting in the front row.

People are congratulating them on their nifty kid-dancers. What a lucky family, she thinks. They're bowing now, and so is Quade. Standing ovation, for sure. Cheering and whistling. A well-loved family.

Helen is starting to leave, and it's not even over. They don't know who won the dancing competition. "Sorry," she says. "I've got a pounding headache. I think I'll just go home." There is some discussion between Helen and Jeannie as everybody else in the audience sits down to await the judges' decision. It ends in Helen going, brushing past people's knees, saying, "Sorry, excuse me"; Duncan going with her; Jeannie looking disgusted but getting up to leave too; and Aggie saying, "Why is everybody leaving?"

At home, there is so much hostility in the air it feels like a war zone. Duncan has gone. If Jeannie's face gets any redder, flames will shoot out her nose; Helen's is corpse-white. Aggie's just waiting for an explosion, for the mother of all cupboard doors to be slammed, wondering how you'd call 911 without a phone. Go out on the street and shout it, probably. She thinks a basic truth is being revealed right now. Two sisters plus one man equals a very long division.

CHAPTER NINE

Aggie was right. She doesn't even want to think about it. It's enough to know that Jeannie fights dirty and Helen is tougher than you might imagine. And Duncan Hill hasn't been sighted in three weeks.

A few days after the bee episode, Mr. Clarke, the bee man, stopped by with two big containers of honey and a check made out to Aggie for fifty dollars – a windfall. All the way to the bank she kept thinking about what a wad that would make in her pocket, especially if she got it all in fives, or better still, a sackful of loonies. She imagined spending it on stuff she'd been longing for – salty chips, sugary pop, chocolatey anything. Then she got home, opened the fridge, rethought the whole windfall concept, and handed over half of it to Helen for groceries. Helen didn't say much when she did. She doesn't say much anymore at all. Her face looks closed. For the season.

Jeannie doesn't have a lot to say, either. Aggie kind of misses the bickering and sarcasm. It showed there were signs of life in their little palace. Feels like we're all asleep, Aggie thinks, waiting for the prince to come along. Helen is still getting a universal thumbs-down on every job she applies for. Not that there are many available. She nearly got a job in an antique store until the woman said, "Aren't you Cam Quade's girl?" Helen nodded. The woman interviewing her paused, cleared her throat, and said she'd let her know. "No getting away from it," Helen reported, "we're still the criminal element."

It's a windy October day. When Aggie goes outside, she looks up at the trees with their branches spread so wide she thinks they want her to applaud their brilliant final act. She would, too, if nobody could see her. Their leaves are pink and red and gold, and off they go like blown kisses while the bare branches bow and bend and sadly wave good-bye. She believes the sky is part of the act, a backdrop, eye-hurting blue, electric.

Leaves crunch underfoot, carpeting the sidewalks of Port Desire. People who live near the water rake them into piles and burn them. A thin blue wisp of smoke rises from a neighbor's backyard. To Aggie, still uncertain about her future, the air smells like the sadness of longing and unfinished dreams and cold empty nights.

She has to cheer herself up. Following a sign with an arrow, she finds herself at a garage sale not far away, at a house down the street. She pokes among the treasures and junk, not planning to buy anything, although there are many appealing little items, and some not so little. For instance, who, she wonders, could resist a giant chrome-plated ashtray on a pedestal, with an airplane taking off from one side of it? Twelve bucks. (Bit steep.) Okay, she thinks, how about this? A real black squirrel, stuffed. It's dead and everything, but why would anyone. . . . She's not even going to check for a price. She stops. *Well, would you look at this!* A music book with no music in it, just narrow little lines where you could put the notes if you knew them. Twenty-five cents (a steal). "I'll take that," she says to the woman behind the table. She pulls a few coins from her pocket, hands them over to the lady, and now she's the proud possessor of a potential sound track symphony. She's feeling pretty darn cheery now.

The next day, Sunday, Aggie drags Helen out of the house for some fresh air. Her long sad face is beginning to get on everyone's nerves. Even though she has sent off three letters asking about admission requirements to university and about student loans, she has received nothing in reply. Aggie is secretly happy about this, but also, she's feeling the tiniest twinge of guilt. She knows, but Helen doesn't, that there is no mail delivery in Port Desire. You have to go to the post office to pick it up. Aggie's sense of fairness gets the upper hand. They go across the street and up the steps, but of course, the post office is locked on Sunday.

They walk along Lake Street following the curve of the lake. As they pass the "bee" restaurant, Aggie sticks her tongue out, but Helen nudges her hard to make her stop. At that moment, the owner, Mr. Skint, pulls up in a truck about to drive in beside the restaurant. Helen and Aggie move hurriedly past the driveway, out of the way, Aggie feeling a little foolish. "Hey, Helen!" he calls through his open window. "I could use some help for the next day or two. Want a job?"

Helen is speechless, so Aggie returns the nudge. "Y . . . yes, I guess so." Aggie nudges her again. "Sure," she says. "When do you want me to start?"

"Right now, if you don't mind workin' on Sunday." He gets out of the truck and opens up the back, which is filled with boxes and crates.

"Me, too?" Aggie asks.

"How old are you?"

"Fourteen."

"Too young. Anyway, I can't afford to hire the botha yez." To Helen he says, "Well, if you're goin' to work, don't stand gawkin'. Give me a hand with these crates." Helen gives a little shuddery sigh and picks up one of the crates. Something pinkish red drips from one corner, and she screams. "Don't worry about it," Mr. Skint says. "I'll give you a big apron to cover your clothes."

"What is it?" Helen asks.

"Blood. It won't bite you."

Helen looks back at Aggie a little sickly, a little white-faced, and that's the last Aggie sees of her until six o'clock that evening.

"Oh, God!" Helen says at six, when she stumbles into the kitchen and flops down on a chair.

"What?" Aggie and Jeannie want to know. "What did you have to do?"

"Look at my hands!" Helen's hands are pink-streaked, with red gunk under her fingernails and around the cuticles. "And this is after I scrubbed," she howls.

"How come?"

"He's got himself a whole truckload of freshly killed chickens that need to be eviscerated and then packaged for freezing."

Jeannie starts to laugh; she howls with laughter as Helen's face takes on the hue of a storm cloud. "So, little Helen has a job ripping the guts out of dead chickens. I love it. All those squishy giblets and squirmy intestines and slimy egg sacs. Didja get any on ya? Is it bags of fun?"

Helen tries to get her blood-streaked hands around Jeannie's neck, but fails. Jeannie dodges and runs into one of the other rooms, hooting her glee. Helen rests her head on folded arms at the table and groans.

"I'm cooking fried eggs for supper," Aggie says.

Helen makes a gagging sound and lifts her head. "How could you?" In a few minutes she drags herself upstairs to the bathroom, announcing that she is from this moment on a vegetarian and for supper will have a lettuce leaf or two, only – if they have any.

Helen's chicken-guts job lasts three days. "Do you realize the extent to which I am going to support this family?" she says to her sisters. "Each day I force myself to face these plump, headless, baby-skinned creatures and nearly throw up when I have to stick my hand up their insides and yank out purple blobs and orange half-formed eggs and yellow gobs of fat. And the smell! I can't stand it. It's a sweetish, bloody, fatty, fresh flesh smell that gets in your hair and clothes and clings to your skin. I'm going up right now to shower."

By the last day, Helen arrives home in a better frame of mind. "I never thought I would, but you can get used to anything," she surprises her sisters by saying. Her face isn't as white as it has been on arriving home other days. In fact, there is a touch of color in her cheeks. "Here," she says gaily, plopping down on the kitchen table a freshly eviscerated chicken packed up for freezing, "a gift from Mr. Skint."

Aggie and Jeannie survey the donation skeptically, mouths turned down. Aggie puts a hand over hers. "After all your descriptions, I don't know. Chicken doesn't have the same appeal." Jeannie, however, takes it into the laundry room to put into the chest freezer.

Helen is standing idly in the kitchen, not, as she usually does, rushing up to have a shower.

"Did you get paid?" Aggie asks.

"Quite well paid. In fact, he wants me to come back to work in the restaurant part-time." She continues to stand in the middle of the kitchen, smiling. "I met Duncan on the way home," she says.

Aggie turns up the heat under the spaghetti water. "What did he have to say?"

"Nothing much." Helen is smiling serenely.

"Did he get close to you?"

"Well, sure, he walked me home."

"How did he feel about the glob of chicken fat clinging to your hair?"

"Oh, my God! You're kidding!" Horrified, Helen runs to look into a small oval mirror attached to the cupboard near the sink. "Oh, my God!" she repeats, pulling something yellow and sticky from her shining dark hair and pitching it into the sink. "I can't believe he saw me like this and didn't say anything."

"He's a real gentleman," Aggie says.

Helen is on her way to the shower, but sticks her head back into the kitchen as Jeannie returns. "Duncan wants to take me out for dinner next week," she announces.

"To the 'bee' restaurant?" Jeannie asks, ready to guffaw.

"No. There's another place not far away, quite elegant, apparently – a resort."

"I've heard about it," Jeannie calls after her. "They specialize in chicken."

If Helen hears her, she doesn't let on.

It's the day before Thanksgiving, and Aunt Lily has arrived to bring them, not one, but two loaves of bread. One they will freeze to have later. "One of these days," she says, "I'll give you a bread-making lesson, but not today." They are in the kitchen where Helen and Aggie are thinking about opening a box of Kraft Dinner. They ask her to stay and have some, and she thanks them as if she wouldn't mind, but she has too many things to do, she says.

Thanksgiving has come and gone. They didn't exactly celebrate it. They considered thawing the chicken, but then, in the end, nobody had an appetite for chicken. Linda invited them to share their turkey dinner, but Helen told her they had made other plans. Aggie regretted not having turkey (her poultry prejudice doesn't extend to turkey), but none of them really wanted to risk another session with the satanic Susie. For Thanksgiving dinner they had vegetable soup and toast spread with honey.

After their own Thanksgiving dinner, Linda came by

with some leftover cold turkey for the girls, saying that they had much more than they could eat. Aggie took her carefully measured share and made some sandwiches out of Lily's delicious bread to eat at school.

Aggie and Rachel are sitting together in the school cafeteria, as they usually do. Rachel scowls in distaste at her single plastic cheese slice between two slices of kapok posing as bread. "Want to try some of mine?" Aggie asks. She tears apart one of her turkey salad sandwiches and gives it to Rachel, who makes appreciative groaning sounds as she chews and swallows. "That is *sooo* good!" she mumbles through crumbs. "It's really delicious bread!"

Rachel's boyfriend, Gordie, looks up from his bag of chips and says, "Wha-a-a-t?" in such a plaintive way that Aggie gives him a bite, too. "Me, too," says the guy sitting next to Gordie, but Aggie pulls the rest of her lunch in close and guards it with her arms. "Trade you a . . ." He peers into his lunch bag, pulls out a tired bruised pear, and waves it at her. Aggie shakes her head. "Twenty-five cents?" he inquires. She narrows her eyes. "Fifty?"

"Sold," she says, wondering if she should have held out for seventy-five. Other kids are looking up from dry peanut butter, stale and nameless mounds of pressed meat, soggy lettuce, all between slices of preservative-laced breadlike substances. And so, before Aggie knows what's happened, she's sold her entire lunch. She doesn't know why she did that because she was starving, but maybe starvation is what inspires ideas. She now believes she could make really great sandwiches for kids and sell them at school if Aunt Lily would make good on her promise to show them how to bake the world's tastiest bread.

Duncan has taken to having coffee in the "bee" restaurant on the mornings Helen works there. Their date to go out for dinner, however, has been postponed indefinitely. The resort is closed for repairs.

Jeannie now works more hours sweeping up in the As You Like It. She still doesn't make much money, but she's allowed to give shampoos – a promotion, she figures. Not only that, she got a free haircut from Lydia, the woman who owns the salon. She looks a little classier than she did, in Aggie's opinion. Aggie actually didn't mind her tarty look because she always seemed to be having fun with it. Right now, with the blonde disappearing from her hair and her makeup all used up, she looks, Aggie thinks, like an insecure young kid wearing somebody else's clothes. After her haircut, she came home and asked Aggie if she knew a guy at school named Tom Ryan.

"What grade?"

"Thirteen."

"Nope," Aggie said, "can't say as I do. Why?"

"No reason," Jeannie said. "He's Lydia's son. Came into the shop today to drop off his books. Kinda cute."

"I'll keep an eye out," Aggie said, adding to herself, "for somebody who looks like a gangster." Jeannie's idea of "kinda cute" tends to lean toward the unwholesome.

Aggie has decided that the best way to approach Lily about moving in is through a letter. She has started one, but it's slow going. She's trying to explain the situation as sincerely and truthfully as she can. It starts: *Dear Great-Aunt Lily, I think our family problem is mostly mine because if my sisters leave, I have nowhere to go except to a group home or something. If you would move in, we could all live here, and if my sisters decide they have to go away, they can, but this would still be their home, and they would come back for holidays, I know. And I would be able to stay right here because you'd be here, and we could, in a way, look after each other. I know it will be hard for you to leave your island, but . . .* And that's as far as she's got. Lily will never leave her island, Aggie fears. She no longer feels like someone in a movie. Her inner projector seems to have shut down.

Speaking of movies, the one being produced by Aggie's English class is progressing at the speed of water evaporating. Somebody read out the first five or six scenes in class one day, and Aggie voiced her opinion. "I don't think people really talk like that, do they?"

Rachel said, "Like what?"

"Like doorknobs."

"Perhaps you could be more specific," Miss Greenwald said.

"People don't usually talk in long paragraphs like that, that just meander on and on. And the way it is now, when they do speak, you can't tell one character from the other. They all sound like the same person explaining things to all the other characters. I don't think there should be so much standing around explaining everything. It's a movie, isn't it? Gotta make 'em move."

Quade piped up with, "Some people talk in long paragraphs." And everybody laughed. Aggie had to laugh, too, because it's not often Quade gets off a good one.

But now, the movie has to go on hold for a couple of weeks while Miss Greenwald is off sick with the flu. Just before she got sick, Miss Greenwald put up signs in the post office and the grocery store and a few other places requesting the loan of a movie camera and projector for the class to use, if anybody in town has such items. A video recorder won't do because they want a big screen production. If they don't get someone to lend the necessary equipment, she told the class, she's going to find out if you can rent it somewhere.

Helen has had a reply to her letter about student loans. Aggie goes around with frown lines creasing her forehead because now Helen's busily writing more letters to see about actually getting one, and also requesting application forms for university entrance if she can get a loan; she doesn't care where. Could be anyplace – Vancouver, Halifax, North Overshoe.

Jeannie yells at her, "Right, so you get to go to university and I'm stuck with –" she pokes her thumb in Aggie's direction "– in Tombstone City."

"You should have thought of that when you quit school," Helen says. "You probably could have gone to university on a scholarship." Jeannie, although she hides it well, was nearly always at the top of her class back in Sudbury.

"I'm not staying in this lame town one minute longer than I have to," she says, and slams the door on her way out of the house to go out and squander some money on a large Coke.

Aggie has just closed her book, turned off her light, and is lying in bed thinking, worrying. Supposing Lily does move in, Aggie muses, and her sisters move out. Will she and Lily get to live in the house anyway? Possibly not, if she remembers rightly, according to the rules of the will. If not, maybe Lily would let her live with her on her island. Aggie shivers at that thought. She'd have to risk drowning every school day of her life.

Worse than anything would be the loneliness, though. She knows she'd miss her sisters in spite of all the fighting and bickering. They all have a lot of rough edges, she realizes. Their mother wasn't with them long enough to teach them how to be nice people, like Meg and Jo and Amy and Beth in *Little Women* – the book she found in the study and which she's just started to read. She and her sisters have never learned even to show each other affection. If they tried, they'd feel like total jerks. If their mom would just come back, all their problems would be solved. At least Aggie's pretty sure they would.

Forget that, she thinks. It won't happen. Her sisters will take off and she'll be stuck in some strange house somewhere with a lot of homeless bums. If she could have her heart's desire, she would like to keep her family together. If she had some money of her own, she could help pay the rent on a place near a university, if that's where Helen wants to be, or down in the States with Jeannie if she'd let her. If she could pay her own way, she wouldn't be a drag. She could stay with one sister half the year and with the other, the other half. That way, they wouldn't get sick of her.

She can't sleep. She has too many ideas buzzing around inside her head, some of which involve making and selling sandwiches to the kids at school. She's listening to the usual creaks and groans of the house, although maybe they're coming from her chronically empty stomach. She thinks Jeannie or Helen must be wandering around downstairs. She can hear something. Maybe she'll go down, too. Have a little bowl of cereal to see her through until morning.

Bright as day out in the hall, almost, she thinks. Well, not really, but it's bright with the moon shining in through the window above the wide front staircase. She's downstairs now without a light on. Doesn't need one. Anyway, the hall light's burnt out. What if they all burn out? she wonders. Will Helen break down and dip into the bank account? Probably not. There are some old candle stubs in a drawer they'll probably be forced to use. They'll be like moles. Probably develop night vision. Already have, she thinks, as she makes her way toward the kitchen.

She thinks she sees somebody on the back stairs. "Jeannie?" she whispers. Nothing. "Helen?" Gone back to bed without speaking, she guesses. Has she done something to them to deserve the silent treatment? Probably, she just can't remember what. She flicks on the kitchen light, has her cereal, and goes back up to bed. She snuggles in thinking about how, with the money she will make from selling sandwiches, the first thing she'll do is take her sisters out for a turkey dinner: crisply browned skin on the outside, and inside, succulent juicy meat, both dark and white, with dollops of seasoned dressing – a little crunchy – and brown gravy, rich, but not too thick, and . . . and for dessert . . . and for dessert. . . . Maybe she'll finish this meal tomorrow, when she's not quite so sleepy. Maybe she'll just burrow right in here and zed off.

Helen gets up when Aggie's alarm goes off now because she has the breakfast shift at the restaurant. "We seem to be going through the cereal pretty fast," she says, looking suspiciously at Aggie, who is trying to pop her toast before it burns and doesn't admit to anything. "And another thing," Helen says, "I thought we had a rule that the last person to bed locks the doors at night. I came down this morning and found the side door not even shut properly."

"Not my fault," Aggie says. "Must have been Jeannie" (who is still sawing it off and not there to defend herself).

CHAPTER TEN

It's Sunday morning – always a sluggish time in Port Desire, in Aggie's estimation. It's cold, but of course it's nearly November. The furnace came on in the night all by itself. They didn't have to do a thing. "Isn't a furnace like that one of the world's greatest inventions?" Aggie says to Helen as she dives into her breakfast, puffed wheat, a welcome change from cornflakes.

"Sure," Helen says, her voice flat, "until the fuel runs out."

"The bank will buy us more."

"Mmm," she says. She has lost a little control over things. She got a statement from the bank saying it had paid the hydro bill. There wasn't a darn thing Helen could do about it except say "humph."

They have been lounging in their usual Sunday style, reading the household books. Aggie is well into and loving *Little Women*. This could be me and my sisters, she keeps thinking, if we were a little sweeter and there was one more of us. The Quade sisters are still clad in their nightclothes – Helen in a well-mended flannel nightgown she's had since grade ten; Aggie in boxer shorts and her T-shirt with the hole in the back, on backwards by mistake, but covered by a pink satin dressing gown trimmed with deeper pink ostrich feathers; and Jeannie wearing nothing but a faded cotton quilt.

About midmorning they hear the side door opening and a voice calling, "Yoo-hoo!" Aggie puts a finger in her book, sticks her head around the living room door, and is greeted by Aunt Lily, who says, "Roll up your sleeves, ladies." She shrugs out of her coat and dumps it on the hall chair. "The secret of the bread is about to be revealed." While they scurry upstairs to get dressed, Lily busies herself searching the cupboards for bowls and pans and whatever ingredients might be on hand. She has brought with her, in one of her many canvas bags, a large bag of flour.

"This is what we're going to need," Lily tells them, when they appear in the kitchen ready to work. She has an errand for each of them – Aggie she sends to a woman three streets away who buys bulk bags of grains and seeds whenever she goes to the city and always brings back extra for Lily; Jeannie is to go shopping for yeast, potatoes, onions, and cheddar cheese to go in Lily's specialty loaf; and Helen she instructs to go to the hardware store to get an oven thermometer because, if Lily's memory serves her right, the oven isn't to be trusted. She offers to provide the necessary funds, but Helen says, "Absolutely not. We'll pay for it ourselves." Determinedly, carefully, she doles out some of her chicken-guts money to each of her sisters and off they go to do Lily's bidding.

When they return, they find Lily poking about in the study, a little out of breath, saying, "I don't know where Cam has hidden all the pencils and paper in this house. I've searched high and low."

The girls pause in removing their coats. Aggie thinks, oh-oh, she's losing it again. She looks Lily straight in the eye and says, "Cam's not here."

Lily shakes her head, looking a little embarrassed. Wearily she says, "Oh, my goodness me! What I meant to say was, there's nothing for you to write the recipe and instructions on."

The girls breathe a little easier, hang up their coats, and Helen says she'll get the necessary paper and pencils. Soon they are busy sifting, measuring, peeling an onion, grating cheese, and scribbling notes.

And now the job is finished. Four fine loaves of bread sit cooling on the kitchen table. The girls and Lily are smudged with flour; the kitchen looks like the site of a natural disaster, but they're all grinning and laughing and the radio's on, and Aunt Lily is putting on her coat, getting ready to go, and saying, "Now I've brought you girls a few things that might come in handy." From the deep pockets of her coat she pulls two tins of tuna, two tins of salmon, and a jar of mayonnaise. "Eee," says Aggie, "we're in the sandwich business!" Helen, of course, would like to pay for the donated items, but Aunt Lily won't hear of it.

They all go down to the boathouse with her, where she left her boat tied to the dock beside it. She looks into the boathouse and says, "That old rowboat's going to sink if we don't bail it soon. And we'll have to get it out of the water before freeze-up."

"Oka-a-a-y . . ." the girls say, with hesitation in their voices. Does she mean "we" as in all four of them, they wonder? "How do we, um, go about this?" Aggie asks reluctantly because she has this not entirely irrational fear of falling out of boats and drowning.

"You know how to do that as well as I do," Lily says over her shoulder as she heads for her own boat. "And Cam, don't forget to cover it with the tarpaulin!" The girls look guardedly at each other, mouths turned down because Lily seems to have slipped out of reality again and they aren't sure what they should say. Aggie has been working up to the topic of Lily moving in. Now the moment seems to be lost.

With her canvas bag beside her, Lily sits down heavily on the dock and unties her boat, varnished to such a high gloss you can see yourself in it. "Don't let me drift," she says, handing Aggie the rope and knocking her bag over, spilling out her wallet and a calendar and some mints, all of which she scoops up from the dock and stuffs back in. "Lucky it didn't fall in the lake," she says.

"Aunt Lily," Aggie begins.

Lily eases herself down into the boat with a grunt, making it tip precariously until she sits down on a cushioned chair behind a complicated-looking engine in the middle. "Yes, dear," she says, as she gets the engine going without much trouble.

Aggie has thought of a new way to ask the question. "When," she says, "are you planning to move in with us?"

"Throw me the rope," Lily says, "and give me a little push off. That's the girl." She looks up at Aggie. "You know, I don't think I can do it. It's such a sad house now."

"It wasn't sad while we were making the bread," Aggie calls over the sound of the engine.

"True," Lily calls back. "But, I can't get it out of my head that it's a bitter house since, well, since Cam grew up. An unlucky house. I'm sorry." She puts on her floppy-brimmed hat, waves good-bye with one hand while she grips a little steering wheel on the side attached to ropes and pulleys, and off she goes, not too speedily, but at a pretty good clip all the same. Aggie's shoulders slump. Even Helen and Jeannie look disheartened.

They watch Lily as she sets out across the lake, her hand on top of her head to hold her hat on, but instead of going straight ahead, she slows down and makes a big circle. "I nearly forgot," she calls, halfway around her circle. "I hear your school needs some movie-making equipment, Agatha."

"That's right," Aggie yells back.

"You have the very thing. It's in the back room behind the laundry room," she calls from the far side of her circle. She waves, straightens her boat, and continues on with one hand on her hat.

"It's not there," Aggie calls back, but Lily doesn't hear her.

The girls watch her all the way to her island, which doesn't seem very far away, now that they know it's hers. They can no longer hear the engine. The boat slows and glides in behind the trees sheltering what must be her boathouse. "Maybe we can change her mind about the house," Aggie sighs.

"Give it up," Helen says. "She's a daft old lady who says whatever pops into her head. You heard her in the boathouse."

"No, but –" Aggie wants to argue.

"The day she moves in," Jeannie says, "is the day I'll pledge my life to higher education and the betterment of mankind."

Helen snorts.

Aggie says, "But she will if we can convince her that the house isn't as unlucky as she thinks."

Jeannie says, "Yeah-yeah, and Santa will bring us a million bucks."

The older girls, shivering now, bustle back up to the house. "Wait," Aggie calls, "we have to get the rowboat out of the water."

Helen stops and calls out to Aggie, "You leave that rotten old boat exactly where it is. It's not our problem. I'm not going to have you nearly drowning on us in this weather. Did you hear me?"

"No," Aggie mutters. She stands in the boathouse door contemplating the half-swamped boat. The water in the boathouse is shallow. She wouldn't drown in there. She hopes. There's a pail in the corner of the boathouse, near the tarpaulin she slept under that first night. She remembers the cockroaches and shudders.

Bailing a boat is not the most fun in the world, but she does it without falling into the drink. By the time she finishes, the sun is going down, but she's proud of her work.

The old boat is bone dry and she's half frozen. *Never mind.* She scrambles out of the boat, puts the bailer back in the corner, grabs the tarp checking for bugs, but they must all have gone wherever bugs go in cold weather. She lugs it over and drops it into the boat. Next she unties the boat, hangs on to the rope, and pulls it out to the end of the boat slip along the catwalk. Still holding the rope, and hanging on to the doorframe of the boat slip, she edges herself around onto the dock outside. "Did it," she says out loud.

"Now, what?" She lets go of the rope, gives the boat a big push toward a piece of sandy shore opposite the boat-house dock, under the now leafless branches of the willow tree, where it stops with a little scrape. She jumps across to the beach, grabs the rope again, and hauls with all her might – pulling it up, up, crunching it over the sand and pebbles – and up it comes, finally, onto the grassy shore. She is out of breath but no longer freezing. She's sweating, but she doesn't stop there. *Nope, not until the job's done.* She hauls out the tarp, stands on one side of the boat until it turns half-over, and yanks on the other side until the boat flips, bottom up, just as she jumps out of the way. Mission accomplished. She covers it with the heavy tarp as Aunt Lily asked her to, and stands back, very, very proud of her work.

That evening she busies herself in the kitchen until she's so weary she can hardly drag herself up the stairs to bed.

At school on Monday, she says to Rachel, "I'm selling sandwiches today. Want to help me pass the word around?"

Rachel says, "Are you allowed to do that?"

"Probably not, so keep it quiet. No telling how the big guy will react to real food being sold in competition with those pseudo-sandwiches decaying all over the cafeteria."

"Right." Rachel nods knowingly. She will use the word "black market," she decides, and keep a finger on her lip.

By second period Aggie is blitzed with orders. She sends a note around to her potential customers, saying they can exchange goods for money at Aggie's locker just before lunch. The buzzer goes, ending the final period of the morning. Aggie saunters to her locker, clandestinely spins out the numbers of her combination, checks over each shoulder for spies, and notices a line beginning to form. "Spread out," she hisses, and they all start to mingle and move. She opens her locker and hauls out a plastic bag with about sixteen wrapped sandwiches in it. Quickly she hands out the first three and pockets the money. She shakes her head at someone with a twenty-dollar bill. In no time at all, it seems, she has the sandwiches distributed and even manages to make change for the guy with the twenty. And she's now forty-eight dollars richer. *Eee, look at me go!* It feels like forty-eight thousand.

She can hardly get her own lunch into her for kids, total strangers, coming up to her and asking to be put on her sandwich list. One of them says he's Tom Ryan and that he knows her sister Jeannie. Aggie adds him to her list. *Talk about your supply and demand!* I think we've got a commercial giant in the making, she marvels. It's like, move over McDonald's!

At home after school there is a beehive (so to speak) of activity going on. Helen has been baking bread all day, using the instructions she wrote down word for word while Lily the Great showed them how to manufacture the world's most popular bread. Jeannie has just come back from shopping with her sweeping-up money and buying more mayo and green onions and fresh dill and lettuce, and Aggie doesn't know what all. Aggie turns her knapsack upside down on the kitchen table and pours out the forty-eight dollars, which she intends to share with them. Jeannie shrieks, and Helen hugs her, getting flour all over her Mary Poppins jacket. Aggie feels like standing dead still to stare at Helen with her mouth hanging open because, believe it or not, that was a genuine, arms-around-her hug. But she doesn't. Instead, she laughs out loud, and pretty soon they're all laughing as if they are insane little capitalists. Which they are.

Life in Port Desire is all they could possibly hope for. The sandwich factory is a total success story. Jeannie took some sandwiches to the As You Like It and passed around a plateful to the ladies under the hair dryers. They couldn't get enough of them. She now has orders for a Christmas party and two bridge parties. They asked her if she bakes cookies as well.

She consults with Helen and Aggie. "Why don't we?"

Helen says, "Not a good idea. We're good at bread and we're good at sandwiches. Let's stick to what we do well."

Jeannie shrugs, but agrees. Aggie shrugs and agrees, too, because who knows? It's probably good advice, and Helen's probably on her way to becoming a corporate goddess.

Jeannie seems more agreeable in many respects. Aggie can scarcely believe the lack of bickering between her sisters. She would like to imagine that the bread-making project has brought about some sort of miracle, and maybe it has, but she also has to take into consideration the fact that Jeannie has a boyfriend. That's right, he's Lydia the hairdresser's son, Tom Ryan. And he's cute and doesn't look even remotely like a gangster as Aggie noted when he introduced himself at school.

"So not Jeannie's type," Helen says out of the corner of her mouth to Aggie, when she sees him for the first time. He has walked home with Jeannie from the As You and she has invited him in. "Great house," he says, looking around in astonishment. "Looks like something out of an old movie."

Aggie pricks up her ears. "Old movie?" she says. "Do you like old movies?"

"Doesn't everybody?" Tom says.

"Absolutely," Jeannie says, smiling broadly. Helen and Aggie glance at each other because if there's one thing Jeannie has always said she hates, it's old movies. "Come on," Jeannie urges Tom, "I'll give you a little tour of the place."

Afterwards, after Tom leaves, Jeannie joins her sisters in the kitchen, where Aggie is making a salad (something new in their diet) and Helen is mixing up ground beef and onion soup mix in an effort to make meat loaf from a recipe she found in one of the household cookbooks (also a brand new dining concept for them). Jeannie says, "Did you ever notice the green-and-gold elephant that stands on a table in the study?" Both her sisters say yes and ask why. "Aren't there supposed to be two of them?"

Aggie frowns and says, "I think so."

Helen frowns and says, "I can't remember."

Jeannie says, "I can't remember, either. Anyway, there's only one."

"Maybe there only *was* one," says Helen.

"Maybe."

"I think there were two," Aggie insists.

"Intriguin'," Jeannie says.

Helen continues mixing up her meat loaf and Aggie continues making her salad. All three look worried. Helen says, finally, "I think there was only one."

Duncan Hill and Helen seem to be becoming an item. It's Friday, and Helen has thawed Mr. Skint's chicken and invited Duncan for dinner. When she sees how little meat there actually is on one bird, she tells Aggie and Jeannie to say they don't want very much and to just fill up on mashed potatoes. "Hah!" says Jeannie, "dream on."

Aggie says, "I'm grabbing a leg, and that's that." The captivating aroma of roasting chicken has removed any qualms they may once have had stemming from Helen's chicken-guts stories. But, when the time comes, they do hold back like proper little martyrs. "*Little Women* ain't got nothin' on us," Aggie says, halfway through her heavy-on-the-mashed-potatoes meal.

"Pardon?" Helen asks.

"Nothing," she says.

Helen offers Duncan seconds. Aggie and Jeannie spend the rest of the meal being amazed by Helen, who is actually flirting with Duncan – smiling with her eyes, coy as some ancient movie queen from the fifties. She's wearing tight black (what else?) pants and a black sweater with a (believe it or not) mauve-and-green scarf around her neck! "Très chic," Aggie said, when Helen was trying it out in front of the mirror. Helen said, doubtfully, "Are you sure?"

Jeannie behaves herself for the entire meal and doesn't once try to move in on Helen's territory. Aggie keeps an eye on her, waiting for her to strike, but the only thing she does that's questionable is tell a couple of off-color jokes. Miraculously, Helen doesn't get peeved. She even smiles. And Duncan laughs like a loon.

It seems to Aggie that everybody has a boyfriend except her. Everybody at school is talking about the upcoming Christmas dance. You don't really need a date to go, she's heard, but a lot of people are going in couples. Her friend Rachel is going with her guy, Gordie. She says to Aggie, "You know a lot of guys would ask you out if you didn't dress so weird."

Aggie says, "What do you mean? I've toned down my costume-wearing to almost zero." Although, from time to time, she can't stand the uniformity of jeans and a sweater and turns up in something spectacular from her third-floor wardrobe department.

Rachel reminds her, "Last week you wore some green feathery thing around your neck."

"Oh, that," Aggie says. "Nothing."

"And yesterday," Rachel continues, "it was that ghastly plaid skirt with the zillion little pleats."

"I like twirling in it," Aggie says in defense. "Anyway, I don't think I'm about to give up my costumes just so some wimpy little creep can get up enough nerve to ask me to the dance. If I didn't have costumes, my soul would wither."

Rachel's eyes are aglow. "That is so profound," she sighs.

One day it's so mild it seems like spring and the next it's snowing. That's December for you, Aggie thinks. It's Sunday and they are all sleeping in, but maybe she'll get up because she has a lot of sandwiches to make for Monday's lunchtime. The house is kind of chilly, but that's the way Helen insists on keeping it to make the fuel last.

Aggie throws on a sweatshirt and looks around for socks. No socks. Down the stairs she goes. Nobody else is up. She looks out the front door to see how much snow there is. Quite a bit, actually, she notices. It's cold on the feet in the hall. She skips on down to the laundry room to see if she did her washing (she can't remember because she doesn't do it very often). "Yup. Here we are," she says, reaching into the dryer. "Cozy socks."

For no reason that she can think of, except that the house is chilly, she decides it would be fun to light a fire in one of the fireplaces. She opens the door of the back room, where the dead plants are, to get some of the old newspapers to start the fire. She turns on the light and lets out a yell. "Oh, my God! What the frig? This is psycho! This is way too spooky!"

Sitting on a table, half hidden by a pile of newspapers, is a movie camera, a projector, and as she looks closer, a box containing the splicing thing that Quade mentioned, floodlights, reels, and an instruction book. *What is going on? Someone's been in our house. Or else there's a ghost. Or else. . . .* She thinks she's going to start to scream. She *is* screaming. Helen and Jeannie are flying down the stairs. "Where are you?" they shout. They find Aggie in the back room and stare at her in bewilderment. "What's wrong?" they say in unison.

Aggie points to the movie equipment. "This stuff just appeared like magic," she tells them. "It wasn't here when we first moved in."

"Don't be silly," Helen says. "It couldn't just appear like magic."

Aggie curls her lip at Helen. She knows that, but on the other hand, how, in fact, did it get here? "How did it get here?" she asks. "Quade and I were looking for it, months ago. We looked in here."

"Well, I guess you didn't look very hard."

"No, wait, this is serious. Someone has got into our house and put this here. We should go to the police."

"And say what?" Jeannie asks. " 'Oh, yes, Constable, someone has been breaking into our house and giving us things.' Right. With our reputation, he'll charge us with possession of stolen property."

Helen says, "Don't worry about it. It'll all come clear in the fullness of time." Typical Helen statement. Like her do-nothing attitude toward the bees. Aggie doesn't know what to do. Maybe she'll get dressed and go ask Quade what he thinks about it. Maybe it was him.

She trudges along through the snow in her trusty combat boots and three sweaters because she's outgrown her warm jacket from two winters ago. It came in the box of their things sent by Mrs. Muntz. Usually she inherits Jeannie's castoffs, but not this year. Jeannie must have stopped growing because she's once again wearing her old puffy ski jacket, even though, as Jeannie complains, it's decades out of style. "Out of style!" Aggie said to her when she dragged it out. "What does that mean?"

It's stopped snowing, and the sun is coming out. Church bells are bonging, and people are coming out of church and heading home to, what? Aggie wonders. Roast beef and gravy? Bacon and tomato sandwiches? French fries? Her stomach is rumbling so loudly, she decides to run so as not to deafen the villagers.

She knocks on the front door of the Bertie and Linda Quade home, hoping rat-faced Susie won't answer. She does, however. She looks at Aggie as if she's roadkill. "What do *you* want?" Susie snarls.

"I want to speak to your brother," Aggie says sweetly, trying to sound as much as possible like one of the Little Women.

"He's not here." *Slam* goes the door.

Knock-knock-knock, Aggie persists.

The door opens slowly, a crack. "What?" Susie growls.

"When will he be back?"

"How should I know?"

Aggie has her shoulder against the door so that Susie

can't slam it again. She's now smiling down at Susie, well sort of smiling, with all her teeth showing, but her lips stretched viciously, and she's hissing at her through her teeth, and on Susie's face is a look of pure, unadulterated terror. And Aggie's loving it.

"Is someone at the door, Susie, sweetie?"

"Waaa!" Susie yells and runs away.

"Oh, Agatha! It's you," Linda says, appearing in the doorway. "Don't mind Susie; she's in a bit of a blue funk, this morning. Anything I can do for you?"

"I was looking for Cameron." There, she said it. *That wasn't so bad, now was it?* Probably lots of people called Cameron in the world, besides her father.

"He's away taking part in a music recital in Ottawa. He won't be back until tonight. Any message?"

"No, not really."

"I'll tell him you stopped by."

Susie appears behind her mother before the door closes. She's pointing at Aggie and saying, "She did it again! She did it again!"

"What, dear?" her mother asks in a sugarcoated voice.

"She beed mean to me!"

Aggie shakes her head dejectedly, shrugs a little, turns sad but patient eyes on Linda, smiles benevolently, and leaves. But not before she hears Linda say, "Now, Susie, sweetie, aren't you exaggerating, just a little?"

At home Aggie decides she'll take Helen's advice and not do anything immediately about the movie equipment, not that there is anything she really can do. Maybe it's not a question of having watched too many movies in her short lifetime. Maybe Quade really didn't bring it back all those years ago, as he said he had. And now he's repented, and somehow sneaked it back when they were all out. It gives her the shivers. Even if it was Quade – someone she knows and, up until today, trusted – it makes her feel defenseless. Someone has been tampering with her private space. She will start insisting Jeannie lock the door because she is usually last to bed.

CHAPTER ELEVEN

It's only two and a half weeks until Christmas! For the first time since almost forever, Aggie thinks, she's looking forward to the holiday. They're still in Port Desire, the lake shows no signs of freezing over, which means they will not have to leave for a while yet, and she has finally finished her letter to Aunt Lily and posted it. She hasn't heard anything back, obviously, because these things take time, but she's hopeful about it. She poured out her heart in it. She hopes at least some part of it will influence Lily to change her mind about the house's bad luck reputation.

The girls have decided to have a Christmas tree if they can find any decorations lurking about the homestead. They are convinced they will because the ancestors seem to have saved everything else. They spread themselves out to go hunting. "Why don't you look down cellar," Helen suggests to Aggie, but Aggie shakes her head. "Why not?" Helen asks.

"For some reason, when I go down there, I get the feeling that this is all temporary."

Helen says, "Well, it *is* temporary. We all know that. Let's just hope they don't kick us out until we all have someplace else to go."

"Someplace all together, or all separately?" Aggie asks.

Helen doesn't answer. She has her head inside a boot cupboard in the back hall.

Aggie's thinking about the cellar. She thinks that by "temporary," it means her own personal life, that life isn't real; it's a movie. And that someday the movie will end. Or maybe the film will break. It's a very fragile, risky thing to be living in a movie about your life because when the film *does* end, she'll have to face the fact that in real life she's nothing special. She's a nobody who wears funny clothes to make herself think there's more to her than flesh and bones. She'll have to face the fact that there are no props. No mother, no father, no family at all, really, except two sisters who are going to live at opposite ends of the world. No screen. No costumes.

No home. Whenever she has to go down cellar, the truth hits her like a slap in the face.

Instead of the cellar, she offers to search the third floor for decorations. Up there possibilities always leap out at her from the clothes storage room, swirling her away from her ordinary life when she twirls in a pleated skirt that flares out like the wings of a butterfly, or when she strides about importantly in an army officer's peaked hat and khaki jacket with brass buttons.

Jeannie is sure she has seen a box of decorations in the room where the mysterious reappearing movie equipment lives, but no such item exists. After searching every likely spot, they finally give up. "Maybe," Aggie says, "Grand-father pulled a Scrooge and avoided Christmas altogether."

Aggie continues to puzzle about the movie camera mystery. When she finally had a chance to tell Quade about it, he looked truly mystified. He wasn't the guilty party, she's pretty sure, unless he's one heck of a good actor, which she doesn't believe he is.

It's Friday, and Quade is ringing the front doorbell because he is going to help Aggie cart all the movie stuff to school. They're going to start filming this afternoon. Miss Greenwald said they could do it in class time because after school a lot of people want to decorate for tonight's Christmas dance. Aggie can hardly wait. To start filming, that is – not for the dance, which she may drop in on if she gets up her nerve, or she may not, because when you get right down to it, she doesn't know how to dance.

Yesterday, Miss Greenwald asked her if she would like to direct the movie. Her heart soared. Besides wanting to write a movie script (which she seems to have failed at, mis-erably), she has always known in her heart that she is a born director. She hasn't the foggiest notion of how to direct a movie, but she's not going to let that stand in her way. She finds it a little puzzling that she doesn't mind tack-ling a directorship, but throwing herself cold onto a dance floor petrifies the life out of her.

"This stuff is heavy," she says to Quade. "Good thing the school isn't far away." He agrees. It's a cold day. She was lucky enough to find a coat to fit her amongst the other stored treasures. She would have gone for fur except for the reaction she got at school when she wore the dead fox around her neck. *Talk about your politically incorrect neckwear!* Anyway, she's wearing a handsome but heavy tweed overcoat that comes down to her ankles. Serious weight problem here, she thinks, as she struggles toward the school with Quade and their burdens. The coat is so heavy she keeps warm just trying to stay vertical.

She's carrying a carton holding the camera, some lights, some film, and a whole raft of sandwiches for the hungry lunchtime clientele. Quade has a carton containing a tripod, the projector, some reels in round flat tins, and the rest of the lights. They're puffing along side by side, their breath like empty cartoon balloons moving slightly ahead of them.

Quade fills up his balloon. "Are you going to the dance?"

"Who, me?" Who else, she thinks, but she's stalling because she doesn't know whether this is an innocently curious question or a lead-in for something more traumatic. "Um," she continues. The balloons are empty again. "Are you?" she asks, to be neighborly.

"Um," he says.

Here we go again, she thinks, twins separated at birth – same droll skill with the English language, same ability to get to the point.

"I might," he says.

After a lengthy pause, she says, "Yeah, me too, maybe."

There's silence, now. Glad we got that settled, she thinks.

Trudge, trudge they go and finally reach the school. Quade holds the door open with one elbow. They get themselves in out of the record low temperature and take the stuff up to Miss Greenwald's room, which is unlocked because she's there already. Aggie nabs her bag of sandwiches and heads off to her locker. Quade is about to head off to his locker, but before he does he says, "The dance starts at eight, so I'll pick you up at a quarter to."

"Huh?"

He's gone. His locker's downstairs. And there stands Aggie, her face all wide-eyed with astonishment, wondering how she got to the point of being picked up at a quarter to eight to go to a dance with a boy. Also, he's her cousin. Is this allowed? she wonders. I mean, couldn't you end up with a lot of idiot children? Although, she reasons, it's just a dance. He didn't exactly ask her to be his lawfully wedded wife or anything. But, jeez, she didn't even know that's how you ask a girl to a dance. I'm so naive, she thinks, I could end up married with five kids just 'cause some total stranger asks me if I might get married someday. Do you ever have to be careful, these days!

Aggie's directing her first film! History in the making! It's actually not going very well. She keeps saying, "Lights! Camera! Action!" and everybody starts dithering around and forgetting their lines and forgetting to move, and then they have to stop. A girl named Lisa, one of the stars, goes up to Aggie and says, "Would you please mind not yelling 'lights-camera-action' all the time because it just makes everybody nervous."

So. She's sitting still on a high stool, mouth clamped shut. She thought lights-camera-action was part of the director's role. But, who knows?

"Hey, hold on. Excuse me," she can't help blurting, but politely. The camera guy stops the camera and straightens up from the tripod with a big sigh. The actors groan. "You've got your back to the camera," she explains to one of the key actresses. "We have to see what you have in your hand. And you all have to speak louder if the tape recorder is going to pick up your voices."

And so it goes. Another star, Tanya, doesn't like her costume, so Aggie pats her on the back and tells her it looks great on her, that black is her color, and all that.

She pretty well stays behind the camera guy, watching the action like the umpire behind home plate. Nothing gets past her steely glare. I am merciless, she thinks, in my demand for perfection. Well, maybe not totally merciless. Right now she's giving them all a break while Lisa fluffs up her hairdo. Her mother let her bleach her hair just for the movie. One must cater to the stars from time to time, Aggie finds.

Miss Greenwald has been rubbing her hands together in glee, saying, "This is great; this is wonderful." A lot of people have brought along props, including Miss Greenwald, for the three scenes – a modern Canadian house, a space-ship interior, and an alien planet. Rachel, who is artistic, has drawn a huge map of the world, which they need for special effects.

The bell goes and so endeth the first reel of film. They'll start a new reel on Monday, after school. Not too many teens sticking around to put things away, Aggie notices. Oh, well, that's what directors are for, she guesses. Quade's helping, she sees. Miss Greenwald says, "I thought we were going to have some background music."

"We are," Aggie says. "I'm hoping Cameron (first name, notice) will figure out how to put some in. We could have him playing his violin in certain strategic places."

Quade gets all frowning and thoughtful and screws his mouth over to one side and taps his finger on his lip and finally says, "Maybe."

They have arrived at the much anticipated Christmas dance. True to his word, Quade came ringing Aggie's bell at precisely a quarter to eight. She wasn't quite ready because she couldn't decide what to wear. Thinking about it, she groans inwardly because it sounds so typically teenagerish, even though she always prides herself on being a little off center in the typical department.

The posters advertising the dance said SEMIFORMAL, which Rachel said meant 'don't rent or nothin'; just wear something good.' (You can rent clothes? Aggie is amazed. Should she be looking into this as a business venture?)

Something good, hmmm, she mused. She suffers, it seems, from a surfeit of good things to wear. Finally she narrowed her choices down to a sort of choir-gownish thing – red underneath with white over the shoulders that looked Christmasy – or a purple velvet long dress with really long sleeves (down past her fingers) and a V neck that would look good if you could provide it with a generous bustline which, she has to admit, she cannot, hers being a trifle modest.

So there was Quade, forced to sit in one of the many living rooms, making polite conversation with Helen and Jeannie and Jeannie's boyfriend, Tom. Jeannie and Tom are going to the dance, too, but plan to arrive fashionably late. "I don't know what to wear," Aggie yelled down, finally.

To cut to the chase, she ended up modeling both creations for the assembled audience and got quite a few laughs, which was not the desired effect. "I like that one," Quade mumbled, as she was about to return the purple dress to her private costume department, having decided on jeans and a sweater, which on Aggie amounts to something rare and even good.

"Really?"

His cheeks and ears were aglow and his hair, which he had earlier combed and parted, apparently, started leaping into corkscrews all over his head, but he was smiling.

"Okay," Aggie said, and bobbed her own curly head from side to side because she was kind of liking the purple herself. "Wait," she said. "I have just the thing for you." Before he could scowl and back off (not really, he did scowl and did back off), she ran upstairs and came down with a jacket for him to wear.

He looked at it doubtfully, his eyebrows up and his mouth squinched to the side. "I don't know about this."

"Just try it on," she said.

In the background Jeannie and Helen were trying to hold in snorts of laughter. Tom sat with his chin in his hand, tilting his head first one way then the other. "You make a great couple," he said, at length, "a matched set."

The coat was a beautiful black number, with long tails

in back and cut short in front. It actually fit him pretty well and looked great with his jeans and checked shirt. Aggie dragged him out into the hall to look in the full-length mirror. He stood in front of the mirror with a little smile on his face and drew himself up tall, his hand on his abdomen and his head tilted to one side.

And so they are at the dance – Aggie in her purple velvet with her combat boots peeking out below, and Quade in a tailcoat and jeans. Really, she thinks, you can't get much more semiformal than that.

The music is blaring around them, but they are not exactly rushing out onto the dance floor. Quade leans over and says something into Aggie's ear. She thinks he said he doesn't know how to dance. She just shrugs and notices that it's pretty crowded out there, but actually, that's good. So there she is, dragging old Quade out onto the dance floor, bumping a few people out of the way and turning her palms up, saying, "So who does?" She makes her shoulders go in time to the music and her hips and she doesn't know what she's doing, but it feels like dancing.

Quade at first stands dead still, looking as though, if he moves, a trapdoor in the floor will open and he'll never be heard from again. But soon, as people jostle and bump against him, he has to take a step or two in self-defense, and before he knows it, he's grinning and bopping here and there and, wow, Aggie thinks, this guy is good. A regular twinkle-toes.

People are staring at them, but mostly at Quade, she has to admit, who cuts rather a dashing figure in *Aggie's* tailcoat. Girls are giving him the eye, especially older girls she doesn't even know. She narrows her eyes. *Back off, babes; he's mine for the moment, cousin or not.*

After the dance they walk home with a whole gang of teenagers, just like in the movies. Some reach their streets and peel off. Aggie and Quade keep going. They can see Aggie's place straight ahead, with the streetlight in front. She hopes this doesn't get cheesy and awkward with Quade trying anything romantic, like kissing or anything, because she's just not into that yet. Maybe someday, she thinks, but at the moment she isn't sure her hormones have properly kicked in because all she feels right now is inadequate. She can't even show affection to her sisters, fergawdsake, without feeling like a complete fool.

Somebody is standing under the streetlight looking up at Aggie's house, which seems bizarre at this hour, midnight-ish. It gives Aggie chills. Shoo, she thinks, go way, don't stare at my house.

"Who's that?" Quade whispers.

"No idea." It's a woman – that's all she can see from where they are on the other side of the street – a woman smoking. Aggie can feel her looking at them as they cross the street and go up onto the front veranda. "So, thanks, eh," she says to Quade, and wonders whether she should offer to shake hands with him as a parting gesture, this being a semiformal evening and all. Suddenly the woman calls out, "Jeannie?"

A little shiver is happening inside Aggie. She knows her, knows her voice. She is a mass of electrical goose bumps.

She's gliding down the veranda steps toward her, not walking, not breathing. This is not a dream, though, she's sure of that, and not a movie, either. "It's Aggie," she says, and her voice sounds like a little kid's voice.

"Aggie!" the woman says. "You've got so tall!"

Aggie is right in front of her, within touching distance, and she can see it's her all right. She thinks, shouldn't we be throwing our arms around each other?

The woman puts her cigarette to her lips briefly, then throws it away, exhales, and puts her hands on Aggie's shoulders. "Let me see you," she says, turning her toward the light. She takes in Aggie's long tweed coat and the little curls all over her head. "You're all grown up. Has it been that long?" Her huge eyes go all wide and soft.

She looks the same, maybe older, pinched, but it's cold and her jacket doesn't look very warm. Her hair is different, longer, Aggie notices.

Quade has come down off the veranda. "It's my mother," Aggie says to him. To her she says, "This is Cameron Quade. Same name as Dad's. He's our cousin."

The woman stares at him. He's curved into a slouch, with his hair covering half his face. "Cousin?" she says.

"Second cousin," he says. "My dad is . . . was . . ." He stops.

"Oh, yes – Cousin Bert. I sort of remember hearing. . . ."

They're all huddling in the cold, their breath freezing in front of their faces. "Come on in to the house," Aggie says.

"Well," her mother says, "just for a minute, maybe. It's pretty late."

"But, you have to stay!" She has a little moment of fear. "You can't leave us! Once you get inside, you'll want to stay." Aggie almost pulls her up the veranda steps. She can't let her escape a second time. She'll tie her to a chair if she has to.

Cameron is plodding slowly down the street, head hunched into his shoulders. He turns and glances back.

CHAPTER TWELVE

Aggie's in bed now, but not asleep. She feels she may never sleep again. In a bedroom down the hall, her mother is making herself comfy. She can hear the bedsprings squeak. She keeps listening. She doesn't want to wake up in the morning to find that she has left. Once was enough.

Helen didn't seem very excited to see her. She was sleepy, though – that's why, Aggie believes. She had to wake her up to tell her that Mom was back. She came downstairs in her pajamas, and they just stared at each other. "Hug her," Aggie kept saying under her breath because Helen knows how to hug. Aggie knows that. But nothing happened.

Jeannie was still out. In the living room, Helen sat down on the end of the couch, and their mother chose a chair a little distance away, where she sat uncertainly on the edge, her knees and hands pressed together like a little kid trying to be good. Aggie had never noticed before how open her face is, and how sweet, with big sad eyes, very pale blue, like Jeannie's, and long eyelashes, possibly false, but that's all right. Aggie sat down on the other end of the couch, close to her mother. Helen started asking questions then, a stream of them, such as: where have you come from, where is your suitcase, how long are you staying, and things like that. Aggie just kept quiet and listened.

It turned out she had a change of clothes in the shiny big handbag she was carrying. She had come from Sudbury on the bus and had got in just before Aggie came along. Before that, she was in the States, all over the place – Boston, Chicago, New York, but mostly in California. "California!" She rolled her big eyes. "Man! That's the place to be."

"There's no bus into Port Desire on Friday," Helen said.

Her mother stopped smiling about California, her eyes looking from Helen to Aggie and back. "So I discovered," she said immediately, defensively. "I took a bus partway and then hitchhiked. That's why I'm so late."

"You hitchhiked?" Aggie said.

"Yes!" she said sharply. "People do hitchhike, you know. Not everyone lives in the lap of luxury."

There was a little silence while they all tried to get back into a nicer mood. She started talking again about California and how warm it was, and how friendly, and how you really got a chance to do things there.

"Like what?" Helen asked.

"Like, you know. Anything. Jobs. You can get a really good job down there, especially in the restaurant business."

"Is that what you did?"

"Mostly, yes."

The whole time she was talking, she kept looking around wide-eyed at the shipwrecks and sheep pictures, and at the swirly-backed chairs and the big silky but faded couch Helen and Aggie were sharing. She's a bit nervous, Aggie guessed, but who wouldn't be with Helen grilling you? She said she hadn't brought a suitcase because she didn't think she'd be staying. She was just going to come and see them and then go back. She hadn't realized how far into the sticks this place was. And then Jeannie came in.

As soon as Jeannie saw her, she started screaming at her and yelling, "Why did you go away and leave us? How could you do that to your own children?" And things like that until Aggie told her to quit it because she was afraid their mom would take off again. But Jeannie wouldn't quit, and Aggie jumped up and tried to push her away from where she was standing – right over their mom, threateningly. Their mother was all hunched and leaning away and looking scared and defenseless. Jeannie finally moved away and stood in front of the fireplace, looking shattered, and right then Aggie could see their dad in her, somehow. Jeannie said, "You didn't even come back when Dad died."

Then their mother's eyes filled up and she blinked them, trying not to cry, but she *did* cry; she couldn't help it. "I'm sorry," she said. "I'm just real sorry." She put her hands over her face. "I don't know what else I can say except it wasn't my fault." She told the girls that she'd been temporarily out of her mind and didn't really understand what she was doing at the time she left home, and then she didn't think they would want her back, especially their father. She'd been afraid to phone, she said. To Aggie, she looked like a lost child. Perhaps it was the way she was looking at them over the tops of her fingers. She hadn't known their dad was sick. They hadn't kept in touch. And, of course, she didn't know that he'd died. "I was in a hospital for a while, you know – the mental ward." Pretty soon they were all crying.

Except Helen. Helen kept looking at her mother as if she were a judge about to bring down a verdict. After a while she looked at her watch and said, "I think we should go to bed and talk about this in the morning." She led their mother upstairs just as if *she* were the mother and got her some sheets and a towel and showed her where the bathroom was and where she could sleep.

"How did you know where to find us?" Helen asked her on the way upstairs.

"From Mrs. Muntz. I went around to the deli."

"How does the deli look?"

"Oh, you know, same old, same old. Haven't you been back?"

Helen said, "Can't afford to go back."

Their mother stopped at the top of the stairs. "You can't?"

Behind her, on the stairs, Aggie said, "We haven't inherited anything."

"Why not?"

"Nothing to inherit, except this house, and we may not even get that."

"That's ridiculous!" their mother said. "I think we'd better get after the lawyer and tell him to get off his ass. There's got to be money."

Helen's and Aggie's eyes met. Helen narrowed her eyes skeptically. Aggie frowned and looked down. She had to admit that she was a little surprised that her mother would say that. But maybe she was right. Maybe they needed a woman of the world to look further into the matter for them. Jeannie was still downstairs blowing her nose.

It's a good morning, sunny and crisp. Their mom's on her way out to find a pay phone to let a friend know where she is. Aggie offers to go with her (she's afraid to let her out of her sight), but she says, "I'll be back; don't worry." She smiles at Aggie with that look she has, her eyes soft, kind, but Aggie is worried anyway. In fact, all three sisters look worried, but for different reasons. They hear the door close as their mother steps out.

They're sitting around the kitchen, eating toast (home-made) and honey (thanks to Aggie's bees). "I don't trust her," Jeannie says. "She doesn't seem like our mother anymore."

Helen says, "Looks like she's here to stay."

"She's been gone too long. You can't just waltz back into a person's life like that." Jeannie's eyes are puffy from crying last night.

"Not much we can do."

"We can tell her to go."

"We're not telling her to go!" Aggie shouts.

"Okay, okay," Jeannie says, "pipe down."

"Let's not do anything rash," Helen says. (What else?) Jeannie rolls her eyes and drums her nails on the table.

"Let's just wait and see what happens." (Helen, of course.)

Tappety-tap go Jeannie's nails. But she doesn't have a better suggestion.

Pretty soon their mom comes back, and Aggie offers to make her some toast, but she says she just wants coffee.

"We don't have coffee; we have tea," Helen says.

Their mom wrinkles her nose, but then says, "Sure, whatever," and smiles.

Aggie pours her some tea while she starts to open a fresh package of cigarettes.

"Um," Helen says, her voice edgy.

Their mother turns narrowed eyes on her – no smile, now. Helen looks a little flustered. After a pause, while their mother gets out her lighter, Helen swallows hard and says, "D-D-Do you mind not smoking in the house?"

Jeannie and Aggie are staring at their mother to see what will happen. She's always smoked for as long as they can remember – in the house, in the car (when they had one, once), anywhere. She was the mom. She could do what she liked. They were only the kids. If they didn't like smoke, tough. "Get used to it," she'd say. "Hold your breath."

"We can get used to it," Aggie says.

Jeannie has pushed her chair back a little. She's staring at her mother with her arms folded in front of her. She's on Helen's side in this, Aggie realizes, even though she, herself, occasionally smokes (although not at home). Nobody says anything. There isn't a sound, yet it feels like a war. Three people have icy looks on their faces, and Aggie's heart is flopping around like a scared bird.

"Whatever," their mother says, at last. She puts her lighter in her pocket and closes the flap on the package of cigarettes and puts it on the table in front of her. Helen sits a little taller, having won a decisive battle.

After breakfast, Aggie takes her mom on a tour of the house. She really seems to appreciate all the knickknacks around the place, Aggie notices, picking them up and looking at the bottoms of things just as if she were shopping in some elegant store. They go into the study. She looks around quickly, but doesn't seem especially interested in the books. "Feel free to borrow whatever book you want to read," Aggie says.

Her mother nods. She glances at the green-and-gold elephant and turns her back on it, saying, "Okay, what else?"

Aggie points out the elephant to her. "Don't you just love this?"

She frowns at it. "Yes," she says. "It's nice."

"There used to be two, I think. We don't know what happened to the other one."

"Let's go," she says.

Aggie has saved the best of the tour until the last and is now taking her up to the third floor. Her mother huffs and puffs going up the second flight of stairs. "Are you sure there's anything worth seeing up there?" she says.

"You'll love it," Aggie assures her.

She takes her into the room where all the clothes are hanging, with the shoes lined up under them and the hats on a shelf above. She always puts things back where they belong up here, even though her own room is in a constant state of chaos.

Her mother is looking at the clothes, and Aggie is watching her face. If she wants to try on a few items, Aggie decides, it's fine with her. "Good God," her mom says, her eyes wide. "Didn't they ever throw anything out?"

"Fortunately, no," Aggie says, "otherwise I wouldn't have much to wear."

"You wear this stuff?"

"Yup."

Her mother shudders. "Look at the dust!" She wrinkles her nose. "They smell like they've been around too long. I wouldn't wear somebody's old cast-off clothes. Never know what you might catch."

This isn't working out the way Aggie had hoped. But then her mother glances at her and breaks into a smile. She says, "I'm just teasing you. This is interesting. It really is." Her eyes sparkle because she's having fun, Aggie knows. She shows her all the rooms, including the one where she found the part of a story in the drawer of the bedside table. Her mother sees the chamber pot and says, "I hope that's empty."

"It is." They both laugh.

Aggie shows her the little locked door in the bathroom, and she nods and says, "Well!" She rubs her arms and says, "It's cold up here." So they go down.

And now the doorbell is ringing; they can hear it on their way downstairs. Helen opens the door and ushers in Bertie and Linda Quade. She hangs up their coats in the hall closet. Bert rubs his hands together to warm them. "We heard that your mother has come back and decided we'd like to meet her since we've never had that opportunity." They glance up at Aggie and her mother as they come down the stairs.

Helen says, "This is our mother, Candace Quade."

"Hi," she says, still on the stairs. "Candy," she says. "That's what people call me."

Bert looks as though he might shake hands, but Candy doesn't go any closer to him. That's okay, Aggie thinks. She's probably shy.

Helen leads everybody into the main living room and they all sit down. They all seem to need to clear their throats. The weather gets a good going over. "We're supposed to get snow," Bert says.

"Apparently not very much, though," Linda adds. "Candy," she asks, "are you going to stay for a while?"

"Yes, I guess so."

Bert asks where she's been for the past six years. "In the States," she says. She's not going into any details, so they stop giving her the third degree. Aggie's beginning to resent their being here at all because it's really none of their business whether their mother is here or not.

Soon they go, and Candy goes up to lie down. Aggie imagines it must have been upsetting for her to have to deal with all that nosiness.

It's Monday, and Aggie's back at school. It was hard to leave her mother, but Helen and Jeannie are there, so she won't be lonely. A man in a car came and brought her more clothes on Saturday, the same day she phoned. She started watching out the window for him in the afternoon around four and ran out to the curb when a car pulled up. They have no idea who he was; she didn't invite him in.

Maybe she'll help Helen and Jeannie with the bread-baking project, Aggie hopes. She tried to get her mom interested in helping her make sandwiches for today, but she said she had a headache and went up to lie down.

Aggie is happier than she's ever been in her life, now that her mom's back and everything's going so well for them. It's an adjustment for them, of course, getting used to having a mother again, after making all their own decisions for so long. Not that she tries to run their lives, or anything. She tries to fit in, although Aggie doesn't think she likes their food, except for the bread. It's funny, but Aggie can't remember her cooking much of anything. She guesses her dad did a lot of the cooking, or they had deli stuff.

When Aggie used to long for her mother, she thought, if she'd come back, my sisters and I would be so . . . well, different. . . . We'd all lie around on each other's beds, telling hilarious and embarrassing stuff and laughing and saying "don't worry," and saying "you're the best," and then going down and telling it all over again to our mom. And she'd laugh and hug us and say "you girls are so great."

It'll just take time, Aggie guesses. The atmosphere in the house seems heavy, somehow, foggy. The girls no longer fight. They don't even talk. It seems that they no longer walk around the house, they drag themselves. They sink into chairs as if they're exhausted, which they are, at least Aggie is. She doesn't know why that should be. Maybe loving her mother so much is wearing her out because she's out of practice.

She doesn't mean to complain, even silently. It's great that she's back because now they're more like a real family. It may take time for everyone to get back to normal, but they will; of that, Aggie is fully confident.

She's at school early so she can tell Miss Greenwald about her mother. They're sitting across from each other on two student desks – Aggie in a sleeveless, faded, wine-colored, short dress from the flapper era, she guesses, that ends in little fabric triangles all around the bottom. She's wearing it with tights and a long-sleeved T-shirt (black, filched from Helen) because it's frigging cold outside; Miss Greenwald is in her ordinary teacher clothes.

"I'd love to meet your mother," Miss Greenwald says.

"Oh, you will! I think you'll really like her once you get to know her. She's a little bit shy."

"What brought her back, at this point?" Miss Greenwald asks.

Aggie begins to frown a little because she notices that her teacher is beginning to sound a lot like Bertie and Linda Quade. But then Miss Greenwald smiles and says, "I guess she's probably really been missing her daughters and couldn't be without them any longer."

Aggie nods in agreement now and is smiling again.

"Seven years is a long time," Miss Greenwald says.

"Only six," Aggie says.

"But still, a lot changes in six years." Kids are starting to drift into the classroom now. Miss Greenwald continues, "But, of course, it's all right for things to change." She stands up, and so Aggie stands up, too, because the bell is about to go. "It's permissible," Miss Greenwald says. She smiles encouragingly at Aggie.

Aggie wanders to the back of the room, where the movie set is, to make sure everything is in place for shooting to begin again after school. For some reason she keeps hearing Miss Greenwald say, "It's permissible." She would like to ask her, "What's permissible?"

The week has gone well, and gone fast, as far as Aggie's concerned. They finished filming on Wednesday. The films are being developed right now and as soon as they get them back, Quade will splice them together into one continuous reel with this handy-dandy splicing thing they have and which he knows how to use, and then they'll show the film next Friday – five days before Christmas – and charge admission. They've put up posters all over town. Everywhere Aggie goes, people are asking about it. There are seventeen hundred people in Port Desire, and she wouldn't be surprised if every single one of them attended.

Aggie's been Christmas shopping. All the stores are decorated with painted frost on the windows, and colored lights on fake evergreen trees that look almost genuine. There are real Christmas trees for sale beside the church and also outside the grocery store, and not very expensive, either. Maybe they'll get theirs tomorrow. Christmas in the village of Port Desire is exactly the way you'd expect it to be in a small place like this, she thinks. The only thing they lack is snow. It's mighty cold, though.

She took some of the sandwich money and bought presents for everyone in her family, especially her mom, and also for Quade's family, and for both the great-aunts. "And that," she tells herself, "is one pile of presents!" She also bought red-and-green tissue paper to wrap them in and a roll of Scotch tape. Bows would have been nice, but she ran out of money.

She has to admit she didn't spend much, which is good, because if they can afford it, she and her sisters might have a little party, probably on Christmas Eve. They'll blow the majority of their earnings on that, probably, if Helen and Jeannie would just show a little more enthusiasm about it.

From the drugstore, Aggie got different kinds of smelly soap shaped like hamburgers and eggplants, and two diamond-studded (fake) clips to put in your hair. She hasn't decided who for, yet. For her mother, she got a glow-in-the-dark ponytail holder. It's a little different. At the hardware store, she bought a rainbow assortment of spray paints because she believes people often have the urge to paint things, but they don't always have the paint. Also, she found some rubber things you stick on your bathtub to keep you from slipping. Those, she decided, will be for Great-Aunt Lily and Great-Aunt Margery (and her husband, whose name she forgets). They have different pictures on them – Bigfoot footprints, famous people's faces like Kramer on *Seinfeld*, and the president of the United States, and things like that.

Outside she notices that it's getting dark. It must be after five. She hurries to the supermarket, hoping to find one more present for her mom. Inside, she pauses by a wire rack of books with brilliant covers, some silver, some with designs cut into them. Aha, she thinks, here's a book she might like. Her mother is not very interested in the books they have at home. This one's called *Vampire Wedding*. Everybody loves vampires, she decides, and everybody loves weddings, so there you are.

She picks up a few other items and stands at the end of the checkout line. At the front of the line, putting her groceries on the counter, is Aunt Lily the Great.

"I guess the lake'll be frozen over soon, Lily?" someone says.

Lily turns around to talk to the man who works in the post office. She has quite a cartful of stuff, Aggie notices.

"Won't be long," she says, reaching into the cart for a bag of oranges. "This has to do me until I can get back to town over the ice."

"Still using your launch?"

"Oh, no. I put it in storage three weeks ago. I'm using my canoe."

"You may need an icebreaker to get back out there today," he says.

"Oh, I'm used to that," she says. She plunks a few more items on the counter. "I just whack away at it with my paddle."

Other people in the line are smiling at each other and shaking their heads. They can't imagine how Lily has the spunk to live out there, especially this time of year, paddling across the lake in a canoe.

"A few cold nights like last night will do it," the man says.

She nods at him. Now she sees Aggie. Aggie smiles, but Lily looks at her as if she's puzzled about something. She looks away without speaking. Maybe she lost touch with reality for a moment, Aggie thinks.

"Hi, Aunt Lily," she says.

Lily turns again and stares at Aggie over the top of her glasses and, after a long pause, says "hello" the way you would to a stranger. Aggie would like to ask her to drop in and meet her mother, but something about the set of her head and shoulders makes her stop. She's paying for her groceries. The checkout lady is putting them into two big cloth bags that Lily hands her, with a green recycle logo on them. Instead of mentioning her mother, Aggie asks her if she's going to come to the movie when they show it in the school auditorium next Friday. "Perhaps," is all she says. She picks up her bags of groceries and leaves.

When Aggie gets to the checkout, the woman says, "I hear your mother's come back to collect her share of the inheritance."

"What?" Aggie says.

"Doubt she'll get a red cent. Why should she?"

Aggie watches dumbly as the checkout lady puts the book, a package of wieners, and a head of lettuce into a bag, along with some packets of yeast. She leaves the store with her groceries and all her bags of Christmas presents. *Is that what they think? That she only came back hoping for some money?*

At home, Helen is taking the last two loaves of their daily bread out of the oven. Jeannie is sweeping up at the As You. "Where's Mom?" Aggie asks, a frightened pitch to her voice.

"At the lawyer's, kicking ass."

"What?"

"That's what she said she was going to do, and I have no reason to doubt her."

"Well, maybe she's right. Maybe we actually have money coming to us."

"Oh, Aggie! You're such a dreamer. You're as bad as she is."

Angrily, Aggie goes upstairs with her parcels and then hurries down, remembering Aunt Lily's strange behavior. She wonders if she has perhaps answered Aggie's letter and is waiting for a reply. Aggie has been so caught up with the excitement of her mother's arrival that she has forgotten to check at the post office. She runs across the street to the post office, but it's closed. Sadly, she goes back home just as her mother enters the house. She dashes in behind her in time to hear Helen in the kitchen sounding superior, as only Helen can, and her mother sounding angry.

"What's up?" Aggie asks, from the kitchen doorway. Her mother brushes past her without saying anything and starts upstairs. "What's wrong?" Aggie calls to her back.

"Nothing," she says.

Aggie goes into the kitchen to confront Helen. Upstairs a door slams – a familiar sound. "She didn't go into details," Helen says, "but I have a feeling Mr. Gorman's ass proved tougher than her foot. She's just learned you can't get blood from a stone."

Dinner is a somewhat silent affair that night. Candy scarcely eats a thing. She keeps fingering her package of cigarettes and finally leaves the table to go and smoke on the front porch. "It's pretty cold out there," Aggie calls after her.

A minute later, Aggie leaves the table. "I'm going to take her coat out to her," she says to Jeannie and Helen.

"You are such a total suck," Jeannie says.

Outside, Candy thanks her and puts the coat around her shoulders. "I'm sick of the tension in there," she says.

"They just find it really hard to get used to having a mother again," Aggie says. "It's because they're older. I'm younger, so –"

"I hate this town."

"It grows on you. You just have to give it some time."

"Everybody's so hostile. They look like they're sticking little daggers into me everywhere I go. And that lawyer! God!"

"Did he say anything about the inheritance?"

"Oh, yeah, plenty. He said, basically, it's none of my business. He said, even if there had been much of an estate, I would get sweet ef-all. How do you like that, even though I put up with the son of a . . . sorry, your father, with all his idiot ideas for all those years, and raised you kids. He said I'm not even mentioned in the old man's will. 'Course he didn't like me, I know that. Treated Cam and me like scum. We sure could have used some money back then."

"What kind of idiot ideas?"

"Who knows? A New Age Robin Hood or something. I never really figured him out."

Aggie's standing beside her on the porch, shivering, wondering what her dad really had been like when he wasn't around his kids. They're both shivering in the bluish glare from the streetlight. Candy blows smoke out to the side so it doesn't go in Aggie's face.

She says, "I don't know how I'm going to survive. It's hard to get a good job when you've got a bad back. I've been in hospital with it and everything."

Aggie says, "Weren't you in a psychiatric ward?"

Candy looks at her, blankly for a moment, frowning a little. She takes a long drag on her cigarette. "Yeah," she says, "that too. Talk about problems! I never know when I bend over whether I'm ever going to be able to straighten up, or when I'm going to have my next nervous break-down. And those two in there are doing their level best to give me another one. I know what'll happen. I know exactly where I'll end up. I'll be one of those derelict bums wrapped in a ratty old sleeping bag on some street corner in Toronto. Nobody gives a damn about me."

"Mom, I do! Honestly! Look, I'll take care of you, for sure. I mean we all will, but I'll make sure of it." This would be an excellent time for Aggie to put her arms around her mother and hug her, but she can't figure out how to do it. What would Candy do with her cigarette?

"Look at you," Candy says. "You're freezing. Go on in. Go on." Her eyes, Aggie can see, are shining with tears, but she's smiling at her. Candy says, "You're a great little kid, and not so little, either. I guess I wasn't a total failure as a mom."

Aggie leaves her out there and goes back into the kitchen, to her sisters. "Let's just get something straight," she says to them. She's leaning over, her hands spread out on the table, her face close to her sisters'. "We are going to look after Mom, now and forever. What's ours is hers. Okay?"

Jeannie shrugs. Helen says, "We'll see."

"No, we won't *see*! She's staying! We aren't letting her run away again."

"We'll see," Jeannie echoes.

CHAPTER THIRTEEN

Last night the world premiere of the movie *Earth Stealers* was held, and Aggie and her classmates are so proud, you'd think they'd given joint multiple births. It was such an unqualified success that they're back at the school Saturday night for a second showing because they had to turn people away at the door Friday night. Couldn't fit them all in. They're just raking in the cash, though. Some of it is going to pay for developing the films, some for a class party, and the rest is to buy new stuff for the school. The moviemakers get to vote on what that will be when they get back to school after the new year.

Aggie's only role last night was to sit and watch the movie with her mom and her sisters, and to radiate glory and celebrate success. "I'll just stand at the back," Candy said, when they got into the gym, which doubles as the auditorium.

"No way," Aggie said. Kids were coming in behind them and dumping their knapsacks on the floor at the back of the auditorium right at their feet, so Candy agreed to come up closer to the front, where the chairs were all lined up in rows. Aggie caught some of her classmates staring at Candy. In her tight jeans and high-heeled boots and leather jacket, and with her really thin figure, especially when she held her stomach in (she forgot sometimes), and with her long red-gold hair hanging down in wisps, she looked almost like a model. Her hair is a little gray on top Aggie has noticed, and kind of unevenly cut, but Lydia at the As You could have a go at it one of these days. A lot of the other mothers looked pretty flabby and ordinary.

Aggie was glad they sat close to the front because she had to go up onstage before the movie started. The movie-makers' names were called and they were each introduced – Aggie as director, the stars and all the actors, the camera guy, the tape recorder girl, the lighting and set people, and Quade, who was the technician (cutter and gluer, that is) and music director (player, actually); they all stood there like a gangster lineup on the stage in front of the screen, while Miss Greenwald told everyone how great they were. Everybody clapped and yelled, but Aggie just kept looking at her mom to see if she looked proud of her.

Everyone loved the movie. There was a lot of laughter, mostly at stuff that wasn't meant to be funny, but it didn't matter. The three sisters, the stars of the show, are crime investigators for the whole galaxy. Aggie has got used to the story and has to admit it isn't as stupid as she had at first thought, partly because she got to put in a few touches of her own. The sisters have been raised by their stern uncle, Drogue, emperor of Earth, because their mother, his sister Serena, has been kidnapped. The three sisters are always searching for her as they go around pulverizing enemy invaders with their special ionic blasters. This was Aggie's major contribution.

She choreographed their shooting scenes so that they move in unison, sneaking stealthily, step-by-step, up to a closed door. Together they kick it open and then, as a single unit, swing their weapons around to point at the enemy. And here's the best part: flames shoot out of their weapons. At least, it would have been the best part if the cameraman had been a little faster. The sisters' ionic blasters are cardboard tubes (disguised) packed with candles. Just after they swing them (in unison) to face the enemy, the camera cuts off; the crew lights all the candlewicks sticking out the ends; and then they start shooting the film again.

At first you see this blaze of fire coming from the weapons. However, and this always upsets Aggie a little, what you see next is one of the cardboard tubes catching fire and dripping wax all over the place before they cut to the next scene, and in the background you can hear Miss Greenwald's panicky voice on the tape recorder, saying something about a water bucket. So people had a good laugh.

The point of the story is that enemy aliens are stealing Earth, country by country. And this was another contribution by Agatha Jane Quade – the aliens come from a planet where they have nothing but water, and so they are trying to build land masses by stealing them from Earth. With a special instrument, they are able to suck the countries right off the map, leaving behind only watery holes. Every so often, the camera is trained on Rachel's hand-drawn map of the world, and each time, some new section, some unsuspecting country, becomes a blank aqua blue space.

Then, in the last scene, the crime-fighting sisters have the alien chief cornered, and just as the sisters swing their weapons around (in unison) ready to fire (literally), the alien chief rips off a mask and reveals that it's actually their mother who has been forced to do the bidding of the enemy all these years. It's a great scene. The mother joins the sisters, and they kill all the enemies, and that's the end of that, except that they also get the stolen countries back by reversing the enemy-land-sucking instrument, which, presumably, vomits them back onto the map. They were running low on film, so had to end the thing without showing how it actually worked.

The background music was excellent, in Aggie's opinion. It was actually live – Miss Greenwald's idea. Quade sat off to the side, where he could see the screen but not obstruct anyone's view, and he made up tunes to go with each scene – quiet and mournful in the sad parts and hip-hop perky in the exciting parts. That boy communicates through music, Aggie can't help noticing. He may not be a great talker, himself, but he can sure get across a message with the fiddle.

After it was over and the lights came on, Helen and Jeannie clapped politely, but they were both looking a little skeptical. "Didn't you like it?" Aggie leaned over and asked worriedly, while the applause was still happening all around them. "Were those sisters supposed to be us?" Jeannie asked sharply. "The one in black and the other one, the bleach-blonde with the big hair?"

"No!" Aggie said. "Not at all. No way. Just a coincidence."

"And the thing about the missing mother?" Helen slid her eyes in Candy's direction and back.

Aggie turned up her palms, shrugging. "One of those things. Life imitates art. You know?"

So they're showing it again tonight. They won't be going up onstage until the end tonight because some of the people can't get here until later. Rachel's on cash again tonight, selling tickets at the door and complaining because last night she didn't get to see the beginning with the title and credits, which she helped design. She had to go up to Miss Greenwald's room to lock up the money after the tickets were sold.

"Go ahead in," Aggie says to her, sitting down at the table in front of the gym doors. "I don't mind selling tickets tonight." As director, she's done just about everything else, so why not?

"Great!" Rachel says. She hands Aggie the key to Miss Greenwald's room. "Don't forget to give this back to her," she says. "Just put the cash box in the bottom drawer of her desk when you're finished here." She picks up her knapsack and disappears into the gym. Aggie plunks hers down on the floor by her chair as the next wave of movie patrons comes through the front door.

Aggie thinks they're probably making as much money tonight as they must have last night. They even have some repeat customers. The gym is getting packed and the ticket lineup is dwindling. Whoa, here's Mom! Aggie notices. "I didn't know you were coming back," she says.

"Not much else to do." She misses cable TV, Aggie

knows. Her mother stands glancing around, not buying a ticket, but why should she? Although, other people who saw it last night are buying them again tonight. But Aggie doesn't care. Candy's looking at the pictures on the wall of classes and teams down through the ages.

"Well, that's the last ticket," Aggie calls to her as the last people squeeze through the door into the packed gym.

"Here's your father," Candy calls back from partway down the corridor.

Aggie goes along to where she's pointing just as someone else comes blustering in out of the cold night. Aggie has to step back a bit to see who. It's her great-aunt Lily!

"I haven't any more tickets, Aunt Lily," she calls to her, "but you can go in anyway. It's just starting." She sees Lily look sharply at Candy. Aggie moves back to her mom and whispers, "Come and meet her!" But Candy wrinkles her nose and shakes her head.

"I'll put my money in the box," Aunt Lily calls. She sounds testy, as if she's cross about something. Aggie wants to tell her she doesn't have to pay because there may not be any seats left, but she hears the box snap shut, and, when she steps back to look, Lily's gone in.

"Here's another picture of your father," Candy says.

Aggie smiles at the picture of a curly-haired geek standing with a lot of other geeky-looking people, who all look too responsible and too serious to be teenagers. "I have to put the money away," she says, returning to the ticket table. She picks up the box, the key, and her knapsack, and the two of them head up the stairs and down the hall to Miss Greenwald's room.

"You like school?" Candy asks.

"It's all right."

"You were always a smart little kid."

"Yeah?"

She puts the cash box in the bottom drawer of Miss Greenwald's desk and closes the door behind her, turning the knob to make sure it's locked. She puts the key in one of the pockets of her knapsack because she doesn't know whether Miss Greenwald is here yet. She said she might be a bit late getting to the school tonight. Her mother is sick, and she had to find someone to stay with her. Miss Greenwald is interested in people's mothers, Aggie is pretty sure, because she lives with hers and looks after her.

When they get back to the gym, the movie has already begun. "Coming in?" she asks Candy. Her mother shrugs, and Aggie opens the gym door just wide enough to let them in. It's hard to see in the dark. They stand at the back, with a lot of other people, amongst all the knapsacks. Kids leave them there because they're not supposed to clutter up the seating arrangements. After a moment, Aggie spots one seat in the middle of the back row and points it out to Candy. She shakes her head. "You take it," she whispers. Then she says, "I'm probably not going to stay for the whole thing anyway." Aggie looks around to see if Aunt Lily has found a seat, but doesn't see her anywhere, so she must have.

After a moment or two, she decides to take the seat. She squashes her knapsack in against the others and tiptoes to the back row. Quietly, she pulls the chair out a bit, sidles in, and sits down. The lady next to her smiles and shifts a little to give her more room.

Aggie has seen the movie five times. She watched it with Quade a few times when he was splicing it together, and then last night. And she's still not tired of it. She bets she could watch it another five times. "Now how often can you say that about a Hollywood flick?" she asks herself.

At the end, the lights go on and, through thunderous applause, all the moviemakers are called up onto the stage and once again introduced, this time by the principal because, as it turns out, Miss Greenwald had to stay home with her mother.

He's looking Aggie up and down pretty sharply because as she well knows, he is a connoisseur of teen styles. She doesn't think he can find too much fault with her antique diamond-patterned, hand-knit sweater, unless he doesn't like the moth holes, which are getting bigger right before her very eyes because the wool is unraveling. *Never mind.* With it, she's wearing a long slender skirt that flares at the bottom and looks fantastic. She was going to wear a bowler hat, too, but Helen hid it on her.

Aggie's sorry to see it all end – they all are – but, end it has. Candy must have left some time ago. Aggie's shuffling along home with Quade and Rachel and a few others. They stop at Miss Greenwald's house to give her back her key, and they all shush each other because her mother's sick and they should keep quiet. Miss Greenwald comes to the door in an old sweatshirt, with her hair hanging down any old way, making her look ordinary – not like a teacher. She asks them how it went, so they give her a detailed description with everyone talking at once.

She says she wishes she could invite them in, but she can't because of her mother, so they leave, still talking about the movie and saying, 'member that part where this happened, and 'member the part where that happened, and falling all over themselves laughing. And they're also talking about making another film because they're so spectacular at it.

At home, everything is quiet although it's not that late. There's a note saying Helen is out, and another saying Jeannie is out. Poor Mom, Aggie thinks, nobody to hang out with. Upstairs she notices that her mother's door is shut. Probably in bed. She decides to head to bed herself because being a movie mogul really takes it out of you.

Brinnng! The doorbell, for Pete's sake! Aggie realizes it's morning, but just barely. Oh, well, nine fifteen. Some people get up that early, even three days before Christmas. She decides to lie there, hoping someone else will answer the door.

Pad, pad, pad, she hears. Swearword. Helen's going down. She can hear her opening the door. A woman's voice. Aggie can't hear what she's saying.

"Aggie?" Helen calls up.

She grabs a sweatshirt to throw on over her PJ's because she doesn't know who it is. She hurries downstairs. It's Miss Greenwald!

Before she can even say hi, Miss Greenwald says, "Rachel tells me that last night you were the one in charge of putting the cash box away in my desk at school."

"That's right." Aggie's looking a little puzzled because

Miss Greenwald doesn't behave like her usual teacherish self. She looks kind of sick. Maybe, Aggie thinks, she caught whatever her mother has.

"I didn't mind," she says. "Rachel missed the beginning of the movie the night before."

"Agatha, the money isn't there."

"Yes, it's there. I put it in the bottom drawer."

Miss Greenwald is standing in the doorway shaking her head, with a stricken look on her face.

"The box isn't there?" Aggie asks, incredulous.

"The box is there, the money's gone."

"Oh, my God!"

"If we sold every ticket, there must have been almost a thousand dollars in that box," Miss Greenwald says.

The gravity of the situation takes Aggie's breath away, as if she's being held down and smothered. She slumps onto the bottom step. When she can breathe, when she can talk, she whispers, "I didn't take it."

Miss Greenwald comes to her and crouches down, her winter coat spreading out on the floor all around her. She squeezes her arm. "I know you didn't," she says. "It's just that you had the responsibility, and you were the last one to see the money."

Helen says, "Did you give the key to anyone else?"

Aggie frowns at her, exasperated. "No, of course not!"

Miss Greenwald says, "How much money was in the box when you took over?"

"I don't know. I didn't look to see. There was some in the sliding drawer that pulls out, mostly change. I didn't count it." She has her head in her hands. She senses that Miss

Greenwald is standing up, now. She and Helen are talking. She looks up and sees that Helen's face is chalk white.

"Well," Miss Greenwald shrugs, her hands open, helpless. "I don't know what to do."

"Maybe it will turn up," Helen says and then looks away because they all know that a thousand missing dollars will not just turn up.

Miss Greenwald starts buttoning up her coat, and Helen opens the door for her. "I'll let you know," she says to Helen. When Helen comes away from the door, she looks like death.

"What's going to happen?" Aggie asks.

"She has to tell the principal. She thinks he'll go to the police."

"Just like with Dad."

"Only worse."

Aggie knows what she means. Somebody else's nightmare happening to you, except that it's real. She goes back to bed because, where else can she go?

Aggie is exhausted. It's been a day straight out of the Spanish Inquisition. This afternoon Miss Greenwald came back with the principal, Mr. Pye. Miss Greenwald kept saying things like, ". . . too much responsibility for a child . . . all my fault . . . should never have . . ."

Mr. Pye said, "Excuse me, Miss Greenwald, but could we just let Agatha tell us exactly what happened?"

Miss Greenwald was huddled on the edge of a chair in the grand living room. Huddled on other chairs were Helen, Jeannie, and Candy. Not a peep out of any of them.

Aggie stood near the window. A grayish yellow sun seeped through the living room windows, stealing color from everyone's face. They looked, she thought, the way they had at their father's funeral – not quite alive.

"Rachel was selling tickets at the door when you arrived at the school," Mr. Pye prompted. "And then you told her you wanted to sell tickets."

"I didn't tell her I wanted to sell tickets; I told her I would do it so that she could go in to see the beginning of the movie."

"You didn't want to see the beginning of the movie?"

"I'd seen it. She hadn't."

"So out of the goodness of your heart, you offered to take over the cash box."

"More or less." Aggie didn't really like the tone of his questioning. He wasn't accusing her exactly, but he made her feel guilty anyway.

"Go on."

"So when the tickets were all sold, I took the box to Miss Greenwald's room, locked it in, came back, watched the rest of the movie, dropped off the key at her house, and came home."

"Did any of the other students sit with you while you sold the tickets?"

"No."

"Did anyone ask for the key?"

"No, I put it in my knapsack, and it was there when I got it out again to give back."

"Why did you put it in your knapsack?"

"Um." She had to think.

"Why didn't you put it in your pocket, for instance?"

"I don't think I had any pockets."

"No pockets," he said, as if he didn't believe her.

"I don't think so. I could check and see if you like."

"Little late for that," he said.

Finally Helen interrupted. "I don't think this is going anywhere. It sounds to me as though you're trying to make out that my sister planned and committed a crime." Aggie liked the way she said "my sister." It sounded as though she wasn't just some stray girl – she belonged to someone.

"Not at all. I'm trying to get to the bottom of this before we have to get the police involved. If she did take the money – and we all know kids make mistakes – it wouldn't be the first time something like this has happened, but if she were to give the money back, I don't think much more than a stern lecture would follow." He looked at Aggie expectantly, as if she might latch onto this bone of forgiveness he had thrown her.

"I didn't take it," she said wearily. She got up and went upstairs and kept on going right up to the third floor.

And that's where she is right now. She's standing in the doorway of the clothes room, looking at all the neatly hung choices and wondering what particular item of clothing would cover this situation. A straight jacket, maybe? Or a cloak and dagger? Maybe a rope necktie. For a fleeting second she remembers the preserved fruit in the cellar, some of it dating back to before World War II. *Just a thought.*

Aggie can hear Helen bellowing at her, but she's not going down. She crosses the hall to the room where she found the story and lies on the narrow bed. She wonders if she's being falsely accused because of her father's reputation, or because she's the only suspect. Or another possibility takes shape in her overly active imagination. Maybe I *did* take it and have blotted it out of my memory. Maybe I sleepwalked, she muses, back to Miss Greenwald's house, stole the key, and then went to the school and took the money. I mean really, I could see myself doing that, as a matter of fact. First she would raid Helen's supply of mourning clothes, and then, dressed in black from head to foot and with a nylon stocking pulled over her head and a sack over her shoulder, snoring her head off, she would. . . . She hears footsteps on the stairs.

Someone is invading her sanctuary. She pretends she's crawled up here and died. Curiosity, however, forces her to open one eye long enough to see a tousled head peering around the door frame. "Mind if I come in?" asks Quade.

So now he's sitting on the floor, giant wrists dangling over bony knees, head against the wall, and Aggie's still on the bed, on her side, folded up, pretending to be an unborn baby. He's not saying much. Too bad he didn't bring his violin, she thinks, to play her some guilty-until-proven-innocent music.

"Do you know what this is like?" she says from the cavern of her imaginary womb. "This is actually like killer bees."

He looks puzzled.

"I mean, killer bees really do exist in South America or somewhere. And they really could be a problem for us, right?"

"Guess so."

"But so far we haven't encountered any, I mean apart from my little fantasy swarm last summer that turned out to be your average honeybee. But, deep in our hearts we know, or feel pretty certain, that it's only a matter of time before those killer bees make their way north through the States up here to Canada to get us. It's like knowing that the worst that could happen is finally starting to happen. And it will be the death of us."

No words from Quade. She wonders if she should ask him to go get his fiddle, so they can converse.

He takes a breath. "Just because killer bees exist doesn't mean you're necessarily going to get stung."

"But the fear is there."

"So you spend your life being afraid of every flying creature between the size of a mosquito and the size of a hummingbird?"

"Basically."

Lots more silence going on. In a while he says, "Okay, look, forget killer bees. Get over them. It's time to fight back."

Aggie unfolds herself enough to lean on one elbow so she can study him because she has never figured him for a fighting kind of guy.

"Tell me everything you did last night, starting from the time you walked into the school."

She's impressed. You could make a movie with a scene like this in it. She begins at the beginning, putting in as many details as possible, which isn't a chore because she has become aware that she likes telling detailed stories about herself, especially if someone is actually listening and cares.

When she finishes, Quade says, "I'm going to try to get professional help for you."

"What?" she says. "A shrink?"

"Of course not. I mean a lawyer."

CHAPTER FOURTEEN

Aggie is about to go out to face what remains of the world. She's been hiding inside since yesterday, when Miss Greenwald unleashed the swarm of killers. Duncan Hill, at the request of her helpful cousin Quade, has been and gone. While Helen fluttered helpfully in the background, Aggie told him the whole saga of the evening before last, just the way she had with Quade. He wrote it all down and told her she should make a list of people they could use as character references.

"What do you mean?"

"People who would be supportive of you, who would swear that you are not, and never could be, a thief."

Right, she thinks, after my sisters (and she's not even one hundred percent sure of them) and my mom, who? Susie the Impaler?

Helen saw Duncan to the door, and Aggie, sitting at the kitchen table with Jeannie and their mother, could hear them having a whispered chat. She wonders if he suspects someone. He seems to have a plan for this afternoon.

Her mom has been really sweet to her since this happened. She looks at her with big sad eyes. Aggie said to her yesterday, "You know I didn't take it!"

And she said, "I know."

Aggie puts on her coat. Everyone else is sitting around looking glum since Duncan left.

Jeannie says, "Way to screw up Christmas! Not you," she adds quickly, looking around at Aggie. "I mean this whole thing."

"It's not screwed up," Helen says. "We're still going to get a tree, and we'll have a turkey. A small one. Just big enough for the four of us."

"No party, though," Aggie says, buttoning her coat.

"No party," Helen agrees.

"Well, you know," Candy begins, and then pauses, "I don't think I'll be here for Christmas."

"What?" Aggie jumps in loudly, "Why not? You have to be here! We're a family, aren't we?"

"I have some business to attend to."

"But. . . ."

"Over Christmas?" Helen sounds disbelieving. She takes a quick glance at Aggie, then locks eyes with Candy.

"Yes, over Christmas!" Candy stares back, beady-eyed. "The world doesn't stop just because of Christmas, you know."

Aggie notices, for the first time, a family resemblance between them. "But, Mom . . ." she starts, then stops because something tells her it's futile.

Helen turns a cynical eye once again on Candy, who retaliates with a sneer. Jeannie for once has nothing to say. Aggie has plenty to say, but no heart for it. A family Christmas! Highly overrated, probably. She wouldn't know.

Of course her mom'll come back again. She knows that.

Still, she'd like to ask her if she wants to come out for a walk so she can talk her into staying, but she doesn't. She's too sad. Too something. Besides, she wouldn't come anyway. She hates the cold; she hates the town. Aggie's glad it's cold. The colder the better. She read once that you could fall asleep in the cold and freeze to death without ever waking up.

"Three o'clock, don't forget," Helen calls after her. She's unlikely to forget. It's her fate being decided this afternoon. Now that she's outside, she doesn't know where to go. It's freezing. She could go to the grocery store and check out the price of turkeys, but she wouldn't be able to put up with the accusing looks of all the shoppers. Turkey. She could learn to hate it.

She could walk around town looking for character references, but that would be a useless and depressing quest. She had thought Rachel might stand up for her, but she hasn't even come over to see her. Nobody has. Not even her sandwich clients. She goes across the street to the post office. It's nearly two o'clock on a Monday afternoon. It should be open, and it is. There are about ten people in there lined up for stamps, or else pulling cartloads of Christmas greetings from their private mailboxes. She feels them all staring at her as she goes up to number 220, the Quade box. Through the little rectangle of glass, she can see that there are letters in it – two. She searches her coat pocket for the key; undoes her coat to search her jeans. No key. Helen must have it.

Now she knows people are staring at her. They might even be whispering. *Never mind.* She bends to peer again into the box. One letter definitely looks like a business letter, probably for Helen. The other one, though, oddly enough, looks something like the one she sent to Lily. It couldn't be.

"Sorry to hear about the trouble you're in."

Aggie straightens and turns around. It's Gordie, Rachel's boyfriend. "Yeah?" she says. "Well, thanks." Everyone in the post office has stopped to stare. In their eyes she believes she sees fear, distrust, hostility. She turns up the collar of her long tweed coat and makes a dash for the door. Out she goes, races down the steps, skids on ice halfway across the street, recovers, and runs into her own backyard and down to the boathouse. She will not go back to the post office with the key. She can't face the aliens. Helen will have to go later.

In the boathouse she's out of the wind, but it's still freezing. She's looking down into the empty boat slip and mulling over what to do. What she usually does is go up to the third floor, slip out of herself, and cover herself with someone else's life. Somehow, though, she doesn't think that's going to work right now. She's stuck with the present circumstances. If this really was a movie about her life, she thinks, what we'd be seeing right now are those holes you see at the end of the film just before it goes blank.

I don't really care who stole the money.

That's ice down there in the boat slip. There are bits of this and that frozen into it. She wonders how thick it is. Sitting on the edge of the boat slip, she bangs at the ice with her heel but doesn't break through. So this is freeze-up, she thinks. The beginning of the ice age. The end of everything.

She drops down onto the ice and it holds. Out toward the open boat slip door, she notices something embedded in the ice. Gingerly, in case she goes through, she creeps toward the door and crouches. It's a bumblebee! A big fat yellow-and-brown preserved bumblebee! How did it get here? she wonders. "Like a little sign from heaven," she tells herself aloud, "only I don't know what it means."

I don't care if they blame me. I really don't.

She thinks the ice must be pretty safe. To test it, she jumps up and down and hears a little boom out beyond the boathouse somewhere. She can see where the ice cracked at some point and refroze. Thick as a plank, she thinks. Thick as the boathouse floor.

Outside again, it's a gray world. She notices the weeping willow and the way the tips of its leafless branches kiss the water. They're frozen right into it. Near it, the overturned boat covered with the tarp looks like the body of a dead giant. Shrinking into her coat collar for protection from the bitter wind, she stands for a moment on the dock remembering Aunt Lily's departure in her motor launch a month and a half ago (it seems like years). She is about to turn from the wind and go back up to the house when something long and black and shiny catches her eye, wedged between two boards in the dock. She bends over to look.

She is able to get her little finger into the crack and, with great care, to push the hefty wrought iron key up to the surface where she can grasp it.

She knows instantly which door it will fit. It's freezing her hand, so she slips it into her pocket. If she had found it a week ago, she would have been excited. She would have started a brand new movie in her head involving a small mysterious door at the top of an old house, blah-blah. But now, who cares? She doesn't have time to try it in the lock, anyway.

She should get along to the school, where Duncan will soon be putting his plan to work. If he can get enough people together at the high school this afternoon to look into the missing money situation, he will turn it into what he calls a kind of kangaroo court. He thinks that if enough people put their heads together, somebody is bound to remember seeing something or someone unusual. "Oh, sure," Aggie said, "who would bother to turn up the day before Christmas Eve?"

"You'd be surprised," Duncan argued. "In my experience, more people confess their crimes just before Christmas than at any other time during the year." Aggie looked doubtful because, when you get right down to it, how much experience has he had? He's not much older than Helen.

She would like a rest, time-out from thinking about her troubles. She doesn't want anyone she knows to be accused. She tramps back through the colorless long grass, stiff with frost, her previous footsteps still visible. She will try the key in the little door after all. It will take her mind off the possibilities that might come up this afternoon. She breaks into a run, bunching her freezing fingers up inside her pockets because she doesn't know where her gloves have got to.

In the house there is no sign of Helen, Jeannie, or Candy, who must already be on their way to the school. The kitchen clock tells her it is twenty minutes to three. Up the back stairs she clumps, flies along the upstairs hall, opens a door, up another flight to the third floor, panting like a chain-smoker. She turns and hurries down the hall to the end. She's getting excited about this, she notices, in spite of everything. She pulls open the bathroom door. And thar she blows, the little door opposite the sink. She crouches with the key and feels a little like Alice in Wonderland. She wiggles the key, says "get in there" to it, turns it, and – open sesame!

"Holy!" she says out loud. "I don't believe this. Wow! There's a whole other suite of rooms out there."

Crouching still, she goes through the door, and immediately down a little flight of four steps. This is nice, she thinks. Crowded, but nice. Homey. Cold, too. Brrr! She looks around and sees a room – a study, maybe – with a potbellied stove in it, a desk, bookshelves; behind it a small bedroom, more bookshelves. Looks like . . . looks like kids' books. Huh! Then out in front of the study, there's another room – a sunroom, she thinks – with a row of windows looking out over the back lawn, with a spectacular view of the lake. She can see Aunt Lily's island out there.

She turns her attention back to the secret new rooms. Books piled up on the floor because there aren't enough bookshelves. Boxes of Christmasy-looking stuff – some of it exactly what they were looking for a few days ago. Pictures in frames are propped on every flat surface and stacked against the walls – photos they are, mostly, taken of people a long time ago. There are also a few painted portraits. Aggie thinks, studying them, that many of them are of her father as a baby, or a curly-haired little boy, and then a gawky adolescent. In many he is with a woman – a younger Lily, probably. There are a few other pictures of old-fashioned kids: LILY, MARGERY, CAMERON, AND BERTRAND it says on the back of one. Huh, she thinks. Another Cameron in the family.

Beside the door she notices a couple of cloth bags sporting a green recycle logo and peeks in. One is full of letters, it looks like, and in the other – snapshots and . . . and . . . movie reels!

"What is going on?" Her brain is whirling right now. She pulls the elastic off one of the small reels, stretches out the film, and holds it up to the light coming through the windows. "A little boy running, little boy running, same little boy. . . ."

She takes a deep breath. So. This must account for all those empty places, where pictures once hung in the study. What is she to think? That it runs in the family? It appears that her great-aunt Lily is a thief. Although, she hasn't actually taken anything away – yet. She's had the key, all along, Aggie thinks, the key to her own private storage space. It must have fallen out of Lily's bag the day of the bread-making and got wedged in the dock when she was getting into her boat. In fact, this might explain the reappearing movie equipment. She must have taken it, and then her conscience got the better of her so she brought it back for the kids to use at the high school.

Suddenly Aggie remembers what is probably taking place right now at the high school. Quickly, she retraces her steps down the stairs and heads outside, racing along the street. With heart pounding, and not just from running, she drags open the front door of the school. I don't want to know who took the money, she thinks. I really don't. In a way, she wishes it had been her.

Through the open gym doors, she can see that quite a crowd of people have come out this afternoon. Duncan must have phoned half the village. The chairs are still in place from the film show, so everyone has a place to sit. She guesses people like to sidle into back rows for something like this; the first few are empty.

It's after three, and Duncan is standing at the front getting things underway. A few people turn to stare when she tiptoes in. She decides to stand at the back and looks around. Rachel is here, she notes, and Quade, of course. Helen and Jeannie. She can't see her mom, but she must be here. All the people from the movie are here. She sees a few sandwich customers. Also, Miss Greenwald, Mr. Pye, and there, she notices, is Bob Clarke, the bee man, and also the soap lady. Whoa! And the checkout girl from the supermarket. And somebody else she's surprised to see – old Skint, owner of the "bee" restaurant. Probably hoping to see one or all of us, she thinks, put behind bars. Give him a break, she thinks. He did take Helen back, after all.

At the front of the room, Duncan says he is going to

rehash everything for the benefit of the audience, telling them the facts, just the way Aggie told them to him. He says his point is to show that there are several ways the money might have disappeared. He's not putting blame on any particular person, he assures everyone.

"Saturday evening, Agatha arrived at the school alone," he says. "She talked to Rachel, who was selling tickets, who said she wished she could see the beginning of the film. Agatha offered to take over selling the tickets to let Rachel go inside the gym, and Rachel, after handing over the key to Miss Greenwald's room, told Agatha to leave the cash box inside Miss Greenwald's desk and to relock the door. Agatha, at this point, noticed only coins in the sliding drawer of the cash box where money is kept to make change. Picture a smallish fishing tackle box," he says. "That's what it looks like. Agatha assumed the rest of the money was hidden under the change drawer. It's possible, however, that it wasn't, that it was already missing."

What? Aggie is dumfounded. Is he suggesting Rachel could have taken it before she came in? No-o-o! Rachel would never have done that! People mumble and whisper. Aggie reasons that the money from the tickets *she* sold would still have been in the box, if that were the case.

Duncan says, "I'm not making an accusation; I'm trying to get everyone to look at all the possibilities. Just before all the tickets were sold, Agatha's mother, Mrs. Quade, arrived. She didn't buy a ticket, but instead walked along the corridor, looking at the class pictures hanging on the walls. Am I right, so far, Agatha?" he calls out to her, where she's leaning against the wall at the back. She tries to say yes, but her voice doesn't work, so she nods. People crane their necks to study her.

He goes on, "After the last ticket was sold, Mrs. Quade drew Agatha's attention to a picture of her father, who had once been a high school student here. Agatha left the cash box open on the table to go a little way down the corridor to see the picture. There was no one else in the vicinity until a moment later when Miss Lily Quade arrived, Agatha's great-aunt. Agatha called to her to go ahead in because all the tickets had been sold. Miss Quade said she would leave the price of a ticket anyway, and seconds later, Agatha heard the lid of the box being shut."

There's another excited buzz from the audience. Agatha scans the room carefully now, looking for Aunt Lily, but she's not here. And there's still no sign of her mom!

Duncan continues, "Agatha then went back to the table and picked up her knapsack, the closed box, and Miss Greenwald's key. Her mother accompanied her to the room while she put the box away. After locking the door again, Agatha put the key in one of the pockets of her knapsack. They then went into the gym, stood at the back for a while, until Mrs. Quade suggested Agatha take an empty seat in the back row. She wouldn't take it herself because, she said, she didn't intend to stay very long."

He looks down at a page of notes. "Agatha left her knapsack at the back of the gym with the other students' knapsacks, near where her mother and about ten other people were standing, and took the vacant seat. She couldn't see her aunt Lily, but assumed she had found a seat. At the end of the evening, Agatha, Rachel, and several others returned the key to Miss Greenwald at her home, and then each of them went home to bed. When Miss Greenwald went to the school to collect the money at about eight-thirty the next morning, she found the cash box in the drawer of her desk, but it was empty. The money was gone. So she says!"

People are gasping. Is he trying to make out that Miss Greenwald would lie, would steal? Aggie frowns. Everyone knows that's impossible. But her next thought is, how do we know that?

There is a general hum as people begin to discuss the case. Duncan lets the whispers and chatter go on for a minute or two, and then, as it begins to die down, he asks if anyone has any suggestions to offer that might shed light on the mystery. No one is saying a word. Aggie sees people looking at their hands, one or two look at the ceiling. No one looks at her.

Duncan says, "Were any of you standing at the back of the auditorium that night?" A few hands go up. "Did many people go in or out while the film was playing?" Duncan asks them.

A girl Aggie recognizes puts her hand up. She doesn't know her name, but remembers she's crazy about egg salad sandwiches. She says, "Mr. Pye went out halfway through the show."

Yes! Aggie's heart lifts as she says a little prayer. Let it be the principal! She can see the headlines. DEPRAVED PRINCIPAL ROBS STUDENTS. FROTHS AT THE MOUTH WHEN ACCUSED.

"I see," says Duncan. "Actually Mr. Pye has his own keys to all the various classrooms, I understand."

Wow! Aggie is aware of a regular hubbub going on, right now.

Duncan holds up his hand for silence and people soon calm down. "Did you see anyone else leaving or entering the auditorium?"

"I noticed Mrs. Quade come in."

"With Agatha?" Duncan asks.

"No, alone."

Duncan says, "So after she came in first with Agatha, she must have slipped out and then come in again. Did you notice what she did when she came back in?"

This is stupid, Aggie thinks. Why is Duncan going on about Mom? God! That is so unfair! Isn't he supposed to be on our side?

"She crouched down to tie her shoe, I think," the girl said.

This is incredible! Aggie's stunned. The girl must be blind. How could Candy be tying her shoe when she was wearing her stylish high-heeled boots that come up to her knees almost? She has to point this out before Duncan goes any further.

"That's not true," Aggie says, louder than she had intended.

"What's not true?" Duncan asks.

"How could she be tying her shoe when she was wearing boots, the kind you pull on?"

"But you saw her crouch down?" he asks the girl.

"Yes."

No one is fidgeting. Everyone is waiting, listening for the next piece of evidence. Aggie can feel her face getting red and her heart thudding. *Why do I blurt things? I've made matters worse for Mom.*

"Could she have been putting a key back in Agatha's knapsack?"

Aggie calls out, "Oh! Come! On!" She's really furious. Everyone has twisted right around to stare at her. "That is so unfair! Why would she steal anything? She's my mother!" She's yelling, she realizes – practically screaming. She can't stay in this room any longer. She bolts through the door and out the front door of the school. She's running and trying to button her coat at the same time, while wild thoughts fly into and out of her head. Anyone could have taken that money. There were lots of people standing at the back and any one of them could have crouched down and removed the key and . . . but. . . . All right, so they didn't know about the key.

However, her mind races on, there is still the unexamined possibility of Aunt Lily. Why didn't Duncan jump on that? Fond of her as Aggie is, she thinks it's entirely possible that she could have scooped the money. In fact, Aggie bets she did. She wishes she hadn't. It's going to make any future relations with her really awkward. But there probably won't be any future relationship. The whole stupid Port Desire dream is over.

While these thoughts boil and churn in her brain, her legs propel her toward home. She has to find her mom. She has to get her to swear she didn't take the money. Because Aggie knows she didn't. She just knows. She pushes open the front door with such force it bashes against the wall. "Mom!" she shrieks. She calls again and again, racing through the living room, dining room, out to the back hall. She is answered only by silence. Maybe her mother was back at the school after all, and she just wasn't able to see her. She calls again, not very loudly. Nothing.

"No, wait!" she says aloud. She's just thought of something. She knows what she has to do. Of course. She knows exactly what she has to do.

Out the side door she hurtles and races down to the boathouse.

CHAPTER FIFTEEN

She should have brought a flashlight in case it's dark by the time she gets back. Except that they don't even have a flashlight, she remembers. It's already getting dark out here on the ice. The sun is low behind a cloud bank. If the clouds break, the moon will show her the way. If there is a moon.

"Yikes! It's slippery. Slow down," she tells herself. What was that? She stops to listen. The ice is groaning. It's holding her though. It must be safe because otherwise, how did Lily get into town Saturday night to see the movie?

"She's got to come back with me," Aggie says, "that's all I ask." She can keep the money, if she needs it that badly. She doesn't care. She and her sisters can pool all their earnings to pay it back. All Aggie cares about right now is convincing Lily to come back and confess that she took the money when she was alone for those few seconds with the box. Judging from the stuff in the secret rooms, she steals things. She probably took the missing green-and-gold elephant, too.

Aggie remembers that summer afternoon distinctly now. She remembers Lily polishing two elephants. She also remembers leaving her alone while she fetched her handbag from the kitchen. She could quite easily have slipped one into the big pocket of her raincoat. If she would confess to taking not only the money, but the elephant and the pictures and the movie equipment, that's all it would take to clear Candy's name. And probably nobody would charge an old woman with theft. She's obviously out of her mind. She's a kleptomaniac. No doubt about it. That's why she occasionally puts things back. Like the movie equipment.

"I hope this ice is safe," Aggie mumbles. A crack echoes behind her.

She's getting closer to Lily's island – almost halfway there, she reckons. The ice is very clear out here, black, with frozen bubbles here and there. She can make out a curled brown leaf frozen right into it.

She hears a boom, and then a cracking sound, coming from the ice. Aggie's heart stops for a few beats and now it's racing to catch up. "Keep going, though, keep going." The sound of her own voice is reassuring. Sort of.

"What was that?" She stops and holds her breath. "Did I just feel the ice shifting a little?" She's shivering and sweating at the same time. "Maybe this wasn't such a good idea." She's sideslipping along now, cautiously, looking down. "Should I be running to get this over with?"

"A-a-a-ggie!" The faint sound of someone calling her. She looks back, squinting through the falling dusk, just able to make out on the shore near the boathouse a crowd of people.

"Aggie-e-e!" Quade's voice. He's calling out something else, but she can't hear what he's saying.

"I want to talk to Aunt Lily," she calls as loudly as she can. A lot of voices now, but nothing comes through clearly. "Aunt Lily!" she shrieks, making her throat hurt. "I need to find Aunt Lily!"

"Come ba-a-a-ck!" A shrill voice. Jeannie's.

"I think she's calling me to come back," Aggie mutters. "What should I do?" She looks around to see how far she's come. Over halfway now.

"Ohmygod!" she screams. "Oh, no!" Three paces from where she has become paralyzed with horror, she sees water. Open water stretches from here to the shore of Lily's island. She watches a nightmare of windswept water lapping at the ledge of ice, washing jagged shards, like broken windowpanes, up onto the very shelf of ice where she stands.

"Run!" she tells herself. She's running back! She can hear the ice cracking behind her. "I don't know what to do!" She knows she's screaming. And screaming. She thinks the ice is moving underneath her. She stops, panting. Her knees are so weak, she can barely stand. Over the sound of her own panting breath, she hears people yelling. She holds her breath to listen. "Lie down!" She thinks they're telling her to lie down. At any moment she could go through the ice and whether or not she can swim wouldn't even matter.

She's lying down now, inching along. "If I take off this heavy coat I'll be lighter," she reasons. She rolls over onto her side to unbutton it, squirming, jerking her arms out. "Eee!" Another loud crack. She stops moving to look around. Something is going on along the edge of the shore.

A large crowd of people now. "Someone's gone in! Gone through the ice! Oh, no, oh, no! It's Jeannie!" She can tell by her hair. "I've got to get to her to help her," Aggie whimpers. She gets up to run over the ice as fast as she can, but keeps slipping. Behind her, the coat lies where it was flung, abandoned, disowned. She nearly falls. People onshore are yelling at her to lie down, lie down.

There is another loud crack. She lies down.

Aggie can hardly focus on what's happening. Somebody else is out on the ice. *Helen! Oh, please, please, please, don't go through!* She's trying to get to Jeannie. People are still shouting, "Lie down, lie down." Helen lies down now and is pulling herself along on her belly. So is Aggie. She can hear Jeannie screaming. She's trying to pull herself up onto the ice, but she can't get a grip.

Farther along the shore, Aggie can make out Quade on the ice with a rope. It's holding him. He is crawling toward Helen. As Aggie gets closer, she can hear Helen sobbing and calling Jeannie: "Hang on, Jeannie, I'm coming. You're okay, we're going to get you, hang on." Quade throws the rope to Helen, but it's out of her reach. He pulls it in and tries again. She's almost got it. She's got it!

Helen gets up on her knees and throws the rope to Jeannie, but Jeannie doesn't grab it. She's still clawing at the ice, trying to pull herself up. "The rope," Aggie shouts to Jeannie, "get the rope." Everybody's shouting at her to get the rope. In a moment she tries for the rope and nearly goes under. Aggie can hear Helen screaming above everyone else. She's close enough now that she can see the same terror in Helen's face that she has in her own heart. "We can't lose Jeannie," Aggie howls. "We can't." She can't see Jeannie's face at all, but she thinks she has the rope.

Helen crawls with the rest of the rope over to Quade. Aggie thinks he has a rope tied around his waist. Other people are out on the ice behind him. Helen and Quade are trying to pull Jeannie out. People behind them are pulling, too. "Oh, no!" Aggie screams. Jeannie has lost the rope! "Don't go under! Don't go under!" She's on her feet and running to Jeannie. She knows she can grab hold of her in another minute. From the corner of her eye, she notices that someone's pulled the boat out onto the ice.

Aggie is opposite Helen now, and they're both reaching into the icy water for Jeannie. Her ski jacket is ballooning around her, keeping her from sinking, but they can't reach her. Aggie's numb with cold. Her throat won't scream. It's full of water. She can't move. She can no longer see.

Many hours have passed. No one knows if Jeannie will survive. Aggie doesn't want to think about this anymore, but she can't turn her brain off.

Jeannie was taken by ambulance to the hospital in Kingston. Aggie and Helen are getting back to normal after being in the water for only a minute or two. Jeannie was in longer. They say she was lucky Mr. Pye was there and knew so much about resuscitation. Also, that the ambulance got there so promptly.

But, poor Jeannie. They say she was in the water a long time. Maybe too long.

Helen and Aggie are sitting beside each other, leaning against each other, really, on the couch in the grand main

living room. There is a lot of to-ing and fro-ing of people –
all the Quades are here including Susie, who is sitting in a
corner looking scared. Aunt Lily is here, too. She's sitting
in the kitchen, elbows on the table, her head in her hands –
troubled, not communicating. Aggie would like to talk to
her, but can't – not yet, anyway. Mr. Pye, Miss Greenwald,
and Duncan Hill are here. Tom Ryan, Jeannie's boyfriend,
drove to Kingston behind the ambulance. Rachel is here,
too. She's been chatting to Aggie, trying to get her mind off
everything. She says her mother's cousin went through the
ice and they didn't find him until the next August. Helen
and Aggie gape, horror-struck, at each other, and Rachel
cups her fingers over her mouth. "Sorry," she says. "I
didn't mean . . . oh, God. . . ." She looks embarrassed
enough to cry, so Helen and Aggie try to comfort her. Linda
made them some herbal tea, which she keeps urging them
to drink, but it smells like cat pee and tastes worse.

Jeannie wasn't breathing when Mr. Pye and Duncan
pulled her from the water into the boat, but they felt a
faint heartbeat. Mr. Pye started mouth-to-mouth on her
immediately, while Duncan hauled first Helen, then Aggie,
over the side of the boat. Several other people went
through the ice, including Quade, but it was fairly shallow
and they were able to wade ashore. Jeannie didn't regain
consciousness.

Helen and Aggie are bundled up in blankets, hugging
their knees, not saying much, just leaning against each
other. Their tea is on a little table in front of them, with
steam rising from it. Candy left before all this happened,

Aggie guesses, otherwise, she'd be worried sick. She'd have gone with Jeannie in the ambulance.

Duncan has been phoning the hospital on his cell phone, but can't get any information about Jeannie. Someone will phone as soon as there is a change, they say. Aggie keeps dozing off and waking up to feel the bottom drop out of her heart. *What if Jeannie dies?* This is her one heart-lurching fear. It pounds at her hard enough to shatter her rib cage.

Some of the people are thinking about leaving. It feels late to Aggie, and maybe it is. Aunt Lily is still here, and so is Quade. He went home to change his clothes and came back again. And Duncan is staying.

Aggie is consumed with guilt because it's all her fault for wanting to get Aunt Lily to confess about the money. She had to, though. It was a question of sparing her mother. She couldn't have people falsely accusing her. As it turned out, though, Lily wasn't even on her island. The Quades had convinced her to stay with them until the ice was solid enough to be safe. No one is even thinking about the money, now.

"If Jeannie dies . . ." Aggie says to Helen, but she stops and doesn't say anything else because she's crying again.

"She's not going to die," Helen says firmly. She unwinds her blanket cocoon enough to put her arm around Aggie. Aggie is trying hard to believe the firmness in Helen's voice, the certainty.

Quade sits on a footstool nearby, his long legs bent like a big *M* in front of him. He holds out a plate of buttered toast to Helen and Aggie, but Helen shakes her head and leans back against the couch. Aggie is staring at the toast he has cut into small pieces and then into his eyes filled with kindness. Tenderness, she might even call it. He picks up a small piece and holds it out to her, and she takes it from him with a hand that is shaking a little. She takes a bite, still looking into Quade's eyes, and it tastes warm. Comforting.

Linda tries to get Helen and Aggie to go to bed, but they won't go. They want Duncan to phone again, and finally he does. He gets up from where he was sitting near the door and goes out into the hall. Aggie and Helen both scramble from their blankets to follow him. The air is thick with tension. Aggie is choking on it, scarcely able to get her breath. Duncan's voice is urgent. "I beg your pardon?" he says. There is a pause. He moves away from the girls back into the living room, but they are both right behind him. "No," he says, "not from here." He looks puzzled. "Yes, I see," he says briskly. "I see. Yes." Aggie is trying to decipher what is meant by "yes," to gauge the tone of "I see," to read the lines creasing his forehead, his closed eyes. "Yes, I see."

Aggie is cold again, colder than she felt in the water. Colder than death. "Thank you very, very much," he says, opening his eyes. For the first time, he looks at Helen and Aggie with eyes full of promise. "She regained consciousness about fifteen minutes ago, and they think she's going to be all right."

Everyone is breathing again, especially Aggie. "She's going to be all right!" she and Helen keep saying to each other. Aggie throws her arms around Helen and hugs the breath right out of her.

"They think they'll be able to let her go home late tomorrow!" Duncan has to shout over the excited babble. When everyone calms down a little, he says, "They would have called earlier except that they thought we had called them and that they'd already told us the news. It was a woman who called, the doctor said."

"Probably Mom," Aggie tells him.

Helen says, "I doubt that. She couldn't care less whether any of us lived or died. Besides, she's long gone, I expect."

"She cares!" Aggie insists. "That would have been her phoning about Jeannie! There are some things you just know. You know?" Aggie is beginning to feel the need of a huge hunk of homemade bread to see her through until morning. What a luxury to have bread! What a relief to be able to eat it.

Helen says, "With a thousand dollars in her pocket, I don't think she'd have stayed around long enough to even know what happened." Aggie heaves a big sigh. She doesn't really want to get into this. She knows her mom did not steal the money. She just wouldn't.

People are sorting out their belongings now, getting ready to leave. Miss Greenwald has her coat on and is patting Helen and Aggie each on the shoulder. Aunt Lily put her coat on, but sat down again on a chair in the living room, still disconsolate, still not communicating. Aggie can't blame her. What is there to say, after all? The Quades are gathering up their coats. Susie fell asleep in a big chair, and Bertie is trying to get her into her ski jacket. Duncan says he's going to leave Helen his cell phone in case the hospital wants to phone back.

They hear *brrring!* as someone rings the front doorbell. Duncan opens the door. In a moment the owner of the "bee" restaurant is standing in their midst, holding out a slim brown paper bag from the liquor store. It doesn't gurgle, it jingles.

Everyone pauses, half into their coats, their scarves dangling. Helen and Aggie have ditched their blankets and are sitting at attention, wondering why Mr. Skint has invaded their privacy. He clears his throat and nervously glances to one side and then the other, at the now-silent audience. "Which one o'yez is Aggie?" he asks.

"I am." Aggie stands up, eyes fastened on the brown paper bag.

"She asked me to give this to you." Aggie steps forward to take the bag and, for a dazed moment, thinks he means Jeannie.

"Do you . . . you . . . you mean Jeannie?" she hears herself stuttering.

"Is that her name?" he asks.

"My sister?" She glances at Helen. "My other sister?"

"No, no, not your sister. An older woman, the skinny one with the fancy boots." Mr. Skint, stoop-shouldered, looks around at the assembly. He doesn't hand over the bag immediately, but feels moved to make a speech. "Y' know, I just have to say, I'm real sorry about all the trouble yez are havin'. Me and the wife there got talkin' about it. We were over to the school this afternoon with everyone else, so we know about how the money went missing. At first we said, you mighta knowed something like this woulda happened. But then we got thinkin' and we said, them girls there, they don't act vicious like what you'd see on the television news. We said, it's like everybody in town's got some kinda bee up their drawers and can't sit down until something happens. And now this goes and happens and the wife, she says, nobody deserves that much trouble at Christmastime. Don't matter what their relatives done. They don't deserve no more heartache than they got. You get on over there with that bag, she says, even if it is after eleven o'clock pee-em at night. So over I come and here it is."

Helen asks, "Who gave you the bag?"

"The woman, there with the boots; she come into the restaurant tonight. She was with some man, fer I saw the botha them drive away in a car. There's a note to explain," he says. "She told me to be sure and tell you to read the note."

The bag is tied closed with a piece of string, which Aggie can't undo because it has about five tight knots in it. Anyway, she knows what's in it. Helen takes it and rips open the bag. A few coins spill out onto the floor and some of the bills drift out after them. Aggie picks them up, and Helen turns the contents of the bag out onto the couch.

"That there's your missing money," Mr. Skint says over the hubbub. Everyone crowds closer to have a look, all talking at once, asking questions, shaking their heads.

From the bottom of the bag comes a folded letter with Aggie's name on it. Helen hands it to her, leaning close to read over her shoulder. It begins:

Dear Aggie,
I'm sorry about this. I never meant to take it. I
don't know what came over me. All I know is, I was

under a lot of stress what with everyone being so
hard on me and everything and making me feel like
dirt. I don't mean you did. I mean I just don't know
how this happened. All I can say is, it wasn't really
my fault because, as you know, I have very bad
nerves, besides having a bad back. Also, I don't
know if you noticed, but you've got your elephant
back. It's in there with the books. You girls should
lock your doors at night. Otherwise, you're just
asking for break-ins.

I'm just real, real sorry. I hope you will under-
stand and forgive me someday, although I know I
don't deserve to be forgiven. I have to go away again
because I know you will be better off without me
around. Plus nobody really wants me, anyway.

Your loving Mom

Tears start coming into Aggie's eyes even though she is
crunching down hard on her teeth, trying to prevent them.
She glances away, blinking, sensing Helen's eyes on her.
Through Aggie's own watery eyes everything is obscure,
nothing is clear, nothing makes sense. But then why should
it? Emotions don't need reasons. If she can't see through
the blur, she thinks, that's her problem. Helen has her arm
around her again and is saying in a soft voice, "She's right,
you know. We're better off without her."

Aggie manages to get her voice going. "It's not true that
nobody wants her – I do." Aggie's memory for recent past
events seems to have become as blurry as her vision. The
recollection of a man steering a small houseboat and a

woman who looked like Candy disappearing into the cabin has drifted into the space where forgotten dreams go. So, too, has the fear she felt when she saw someone peeping through a window one afternoon. She knows it wasn't Lily, yet she's unable to look with clarity at who it might have been. And she has almost forgotten that she sensed someone creeping around the house one night because, what does it matter, now?

Nearly everyone has left. Linda and Bert tried to coax Aunt Lily to come with them. "I'll be along," she says. "Go ahead without me." She's hunched, sad-faced, in the chair opposite Aggie and Helen, knees akimbo – her coat pulled down almost covering them, but not quite. When the others have gone, Lily rouses herself, a little. "I suppose you've been to the post office, have you?" she asks Aggie.

Post office. Aggie has to think about the faraway world where post offices exist. "I didn't have the key with me. But from what I could see through the window," she says to Lily, sadly, "it looks like you're returning my letter. And, oh," she says to Helen, "I think there's a letter for you – business-type thing."

Lily is looking up, her face brightening. "Well!" she announces. She sits higher and draws her knees together primly, like a respectable maiden great-aunt. "Well," she says again. "Perhaps all is not lost." Aggie looks baffled. Lily continues, "I might as well confess. I read your letter very carefully, and the part that really hit home, really swayed me was . . . well, there were two things. . . . Luck being an hourglass was one – you know, if your luck runs out you can always turn it over. You said it was something your dad used to say. Well, do you know something? He got it from me. It's exactly what I used to say to him when he was a child and things weren't going well for him. And of course, the other thing you said in your letter was that a house with hollyhocks can't be all bad. That, too, was an expression of mine. Isn't it a marvel how something like that – expressions, people's little theories – survive and get handed down? I really felt, well, tied to you girls through Cam and the house, and that was when I started a letter saying that I would be pleased and honored to move back home and live with you as a family and be a proper great-aunt to my nephew's children."

It's all Aggie can do to keep from throwing herself at Lily and planting a slobbery kiss on her, but something makes her hold back. Lily looks troubled again, and so Aggie waits, listens.

Lily says, "And then that woman arrived before I had finished my letter, arrived and moved in, and I thought, well, that's that. She was Cam's downfall and the source of all our sorrow and our bitterness and our anger. I can't forgive her." She looks at Aggie helplessly. "I can't."

Aggie frowns at the faded carpet, not able to meet Lily's eyes.

"So, it was in a fit of anger, I admit, that I wrote on the back of your letter that I couldn't share the house with that woman, readdressed it, and there you have the whole sordid truth."

Aggie's still frowning, but pacing now, back and forth across the worn carpet, wondering what she can say, wondering what point there would be in saying anything.

"But," Lily goes on, "I noticed something today – it came through very clearly and cannot be denied or over-looked." Helen and Aggie both become still, their whole attention on Lily. "Lily, I said to myself, these girls took that woman in, in spite of the wrongs she's done them. Accepted her right back into the family. The very thing I was always urging my brother to do. 'Take Cam back,' I used to say. 'Give him another chance.' But, no sir! Bert would not. He felt he'd given Cam all the chances he could. He closed the door on his heart one day, threw away the key, and from then on lived each day as though there had been a new and sudden death in the family."

Lily pauses. Aggie swallows. She's looking expectantly at Lily, her mouth open a little. Helen is almost smiling. Lily says, "I wonder if I could have a second chance."

CHAPTER SIXTEEN

So, thinks Aggie, this is what a typical family Christmas Eve is all about. Jeannie is back with them, looking pale and – Aggie can only define her as – diminished. Tom drove her home from the hospital this afternoon. The way Helen has her tucked up into one of the big wing-backed chairs with a blanket, she looks like a little lost child. Aggie wonders if having death stare her in the face might have rearranged all the sharp edges that make up Jeannie, shattered her and shook her up, and now she doesn't know how to put the pieces back the way they were. Aggie misses her smart-ass, rebel sister.

Tom is still here, but keeps saying he should go home. Helen has made tea and is perched on the edge of her chair, ready to leap up to pour more or to pass the plate of cookies – a real little hostess. Aggie doesn't know how she knows how to do that. Helen gets lines above her eyebrows whenever she looks at Jeannie. "Do you want me to get you a glass of milk?" she asks her.

Jeannie's voice is little more than a whisper. "No, thanks."

Tom has just left. Jeannie says in a thin voice, "I sort of

invited Tom and his mother for Christmas dinner. Hope that's all right with you."

Helen and Aggie both say, "Certainly, of course, whatever you want."

Then Helen wonders if Duncan might come instead of going to his sister's in Kingston. She phones him on his cell phone and nods excitedly at her sisters, indicating an affirmative reply. After a lengthy good-bye to Duncan, she looks at her watch. "Oh, my God," she says, "it's five-thirty and they close at six." She throws on her coat to race across to the grocery store because with the stolen money situation and Jeannie's near-death experience, they still haven't got a turkey.

"Get a big one," Aggie calls as Helen flies out the door. "I'm inviting Quade."

Jeannie says very quietly, "What about his family?"

So Aggie runs outside and yells at Helen as she scurries across the street, lit from above by the streetlight. "Get a hugie! A monster!" Helen waggles both hands in the air in a distracted way without looking back, which could mean anything from *get lost* to *your wish is my command*. Maybe, Aggie thinks, we should have asked to borrow some of the stolen money before Miss Greenwald took it home for safekeeping. Turkeys are expensive.

Helen is back empty-handed. "Closed!" she says. She presses her lips together in defeat. Jeannie shrugs her lack of interest, so Aggie feels she has to do a little ranting on Jeannie's behalf. "What do you mean 'closed'? It's only five-thirty and they usually stay open until six. Go bang on the door; they can't do that to us – it's Christmas Eve."

"Exactly," Helen says. "Their sign says they're closing at five on Christmas Eve."

"I phoned and invited the Quades," Aggie says.

"Aggie!" Helen's agitation is showing. "We'd be delighted to have them, of course (she is now in her shrill-but-polite mode), but that makes ten people!"

"And," Aggie reminds her, "they have Aunt Lily with them."

"Oh, dear God." (This could be a prayer.)

"Quade said Aunt Margery usually comes, too, and her husband."

"Could we possibly invite anyone else?" Helen is becoming cynical, but Aggie prefers not to notice.

"Actually," Aggie says, "it would be nice to have Miss Greenwald and her mother." She leafs through the phone book, looking under G.

Helen throws herself into a chair, gasping and sputtering and counting people on her fingers. "Are we expecting some sort of miracle here? I mean, I know it's Christmas and everything, but good Lord!" Slouched down, legs out in front like two sticks, she flattens the back of her hand against her forehead and closes her eyes. Aggie surveys her critically, sizing her up for a role in some future movie. Then, sadly, she looks at Jeannie, the would-be actress, bundled like a mummy and just as quiet. Jeannie glances from one to the other as if she doesn't understand what's going on.

"What's wrong, Jeannie?" Aggie asks.

"Nothing."

"You're so quiet."

"I know." Aggie waits, thinking she'll explain. "It's because I'm noticing things. Observing."

Aggie and Helen exchange a puzzled glance. "You mean us?" Aggie asks.

"Yes."

Aggie wants to hear the truth from her sister who lost touch with the conscious world, who defied death. "Wh . . . what do you think?" Jeannie looks at her, not comprehending. "Of us?" she adds.

Looking sad and wise and as if her life depended on the answer, Jeannie hunches forward. For a moment she seems perplexed, searching for the right words. Helen is sitting very straight, looking at Jeannie as if she might reveal a great truth. "Of you two?" Jeannie says quietly, thoughtfully. She pushes the blanket away, watching it until it falls to the floor. She takes a breath. "I think," she says, and now she yells, "You're both out of your friggin' minds!"

Aggie's laughing; Helen collapses back into her chair, laughing; and Jeannie's laughing and coughing and crying. Tears are pouring down her cheeks, and now they're huddled around Jeannie, their arms around each other, and they are all one hundred percent hysterical for about a minute and a half.

After they gasp breath back into their lungs and wipe their eyes on their sleeves, Aggie says, "I have no idea why I keep inviting people to a nonexistent dinner." And that sets them off again.

"This is going way beyond madness," Helen says. She snatches the phone from Aggie. "Guard this with your life," she tells Jeannie. "No more invitations."

Helen goes out to the kitchen to gaze into the open fridge. She calls out, "One and a half bags of skim milk, not quite a pound of butter, some eggs, three apples, a dish of leftover Kraft Dinner, two onions, several rubbery stalks of celery, and a head of rusty lettuce. Oh, and a dead carrot. That's what we have on hand."

Aggie joins her in the kitchen and catalogs the contents of the can cupboard. "Three tins of tuna, a tin of salmon, two tins of soup, a jar of spaghetti sauce, and a jar of mayo. And a few questionable things at the back."

"All right, we've had our little jokes," Helen says. "This is serious. How are we going to feed the multitudes?"

Jeannie is in the kitchen now, a little wobbly, but with color in her cheeks. "With sandwiches, of course, what else?"

Their little conference is shattered by a sharp ring of the front doorbell – very short, very businesslike. They look at each other frowning until Helen goes to the door. Jeannie and Aggie stand in the hall, curious. Helen opens the door to Mr. Gorman, the lawyer. He takes off his hat and comes in.

"Can't stay," he says. "This is more of a business call than anything else, although I did want to check on the young lady who had the misfortune to go through the ice." He nods at Jeannie, who has moved closer. "Right as rain again, are we?" Jeannie nods yes, and he shakes his head and says, "You won't be wanting to try that again, I shouldn't think." Jeannie shakes her head no, and now he's nodding his head at all of them. "The good news is," he says, "your aunt Lily has agreed to the specifications of your grandfather's will and would like to move in early in the new year, as soon as she can close up her island home and make it secure for the winter. I trust you are in agreement."

Smiles and words of agreement all around.

Mr. Gorman bids them a merry Christmas. He takes each of them by the hand, fractures the small bones of their knuckles, and leaves.

"And that, as they say," Aggie announces, "is that." They stand in the front hall, massaging feeling back into their hands, taking deep breaths.

"I can't believe it's actually going to happen," Helen says.

Jeannie says, "I didn't know I cared so much. I think I'm going to cry again."

"Don't!" say Aggie and Helen together, knowing she'll set them all off. Helen bustles Jeannie back into the living room.

Helen and Aggie have made a whole whack of sandwiches (they made Jeannie lie down), although not enough to make anyone groan from over-fill. They had a few home-made loaves of bread in the freezer and one loaf on the go, so that's what they used. Aggie bets the guests will bring cookies and things to fill people in around the edges. "And," she suggests to her sisters, "we could have a pasta course." She forgot to mention that they have several boxes of spaghetti and Kraft Dinner. "It's all going to work out, don't worry," she keeps telling Helen.

Jeannie is lying on the couch not worrying at all. "I'm too knocked out to eat anyway. You can dish up roast rubber boots, for all I care."

This is more like the Jeannie they know and love.

"But you have to eat with us," Helen protests, "it's Christmas."

"Last Christmas we worked in the deli most of the day and ate deli leftovers for Christmas dinner because Mrs. Muntz was off visiting her sister," Jeannie reminds her.

They turn out the lights and are on their way upstairs to bed. "It doesn't look like Christmas. We don't even have any decorations." Helen seems determined to force them all into a state of psychotic depression.

Aggie stops halfway up the stairs, a look of glee in her eyes.

Helen and Jeannie, suspicious, want to know what diabolical idea has just struck.

"Nothing, nothing." Aggie clamps her lips mysteriously. Her idea will be a little surprise for her sisters. She waits until they've each been to the bathroom and finally closed their doors for the night. Off she goes now, up the stairs to the third floor. The costume room is not her goal, but she turns on the light and gazes in anyway at the rack of preserved clothes – vestiges of other lives, other eras – boots and shoes in a neat row below, hats, some in boxes, above. It's like a museum in here, she thinks, a place to visit, to poke around in, to study. *But you don't live in a museum. You can't be an exhibit.* She goes in and straightens a pair of army boots – left on the left, right on the right, laces tucked into the top.

Standing back from the display, about to turn out the light again, something occurs to her: she suddenly knows something new. She'd rather create a character than be one. She smiles, her hand on the light switch; she has just made that discovery about herself. She turns out the light. She can do that, she thinks. She can make up and write a character out of nothing but her imagination and a few beads on a blouse, or an old glassy-eyed fox head. She knows somehow that she can people a world with characters, that they are all there, just waiting to be imagined. She walks silently, happily, along the third-floor hall, not wanting to waken her sisters.

In the bathroom she turns the key in the little door, crouches through, descends the few steps, and there is the box labeled CHRISTMAS DECORATIONS beside a pile of books. She spied it out of the corner of her eye when she was here yesterday (if that *was* only yesterday). She picks up the box, blows off the dust, sneezes. Oops, she thinks, better be quiet. Down she goes, all the way down, tippy-tippy-toe. Regular little Christmas elf.

Downstairs she opens the box. No wreathes or garlands, she notices, no crèche scenes. Not even a plastic Santa Claus. *Hmmm*, she is pressing her lips together thinking. An idea lights up the inside of her brain.

And so it's Christmas morning. They all slept in, although Aggie has to admit that she's been lying in bed waiting to hear her sisters getting up. And now she hears them. She wants to go down with them to see their faces. Out in the hall her sisters are yawning, scratching, starting downstairs. Aggie rushes ahead of them, scaring them witless. "Knock us down the stairs, why not!" Helen says crossly.

Aggie dashes into the living room, dark because last night she pulled the drapes closed in order to provide the full effect this morning. She plugs in the tree lights with a little spark, and voilà!

Helen and Jeannie are agog. "Wow," they say, "holy!"

"Yup," Aggie agrees.

The glorious object in front of them is one of those trees in a big pot you see in shopping malls and airports, although smaller. Still, it's nearly as tall as Aggie. But absolutely dead. She dragged it and lugged it all the way from the little back room full of dead plants (where they found the movie projector and camera) into the living room. She has decorated the dead tree with what she found in the box in the secret rooms – some spear-shaped things like icicles, old-fashioned painted glass balls, some egg-shaped, some with holes in the middle like doughnuts. They hang elegantly from the tree from which she has removed all the dead leaves. A string of red berries (some have crumbled off) winds its way among the branches. And the whole thing glows softly – yellow, red, green, blue – with a rotting string of ancient lights that she hopes will not short-circuit and set everything on fire. The three sisters just stand there admiring the tree and telling each other how beautiful it is. Under it, Aggie has placed the presents she bought every-one, except the ones for her mother. Those she's saving for next year because, who knows, she may be back by then. Or she may not.

While the girls are eating breakfast, Quade drops over to spy he says, sent by his parents and Aunt Lily to find out what the girls have and what they might need for dinner.

"Can't think of a thing," Helen says. Jeannie and Aggie grab her and shake her in horrified disbelief.

"How big is your turkey?" Quade wants to know.

"Tiny," Helen says. "Well . . ." she begins, eyeing Jeannie and Aggie.

"To the point of being invisible," Aggie says.

"Oka-a-a-y. . . ." Quade is taking mental notes. "Veggies?"

"Not a lot."

"Hmmm. Dessert?"

"We think some of the guests are bringing it."

They know now that they can get fifteen people around their dining table without any trouble. They have to keep their elbows in, but they're coping. They end up with two turkeys. Linda cooked hers to perfection and brought it, and so did Tom's mother, Lydia (a smaller bird, but just as perfect – the turkey, not Lydia, who is actually a good hefty size). They have piles of vegetables, brought by various other people, also gravy, dressing, cranberries. They even have champagne, which Duncan kindly donated. Aunt Margery and her husband (his name is Philip) brought a plate of canapés that smell like cat food, and look as if a number of small creatures have died on top of circles of melba toast.

Aunt Lily brought Christmas crackers containing paper hats and fortunes and really neat little gifts. Aggie's is a miniature deck of cards, Helen's a sewing kit, and Jeannie's a fake diamond ring. "Trust Lily to go for the expensive crackers," Margery mutters. Lily gets a magnifying glass and Quade has the same as Aggie – cards. Susie has minia-ture handcuffs. "These are stupid," she says.

People have brought cameras and keep jumping up from the table to take pictures of everyone in small bunches wearing their ridiculous paper hats. Susie scrunches hers into a ball and throws it under the table. Pretty soon pieces of broccoli from her plate join it.

And Aunt Lily makes a rambling but heartfelt speech. She starts off saying, "You know, when I was a child we always had all our relatives with us for Christmas dinner, a huge number of people, along with a lot of friends, why, I remember Christmases where we'd sit down with twenty or thirty people, of course we had servants back then, and I remember little Cammy in his high chair eating with a fork just as smart as you please, although, mind you, that would have been a few years later. And it was right here in this very dining room where my fondest memories took shape. And I have to say that those were the days, all right, and it makes me sad to think they're all behind us, and that we had to go through those years of bitterness and emptiness, months of silence, and everywhere in the house locked doors. But, you know, this is so much like old times, the good old times, that I feel, well let me see, how do I feel? Happy, of course, and grateful, and, well, I could almost shed a few tears, I'm so overcome with. . . ."

"Hear! Hear!" Bertie says loudly, and everyone else says it, too, so that Aunt Lily doesn't get a chance to shed any tears, and they all drink a toast to Christmas and to families and to friends, and then they have dessert. They have been furnished with enough sweets to put them into orbit, or would, if they weren't all so weighted down with turkey they can barely get up on their hind legs to walk.

They had to, however, because now they have regrouped in the living room to open presents. The handsome little dead tree is the center of attention, even though Aunt Lily and Aunt Margery have just been outdoing each other with detailed descriptions of the forests of spruce and pine chopped down and hauled inside to bring them joy each and every Christmas of their childhood.

There are other presents besides Aggie's little pile. Soon there is Christmas wrap all over the place and quite a cheerful little hubbub of my-my's and look-at-this's and one or two well-now's.

The great-aunts and uncle are happy about the antislip things for the bathtub. Aunt Lily says, "Why, they're the very thing! Exactly what I wanted!" Aunt Margery seems a little skeptical about having the face of the president of the United States staring up at her while she showers, but her husband (Philip) says, "I'm sure, if he knew, he'd be delighted." And everyone is laughing, so that's that.

Now Helen and Jeannie and Aggie are opening little presents from Lily, which turn out to be pieces of jewelry that had belonged to her mother. They look at each other, mouths open, because they can't believe it. They are – Aggie would have to say – overcome, their eyes a little watery, going *blink-blink*. Aunt Lily pretends it's nothing, but Aggie can see her biting her lip as if she's pleased that they're so astonished and just plain touched.

Susie shrieks, "Spray paint! Wow! My very own spray paint! It's from Aggie!" And Linda looks worried and says, "Maybe we'll put that away, dear, until you're a little older." But Susie isn't listening to her. She's shaking it up and trying to figure out the childproof stopper on it. She's managed to squeeze herself in between Aggie and Quade, sitting beside each other on one of the small couches, and she keeps saying things like, "You're the best, Aggie!" and, "Can I come over to your house to play tomorrow?" and, "Do you want to come to my house and see all my stuff?" And things like that. And Aggie's thinking, what have I done?

Quade and Aggie are unwrapping gifts from each other with Susie in between, testing the springs of the couch, saying, "This thing isn't very bouncy, is it?" Quade and Aggie have given each other books to further prove that they are actually twins in disguise. Aggie's to him looks like a school notebook with a coiled back, but on the cover is a picture of a violin, which she found and pasted on. It's the music book she bought at the garage sale in the fall, with page after page of narrow lines for writing down musical notes. She's very proud of herself for finding it because she thinks Quade loves it. The book he wrapped up for her is called *The Keeper of the Bees*. "It's a pretty old book," he says. "It was given to my grandfather when he was a boy living right here in this house."

"Good title," Aggie says, although it looks like a sluggish read.

It's getting late, and people are sitting around relaxing and thinking about going home, but not quite ready to make the effort. They insisted on doing the first load of dishes, which in no way offended Aggie or her sisters. While they were clearing the table, Aunt Lily, with the help of Susie and Quade, brought down all the pictures that she had put upstairs in the little back rooms for safekeeping. It seems that just before her brother Bertrand went into the nursing home, he threatened to take every photo and every portrait out to the backyard and burn them. Afraid that it might not be an empty threat, Lily snatched them off the walls one day when she knew he was out, swept them off dressers and mantelpieces, and taking the key to the suite of rooms at the top of the house, put everything there, including the movie reels, camera, and projector, and locked them in. He was fit to be tied, but she would not let him destroy her precious memories.

"You know, I meant to tell you about the movie para-phernalia the day I brought it down from the third floor, but I forgot," she said, a little shamefacedly. "You were all out running errands or something. Can't think why. Oh, the bread! Then I got all fussed up about something else – pencils, was it? Cammie used to hide things, you know. He was a scamp."

The dishwasher is humming in the distance. Aggie glances around the living room, noticing that people have moved into little clusters, for the most part. She and Aunt Lily sit close to each other, looking at a stack of snapshots from the canvas bag she brought down from the third floor. Aggie asks her about the funny little rooms.

"They were the maid's quarters, at one time," she says, "long ago, when I was a child."

Aggie says, "You mean, the maid had to duck through that little door in the bathroom?"

"Oh, no," she replies. "There was a larger door. It was boarded over when the tub was put in on the third floor. Those back rooms haven't been in use for fifty or sixty years. When your father was a boy, after his mother died, he and I spent many a happy day out there. I read to him and played games of let's pretend. We had a good view of what is now my island, but back then, it was a magical island. It was great fun. He liked to imagine he was in a sailboat sailing to an island of treasures. And I liked to imagine he was my son. I'd have forgiven him anything."

Margery has just been having a wonderful time telling Miss Greenwald and her mother about what an upstanding citizen her father was, and how old and renowned the Quade family is, and now old Mrs. Greenwald is getting in her two cents' worth, regaling them with a tale about how wonderful her husband was and how important his family is. Miss Greenwald is knitting something blue and white on big needles and smiling serenely. Margery's husband is not in a group, but is reading a 1953 *National Geographic* and getting a lot of enjoyment out of the bare-naked Africans. The Quades (Bertie and Linda) and Lydia are discussing politics. Susie is pretending she is temporarily blind and is walking around with her eyes closed and her arms out in front of her, bumping into furniture and tripping over people's legs and feet.

In a far corner of the room sit Jeannie and Tom. Jeannie is having second thoughts about running off to the States. Instead she's thinking about going back to school after the new year. They have their arms around each other, kissing and nuzzling, but looking around first to make sure no one is noticing. Of course, everyone does notice. Hard not to. Their little corner of the room fairly throbs with desire.

Duncan and Helen are near the door, gazing longingly into each other's eyes. Helen is hoping to get into university in Kingston, less than an hour away by car. She'd like to try to resurrect the heap of scrap metal they once called a car, if she can, but she'll have to get her license first. Duncan thinks he should be on his way to his sister's, but he doesn't leave. Around them the air seems almost flame blue and crackling. Suppressed desire, Aggie imagines you might want to call it.

If she were making a movie about this, she would have the camera take in this whole scene, bit by bit. The camera's eye would finally, for a moment, fall on Quade, sitting on a low footstool, his favorite perch it seems – a mass of bony arms and legs pointing in different directions, like something prehistoric, or newly evolved – a ptero-dactyl or a heron at the moment of landing.

He's looking at Aggie with his head on one side, as if he'd like to know what she's thinking. She smiles enigmatically, and he laughs at her because she doesn't know how to smile enigmatically. He's still looking at her, though. She could be wrong, but she thinks his eyes have a soft little glow of longing about them. Dare she say budding desire? If she were to look closely into his eyes she would see herself reflected, but she won't. She prefers, for the moment, to remain a mystery, even to herself.

The camera backs off slowly, until the people and their passions and hopes and quirks become very small and indistinct. Softly, subtly, one hears the strains of a violin. The living room becomes hazy and dissolves into an exterior view of the redbrick house on Lake Street, sitting, as it does, so close to the sidewalk that it seems to want to be part of the bustle and spirit of the town. Nearly all the windows are warmly aglow, and through one can be seen a dead tree, alive with colored lights reflected in glassy ornaments. Across the street, in the shadows cast by a streetlight, one imagines a solitary figure flicking ash from a cigarette, contemplating the house and all it contains. The camera's eye lingers, hovers wistfully, reluctantly moves on.

Now the windows' muted glow blends with the glimmer of stars above. It is as though we are soaring, beating our tiny transparent wings in the rarity of height. We see an overview of the small town – a village, really – sitting so close to the shores of a lake, we know it wants to shake off winter and night and welcome the splashing waves and dashing boats. The lake is covered with a sheet of ice and a blanket of snow, but in a moment we see the day brighten and the snow magically recede and disappear as the ice begins to thaw in the sun and melt. The lake is brilliant in the sunshine, its grasping weeds, its oozy bottom deeply hidden, forgotten beneath the glitter. The wind whips it up into frothy peaks and, in the distance, a speck becomes a sailboat heading for a tiny island.

The music of the single violin envelops us now, as lake and sky fuse in a mix of whitecaps and clouds. It sings to us in a language we are learning, telling us something we are beginning to understand. Our heart's desire is within our reach, almost, if we stretch a little farther, and hope a little longer. And we do.

The End